PRAISE FOR

She Never Told Me About the Ocean

"I've always admired the writing of Elisabeth Sharp McKetta, and her beautiful, ambitious first novel demonstrates why. *She Never Told Me About the Ocean* is a heroine's journey through forgiveness, birth, and rebirth, all the while treading the line between honoring the dead and feeling paralyzed by them. She has offered us a complicated portrait of mothers and daughters, cupped inside one another like nesting dolls."

ARTHUR GOLDEN, author of *Memoirs of a Geisha*

"*She Never Told Me About the Ocean* is a tidal and intimate book, brimming over with wonders and terrors and the watery echoes that bind generations of women. What a pleasure this book is from start to finish. McKetta maps the dark portals through which her women continuously reinvent themselves, newborn at every age."

KAREN RUSSELL, author of *Swamplandia!* and *Orange World and Other Stories*

"A superb enchantment showing the richness of ordinary life and the permeability of life's margins. We meet those who help us enter into this world and those who can hinge into the world beyond. With stunning perceptions and captivating language McKetta brings us a brilliant reimagining of the myth of Charon along with much forgotten knowledge from the provinces of healing and herbalism."

GRACE DANE MAZUR, author of *The Garden Party*

"*She Never Told Me About the Ocean* is an aria for mothers. There is a kindness and love that runs through this story; it just sits in the background and breathes."

LESLEY BANNATYNE, Bram Stoker Award nominee

"With luminous, aqueous prose, Elisabeth Sharp McKetta tells a story of healing and resilience through relationships, work, and a journey of self-discovery. Readers of all ages will be enchanted."

KIM CROSS, author of *What Stands in a Storm*

"A kaleidoscopic story of mothering and daughtering, wrought with all the myth and wisdom and flaw and singularity that accompany them. *She Never Told Me About the Ocean* weaves everything I thought I knew about these sacred relationships into a something else, a glimmering tapestry revealing a truth so difficult to keep hold of in the waves of our days: that every one of us is at once mythic and startlingly human."

CL YOUNG, author of *Rose of No Man's Land*

PRAISE FOR

Elisabeth Sharp Mcketta's

OTHER BOOKS

"For some years now, I have been reading and appreciating Elisabeth Sharp McKetta's exceptional *Poetry for Strangers* project. With generosity, inclusiveness, and openness to the wonders of nature and the human spirit, McKetta reaches out to those strangers, encountered by chance, inviting them to participate in an art form that non-writers so often consider alien territory. She is a bridge-builder of the most original kind. And, equally admirable, from this unpredictable starting point she writes many amazingly good, complexly developed poems, imbued with her own intelligence, wit, and kind perceptiveness."

LYDIA DAVIS, author of *Can't and Won't*, on *Poetry for Strangers*

"Elisabeth McKetta taps fairy tales, and, presto, they transform themselves into living things that reach out and tug at us, reminding us of the exquisite fragility in 'once upon a time.'"

MARIA TATAR, Harvard Professor and author of *The Fairest of Them All: Snow White and 21 Tales of Mothers and Daughters*, on *The Fairy Tales Mammals Tell*

"Elisabeth McKetta grapples with the bedrock basics of being human. All of the imperatives of flesh—love, lust, the making and breaking of hearts, marriage, children, and all the rest—get full play in her writing."

BEN FOUNTAIN, author of *Brief Encounters with Che Guevara*, on *The Fairy Tales Mammals Tell*

She Never Told Me About the Ocean

a novel

ELISABETH SHARP McKETTA

PAUL DRY BOOKS
Philadelphia 2021

First Paul Dry Books Edition, 2021

Paul Dry Books, Inc.
Philadelphia, Pennsylvania
www.pauldrybooks.com

Printed in the United States of America

ISBN 978-158988-153-2

Library of Congress Control Number: 2021931197

Dedicated to all my mothers before and all my daughters after,
& to Paula, who gave me the first seed.

Contents

She Never Told Me About the Ocean

The ultimate meaning to which all stories refer has two faces: the continuity of life, the inevitability of death.

—ITALO CALVINO

"Oh no," my mother says, stopping suddenly on the side of the road in a patch of dry grass.

"What is it?" I ask. I look down at her feet to see if something has stung her: an insect or a fox-head. But she is clutching her belly.

I kneel down next to her and put my cheek to her drum-tight navel, as I have seen Ilya do many times. "Baby," I whisper to the moving thing I feel. "If today is the day, please come quickly. Come easily. Work with your mother. Make this a safe journey for you both."

I never expected to be the one here with her. But then it may have been inevitable. This story has been going on for so long and each secret has a thousand more secrets seeded inside like nesting dolls within nesting dolls, making it impossible to locate a beginning or an end.

One

1

Sage

AUGUST

Sage is the name she gave me, but she never calls me that. I suppose that's fair. I've never called her mama.

Mother is both noun and verb—a word like love, need, water, and lie. Rock, too: the island where we live, what you do to a baby.

Something else I know about mothers is that the stories that shaped them took place before their children were born. Mothers are myths. Mothers live on islands of their own sorrow. When something hurts them, they sit with the grief for a long, long time.

Here is what I know about fathers: their laughs ring in the trade winds like bird cries. They have beards that smell of boat oil and fish blood. They are full of love and easily distracted. When fathers are at sea, they forget their children's nicknames or remember nicknames that no longer fit.

If you look out past the coral reefs your eyes will find brown and blue motes on the water, tiny dots of fishing boats as they troll the deep with their nets and lines. One of these boats holds my father. My sea turtle father who beaches to fill his food satchels and replenish his hooks and fishing line, and then returns to the water where he belongs. My father, who once was a poor graduate student studying whales, and then started Big Mouth Fishing Company so that he and my mother could have enough money to have a baby. You could always tell when it was time for my dad to return to sea. His gestures became panicked and dry and clumsy. He cleaned out the pantry too many times. He loved being at sea where his only link to land was a radio. He loved us too—it was not that—but he did not seem to know what to do about us. I grew up hearing his crackling voice over the wire saying, "I don't know when I'll be back," and "You can't make promises with the sea."

Even though my childhood was not perfect, it was good enough: I could trust the adults to play their parts, and I knew what was expected of me, and I did it. I could trust the landscape of the days; I could separate fact from fiction. Then came a year that changed all that, and suddenly secrets appeared like bats from under a bridge, flooding our world with their smoky wings. It was as if the secrets had been sleeping during the daylight for centuries, then the summer I turned eighteen, the world turned dark—and all the bats woke up, hungry.

For as long as I can remember, my mother Marella has been a noun, not a verb. She would sit all day on the sofa, pretending to read a book, trying hard to look away from the ocean while the tea in her mug grew cold. This was her position when the hospital called with the news about Nana.

Nana had always lived with us during the months when my father was at sea. She slept on the fold-a-bed sofa and rolled it up neatly each morning before I woke. Nana did the work of raising me, teaching me to read, dress myself, and behave at home and at school. She cooked our meals and tidied our rooms.

While my mother and I drifted around the small apartment like bottom-dwelling fish, Nana was the steady anchor in our aqueous household. Under Nana's watch, I finished high school. Under Nana's watch, I sent out application after application until I got accepted into a university on Blue Island where I would go to become a nurse or a teacher or somebody who didn't make her living off the sea.

But then in May Nana broke her knee, and in June her hip, and then in July the doctors found a large benign tumor in her left breast, and a miniscule quick-spreading malignant one in her right. When Nana went into the only hospital on her home island, I wrote the university a letter asking to defer a year. The counselor who called me back sounded spooked that I would give up college for a grandmother.

For the weeks Nana had been getting treatment, my mother and I had been staying inside, eating packaged food, keeping quiet and waiting. And now the call had come. The verbs in our family, my dad and my grandmother, were respectively at sea and dying, and we were going to be lost now, more lost than ever before.

"Are you going to do something?" I asked my mother.

She swirled her mug in slow circles with one hand and with the other she twisted her hair into a knot, her habit when an action that she does not intend to do is required.

"You should call Dad," I urged her.

She bowed her head to her cold mug. "Will you?"

I was used to her, but there were still times when I found myself waiting for an adult to act, then being wave-crashed by the realization that my waiting would produce nothing.

I lurched toward the kitchen, cupping both the phone and my anger close. I pushed the call button and waited. I would handle this quietly, like an adult. Nana always said I held my cards close. You have to with a mother like mine.

"Hallo?" My dad's thunderclap baritone voice crackled over the wire.

"The Dragon Island hospital called. Nana is..." I couldn't bring myself to say it.

"Haaaaaaaallo?"

"Dad! You need to come home. *Now*."

"Haaaaa—Sage?" There was a crackle and then a deep silence and I thought I had lost him. Then his voice boomed back as clear as water, and it spoke one of those two sentences I had heard most from him throughout my life: "Don't know when I'll be home!" Then static diced his second most frequent sentence: "...can't make promises with..."

Then dead sound. I stepped back into the living room and threw the phone into the warm cushion on the other side of Marella's sofa.

This was how most of our conversations ended—minus the throwing of the phone.

I turned to my mother. "Well," I said. "We're going to Dragon Island."

"I don't want to go," she said, not moving her eyes from her mug.

I left her on her sofa.

When you live in an apartment not much bigger than a boat, it doesn't take long to pack your entire life into a suitcase. I finished mine in minutes, and as my mother had not made a single move, I went ahead and packed her suitcase too. Even though tiny Dragon Island, with Nana's house and the hospital, was only a ten-mile ferry ride from where we lived on Blue Island, the most industrialized of the Charon Islands Archipelago, I had never been there. It was not that I hadn't had the chance—my nana had invited me many times—but she could never win in an argument against my mother.

Our sixteen-story apartment building stood smug and

landlocked in the middle of a hundred other buildings just like it—like my mother, our apartment was in utter denial that it existed on an island. When I was a child and she was in a rare talkative mood, my mother told me scary stories about the island where she grew up: *Dragon Island is haunted. It is water-cursed. Things happen there to people that scar them forever.* To which I'd look at Nana for confirmation or denial, and Nana would shake her head. My mother also used to tell me stories about the old rulers and I remember my astonishment upon learning that my mother—and I—had descended from them. I wanted more, but Nana shushed the stories, saying, "It is an old social system that fell because it was rotting. Read her the modern classics instead." With Nana alive, her feet firmly situated in the real, I did not have to be afraid of my mother's shadowy fears.

But that was in the old days. There were no stories now. Now, my mother hardly spoke at all.

When I came back into the living room, Marella still had not moved. "I will never set foot there again," she said in her beautiful voice that echoed like the inside of a seashell.

"The ferry leaves in exactly one hour. Up," I demanded, yanking her arm, which was as thin as a child's, its bones as delicate as those of a fish. I handed her a dress and shoes. Finally, reluctantly, my mother dressed herself.

In the absence of Nana, I was now in charge; I knew it and Marella knew it and for that reason, she did not fight. Somebody has to play mother when the real mother won't act.

To my surprise, my dad made it to the hospital before Marella and I—the hospital radioed him and had better luck: he wrapped the fishing trip early and took a fast boat back. He was still wearing his rubbery fishing overalls and his ridiculous orange boots. He greeted us on the hot curb, under the patchy black awning underneath the words DRAGON ISLAND HOSPITAL. When he saw us, he picked me up, even though I am nearly his height, and for that moment the only smell in the world was his wiry, fishy-smelling beard.

"Put her down, George, she's too big for that!" Marella scolded.

"Seabird," he said, his searchlight eyes taking in every detail of my face. "I missed you."

"I always miss you too," I told him, while the ugly thought flashed inside me that Seabird was his baby name for me and anyone could see that I was no longer a baby.

He held my hand as we three walked into the dingy hospital lobby with a depressing gift shop that sold wilting bouquets and a few pathetic leis. We bought a bouquet and stood uncertainly at the front desk. I asked for my grandmother's room; they told us the third floor.

The first thing I noticed was that Nana's hospital room had a window that looked toward the ocean but was decorated along the wall with framed paintings of crisp pine trees, of all ludicrous trees. We live on an archipelago in the Pacific Ocean, over two thousand miles south of Hawaii. Nobody I know has ever seen a pine tree except in a movie or as a cartoon. My first thought on entering the room was to despise those trees, their implied lie that anyone could stay evergreen.

And there sat Nana with a weak smile on her face. She was propped up in a hospital bed that roboted up and down, and she held in her hand James Joyce's *Ulysses*.

"It'll keep my brain operating," she said, shrugging at my mother's blank face. (*What are dying people supposed to read?* I wondered but did not ask.)

"All right, mother-in-law?" My dad put one hairy hand gently on the sheets that covered her legs. With the other hand, he held out the flowers like a torch.

Nana blew him a weak kiss.

Marella found a stiff vinyl visitor's chair in the corner and sat in it, pulling her thin legs up to her chest in fetal position. Her hair fell around her shoulders like a black cape and her eyes fixed on the floor. I settled into another chair just like hers, pulling it close to my Nana, its metal legs screeching in protest. Nurses milled in and out, fidgeting with the machines, shooting my mother worried looks.

"Nana," I said, "How are you?"

She shook her head, then turned to the wall. So this was it. The end. Or close enough to it. I rubbed her blue-veined arm while my mother faded into the wall. A nurse explained to my parents the facts of Nana's illness, how the tumor was huge, everything was metastasizing, the surgery had not gone well, mostly due to her age. Things do not look good and we had better stay close. My parents left to eat dinner and sleep at Nana's house. I spent that night with Nana, wishing her to get better, but watching her hourly get worse.

The next morning I woke up with a hurting back from sleeping in the chair. The room was muggy and my bare skin peeled off the chair like a band-aid. Dreams had haunted my sleep; in the one I could remember, my dad was swimming with whales, and he kept becoming a whale and singing for me to join him in the pod, but I couldn't recognize him and even if I could, I was afraid to swim. I was huddled on a tiny boat all by myself, I could see nobody, just ocean forever, and my father's voice kept urging me to jump.

Waking from such nonsense always feels worse when parts of the dreams are recognizable: how after a lifetime of hearing my mother worry about the dangers of water, I was the only eighteen-year-old in the world who had never learned how to swim.

In the bed, Nana lay motionless. I wanted to tell her about my dream and have her reassure me that I was not alone, I had her; or else remind me that I could still learn to swim, I was brave, it was not too late. But I knew there would be none of that today. The only real thing in the room was limbo: not quite life, not quite death, and in my heat and exhaustion, I had the grim nauseating feeling that it almost didn't matter.

Nana stirred, attempted to say my name. I picked up *Ulysses* and asked if I could read to her.

"Hades chapter," she said in a voice that sounded as if she had swallowed sand.

I sat next to her and read all morning, sliding down in my chair, feeling the knots in my spine rub against it. Just before noon my parents appeared. My dad bumbled around the room, looking for things to clean up—he looked and looked and looked, finding nothing between Nana's tidy luggage, her untouched breakfast dishes, and the machinery. His panicked caricature of usefulness gave him away: he wanted to return to sea. My mother just sat in the chair like mine, looking away from the ocean-view window at the stupid pine tree artwork, sitting in silence while Nana labored to breathe. Something seemed to be trying to escape her body.

In the window, the sun had risen high in the sky and settled there. It didn't surprise me when a few minutes after arriving, my parents left for the cafeteria.

The flowers we had brought were drooping in their sad vase, and I put down the book and picked up the plastic hospital pitcher to give them a drink. Nana sat up in her bed and snapped into sudden aliveness, giving me a shock—she had been silent for so long.

"Water!" she called out hoarsely.

I refilled her cup. She tried to drink, but the water fell down her chin. I brought the cup to her mouth, my hands shaking all the way. I blinked back tears; I could feel the tide of her leaving and I was powerless to stop it. *And then*—I couldn't stomach the thought. And then—once she was gone, once the wave of her aliveness crashed and vanished, there would be only the endless expanse of being alone.

Suddenly, shakily, Nana leaned toward me.

"No, no," I said, "keep resting. Please."

Her hair looked so white, her face a dry sand dollar—she looked ancient.

"Before...." she began to say, then she descended into a scratchy cough.

"Before what?" I echoed, foolishly. Her lips moved but the words seemed caught in her throat.

"Before you, a brother—Adam." These words a mere whisper. She began rustling her legs under the scratchy blue sheet, sending *Ulysses* tipping like a canoe over the ripples.

I could hear the voices of my parents in the hallway.

"Nana," I said, "what do you need to tell me? Who is Adam?"

Nana gripped me with her eagle-fierce hands—where had this sudden strength come from?—her papery lips hardly moving. "Sage," she said, "He drowned. Marella—tried."

We stared at each other for a weird, sad moment.

"When?" I asked. Then I began to cry.

A gust of wind rustled the dry petals as my mother opened the door.

"Who's Adam?" I looked up at Marella. "Nana said..."

My mother turned sharply to the bed, with all those pine trees staring down and promising immortal life, even while the woman on the bed had already taken her final breath. But Marella hadn't noticed yet. "Oh, Mother!" she said. "Why would you upset Sage?"

Nana's eyes and lips were closed lines; no more words were coming.

I put my hands over my face and cried and cried. My heart hurt, and my whole body felt clogged, swollen with so much saltwater that it would take weeks, months, my entire life, to drain it all out. I sobbed until my stomach hurt, until the rage in my belly threatened to rise into my arms and pull the pine tree paintings off the wall and hurl them at my mother.

"Stop howling," hissed Marella, closing her hand like a claw around my wrist. "You are acting like a child who's lost its mother!"

But I would not stop and I didn't care how I was acting. The wires connected to Nana must've alerted the doctors to the stopping of her heart, for suddenly they seagulled in, flapping their white coats and stethoscopes, and my father whisked me away.

After my hysteria and anger died down, my mind felt empty, as if all the life I had known had been flushed into deep water. I felt newborn, pink, skinned. Yet what I chose to cling to in the aftermath of Nana's death were the clues she had left me. I had two: the noun "Adam" and the verb "drown." They seemed the only real way forward.

While my dry-eyed mother filled out paperwork at the hospital front desk, I faced my father on the bench where we sat. "Who is Adam and how did he drown?" I added for good measure: "Please tell me, Dad."

But it was hopeless because I knew well what he would say: *Some things are hard for your mother to talk about, Seabird. This is one of them. But you can try asking her.*

And he said exactly that. My father is as predictable as the tides.

He shifted around on the bench, looking like a nervous and helpless bear. In a tone of casual, manly trepidation—his usual way of approaching members of our three-generation house of women—he asked, "Why do you need to know?"

Why did I need to know?

Was it just because these were Nana's last words to me, and only to me? Was it because for my entire life our house had curled around topics that Marella refused to discuss, like a misshapen shell protecting the soft underbelly of a crab? It was this, but it was more. Most of all it was that my mother's anger had proven a third clue. Somewhere deep in my bones I felt certain that the words "Adam" and "drown" were breadcrumbs toward a cure. Like a fairy tale beast, my mother seemed to have a thorn that had punctured her and left an infection that had spread deep, and I believed that these words—somehow—were the secret key to her healing. If I could only decipher the story I could draw out the thorn, clean the wound and let sunlight heal it, and then we could finish our story in some other way.

At that moment, Marella glided over to us.

"Bathroom," said my father, pointing with both thumbs and scooting off. We watched him walk away, and a silence settled on us: the usual eerie silence born from being alone with my mother.

"Let's wait outside," I suggested. She followed me to the courtyard of the hospital. The windows that overlooked it had been flung open. We stood in the sunlight right next to the chapel, within hearing range of the maternity wing where the newborn babies slept; their tiny voices fluttered through the open windows and mingled with the mournful notes of rising prayer.

"So—who is Adam?" I asked her, trying to balance my tone so it didn't sound like begging.

The sun was setting behind her, flanking my mother with angelic purple wings.

"Don't ask questions whose answers will horrify you." She pulled her heavy hair into a knot, tying up the ends of the conversation.

2

Sage

AUGUST

It felt strange to wheel my small suitcase into Nana's house the night after she had died, stranger still because I had never actually been there before, even though she had owned this house since before my mother was born. A sad, icy feeling tingled in my hands and feet, the grief that I would never be in her house with her alive, never get to see how she lived here, inhabiting her own dwelling.

The giant house gaped around us like a whale. I gave myself a tour and twice got lost, because for some absurd reason, even as a widow, Nana kept this house with seven bedrooms. The house had crow's-nest lofts in each bedroom, daybeds jutting out of the walls, a dining table for twelve, skylights cut in geometric shapes throughout the ceiling, and it was made of wooden everything. Ladders clung to random walls like broken vertebrae, and the great staircase in the entry hall rose, seemingly, into the sky. It had a pleasant, nautical feeling—basins of shells next to every bed, bright light bulbs hanging in the centers of rooms from hardy lengths of rope.

"Pick a room," my dad said, and I carried my luggage into the smallest one, on the first floor beneath the grand staircase. The room was enormous compared to my room in our apartment. It had a too-big closet, several sizeable rugs on the floor, and a ladder rising up the wall to a loft.

Above me, I could hear the shallow whine of my mother complaining, then a sound of booming consolation from my dad. Across the room was a round window, like a porthole; I opened it to drown out their noise.

At least outside I could hear the birds. Nana loved birds and I found their sound comforting too. I could see them puttering around on the coconut trees, quarreling over insects. From my window I could see the entirety of Dragon Mountain, a long green and black mountain shaped like a sleeping dragon—it had a tail of black rock that flicked up like a spike and trees on either side that feathered out like wings. Nana's backyard was a field of green, stretching all the way to the ocean where an old wooden pier planked into the shallow water of Dragon Bay.

I lay on the bed, closed my eyes—the old wooden pier floated into my mind, then floated away. Something about it seemed familiar. Something from one of my mother's stories, probably.

Then I heard a sharp knock on my door, followed by Marella's voice. "We need to clear out her things. Then we can go home."

I considered pretending to be asleep. The last thing I wanted to do was spend another night awake, watching my mother—who abhorred clutter—throw away Nana's treasures. If she would only wait a week, I knew I would enjoy looking through Nana's house as she had kept it, trying to get to know her life as it existed away from me, before my mother swooped in with a roll of plastic trash-bags. It seemed that tonight would be my only chance to see what things Nana had cherished and—the mystery reared its head again—to investigate if any of them had to do with Adam.

"I will help!" I called, an agenda in my voice, as I ran into the hallway, the old house creaking beneath my feet.

After a quiet scavenged dinner of pickled things, we got to work clearing out Nana's house. We each picked a bedroom to start with.

She had so...many...belongings. Objects spilled out of cabinets in every room, every closet. We picked up papers and objects and put them into one of three bags: toss, donate, or store. I made quick headway on my bedroom, emptying the closet of several boxes of men's shoes, presumably my dead grandfather's, and putting them gingerly into several donate bags. Such bounty was a version of Nana I had never seen; when she stayed with us, all she brought with her was a small rolling suitcase. I tried to feel her in each object I picked up.

"Are you still not finished with that room?" I heard Marella's voice from the doorway. Had it been hours? How many? Probably she was just impatient, as usual.

Still, I sped up, finished the room, moved to another.

Animal noises from outside spooked me at first, but quickly faded into the backdrop. In the quiet night, I could hear my parents in the other rooms.

I felt a small chirp of comfort in being awake in the darkness with them, all three of us wandering like ghosts around Nana's enormous house, worrying, disbelieving, sorting through boxes, not wanting to turn off lights. For a brief spell, my loneliness abated: at least we three were together in having lost her. It would be too much to ask for one of my parents to ask how I was doing or invite me to talk. But standing in the night together counted—it was a version of enough.

It was late, sometime in the middle of the night, when we wandered into the hallway for a break.

"This is all we've got," my mother muttered, leaning into the curve of the staircase banister, which enveloped her small body like a wooden sea-serpent.

"Yes. We knew that before, Marella," said my dad. He stood in the center of the staircase, suspended between going up or down. "We knew she didn't have money, just the house."

"But I thought by the time she died, we'd be more…secure. That we wouldn't need it."

"Don't we all think that," my father answered, shrugging lightly. "Welcome to the human species." Things like money didn't bother him. Fish meant food and any boat meant shelter.

"This house…" Marella said slowly.

I knew how she felt about the house from the stories she told me when I was a child. It was the house where she was born, a giant house whose size always made her feel small and afraid. It was the house where she had stood in the backyard when her brother almost drowned, and where worse things happened that were alluded to, but never spoken of. Things, I suspected, like Adam.

My dad walked a few steps down and opened a small cabinet in the hallway, then exclaimed, "Oh my!" He pulled out a silver tray of taxidermied hermit crabs.

My mother twisted up her hair and looked away.

I waited until they moved into the office. Then, with a folding knife in my pocket and a flashlight in my hand, I snuck upstairs into the attic.

The attic was easy to get into, though not easy to find—just a small child-sized door in the back of the master bathroom, and behind the door a cardboard maze of boxes. I shined my flashlight into the tunnel and dropped to my hands and knees. I crawled through the maze of boxes, all labeled neatly with practical words such as *Taxes, Medical Papers, Beach Supplies.* These boxes made more sense than taxidermied hermit crabs, for this was Nana as I knew her: always organized. An image flashed in my mind of our apartment kitchen full of neatly labeled jars of rice, beans, dried peppers and kombu, lettered in this same script.

Stop thinking of those, I told myself. *Stick to your job.*

I moved through the boxes, and soon the attic ceiling rose to the height of a normal room, and I saw more objects: a wooden rocking horse, a patch of dusty surfboards, trunks of old romance novels. Then in the far corner of the attic, near another porthole window, I found something promising: a box with my name written in Nana's elegant penmanship: *Sage Brouge,* the letters of my name curled into elegant wisps.

I knifed it open, rolled the tape into a sticky ball, and put it into my pocket. Inside were the things she had promised me: a box of jewelry, two dolls she made for my mother, a recipe box, her sealskin jacket. And then at the very bottom, two books, both wrapped in fading linen scarves, one with a black squid woven into the white thread, the other with a whale.

I opened the squid first. It held an old medical dictionary, its brown leather cover dissolving at the corners and crumbling into my hand. A silver bookmark had been placed a quarter of the way in. With extreme care, I opened to it. On that page, in blue pen, a section had been circled. I read:

Bradycardia occurs in mammals when the heart-rate slows 50% and blood re-routes to vital organs, especially the brain, to give the drowning mammal a window of time to stay alive until rescue. The thoracic cavity, through this blood-shift, stays intact without collapse, and the mammal can stay alive without breath for longer underwater than it could in the air. Hypercarbia are the high levels of carbon dioxide in the blood triggered when the mammal reaches either loss of consciousness or the breath-hold breakpoint, and either way the victim inhales.

I read it twice before I understood; then I got chills all over my arms and legs. The optimistic lungs working hard to stay alive until the very end, even while the rest of the body has given itself up to the water. *Either way the victim inhales.* Nana had left me a description of how to drown.

I closed the pages and looked again at the cover. In the leather, thinly etched, was a name I could almost decipher: it was the name of my mother's father. All I knew about him was that he had worked as a doctor on Dragon Island and that he had died before I was born.

I unwrapped the other book in the whale scarf. It was a baby book. It had a blue and white soft cover on which a name was written in my mother's handwriting: *Adam Brouge.*

To read the baby book of somebody I'd never known was almost too intimate, but I sat cross-legged on the creaky attic floor and read it anyway. I didn't know him, but I knew that his first word was "tickle." At six months, he giggled at the ceiling fan. His favorite food: roasted seaweed. His favorite animal: a dog named Julep (I remembered Julep, a crotchety one-eyed boxer). A single curl of his hair was as long and dark as a scorpion.

There were pictures too: a slimy pink newborn in my long-haired mother's arms. A picture taken underwater of him swimming in a blue wash of bubbles. Smiling with fat cheeks and enormous thighs. A picture of my father—looking peach-faced and beardless—holding this baby horizontally like a big fish. He was born to Marella and George Brouge on July 17, almost two years before I was born.

When I looked up from the book an hour—many hours?—later, dawn light was just starting to glimmer through the attic window and I sat paralyzed on the floor, both of my legs asleep.

I had a brother. I had had a brother. I had had a brother, and I had lost him.

Either way the victim inhales.

I could bring this book to my mother—downstairs I could hear the crashes and rustles of her and my dad, still sorting through Nana's things, no doubt raising a mountain of trash bags. But I did not want to share it with my mother. Adam was only one secret. I wondered what other secrets would appear on this watery and mysterious island, washed up in the tide like a message in a bottle.

I creaked downstairs.

"Hi, Bird!" chirped my dad. "Find anything interesting up there?"

"No," I lied.

"Well that's good, I guess. Makes it easier to give things away."

Nodding mildly in order to discourage further conversation, I walked into Nana's office and resumed work, this time with a ferocious new hope and an even deeper curiosity.

As I emptied her file cabinet drawers, sorting papers into piles, my mind was racing: Adam's baby book was a fact. Proof existed. No matter what lies my mother told me, I had an object that told a story. Nana had left me evidence that I had a brother and my brother had drowned. This was not much information to go on—but it was something.

As I drifted through these facts and questions, I clung like a shipwreck survivor to a single hope: that Dragon Island would be small enough for me to find out everything if I waited and listened. There would be stories, I felt certain. It seemed likely that here my mother's secrets would be washed out by the current, turned over and salted and refreshed. Oceans and death, it seemed, eventually reveal everything.

I worked with terrific focus, stuffing old bills and grocery receipts into trash bags, working as hard as I could so that the words treading water in my brain would be drowned out: *Either way the victim inhales.*

We stumbled into the next morning, squinting in surprise when the sun brightened the house, which now felt like a graveyard of Nana's objects, strewn out of gaping cabinets. As I looked at it all, exhaustion and sadness welled up and I suddenly began to cry once more and had to go lie down on a bed so I wouldn't panic my dad or anger Marella.

When I came back a while later, my father was making coffee and the phone was ringing.

"Will you please get it?" he asked Marella, his hands full of the dust of the ground beans.

She gave him a tragic look, answered the phone, listened briefly, and said, "Not me." She passed the phone to my dad.

He hoisted it onto his shoulder awkwardly and, not finding a kitchen rag, wiped his hands on his pants. He listened for a moment. "It's about the what?" His voice took on a sadder note, and he simply said, "Oh."

He listened longer, first politely and then with slight impatience. "Yes. *Yes*. I know. You don't have to explain. I know about them—Why today?—Now we are in the—Oh God!—Sure. Right. Right-o."

"Seabird," he said in a strange voice when he hung up the phone. "You and I have a boat errand to do."

Neither of us looked at my mother when he said this, for Marella would have nothing to do with boats or water. She surveyed us with her faint smile, as if pleased that we had so wordlessly acquiesced to her wishes. She swept away to a purple armchair and swiveled it to face away from the ocean. She still looked regal, but the shaking of her shoulders showed that it was a pretense. Dad and I watched her, then each other. Then Dad resumed the coffee and I made us a mediocre breakfast that we ate in tense, tired silence.

Then I cleaned up the dishes and Dad looked all over for Nana's car keys, which it turned out she kept in a giant conch on the dining table. Marella did not look up once or offer to help. Dad fluttered around her for a few minutes, seeing if she needed anything and trying to make sure she was okay. Naturally this only agitated her, and at last I succeeded in ushering him into Nana's car.

He was on the phone with a fisherman from his company for most of the drive, directing him kindly and inefficiently on some boat business, so I wasn't able to ask him what we were doing.

We pulled up to the Dragon Island Hospital—an unwelcome sight, for I had not even been twenty-four hours away from it. But instead of going in the front, where we had entered while Nana was alive, Dad drove around to the back, idling in front of a smaller concrete annex that looked newer than the main building. Its windows all blinked shut under awful black awnings like stubby fake eyelashes.

As we waited, two workers emerged from beneath the awnings. They were wheeling a small blue-shrouded figure on a gurney out to our car. They asked if we might put down the backseat to make more room.

"Is that Nana?" I gasped.

The workers looked at me. My dad put the backseat down. Nobody answered.

"Dad, what is going on?" I demanded when we were in the car again.

"Seabird..." He fumbled. "It's not like Blue Island here. They don't use coffins. Or cremation. They have something here called the Ocean Funeral. So basically in this place where your mother grew up, the dead get dumped out into the ocean where they become shark food."

We both winced at this.

"Sorry," Dad added.

I vaguely understood from my mother's old stories that the Dragon Islanders believe that the ocean is where souls come from and where they go. But it seemed impossible that Nana's body would simply be dropped off the side of our boat. There was no reason why two islands that shared a small swath of ocean should differ so much: how one island could be so advanced and urban, and the next one over could be so far behind, so superstitious in its customs. I said this in a few words to my dad.

"They say the same thing of siblings," he responded, then began a tuneless whistle.

We arrived at the big public dock where my dad had hired someone to haul in and moor both his Big Mouth Fishing boat and his small skiff. We were the only people parked in the lot, for it was still early morning, too late to see the first-light fishermen, too early for Dragon Islanders to have any fun on a boat.

I couldn't watch as my father lifted Nana onto the bottom of the skiff, and I was nearly in tears by the time he took my hand and led me on board.

"Here's your oar, Seabird," he said, swallowing. He gave me a quick lesson on how to row.

We rowed, a bit clumsily, in silence. The waters felt dark, deep, ominous. I could not shake the thought of so much world below us, and a fear kept rising its humped back, a recurring vision of something coming up and tipping our boat. I rowed faster. I was ready to get this over with.

It seemed my father knew these waters perfectly and was happy to take his time. We rowed around the curve of the island to a strange rock formation: a cluster of tall tulip-shaped rocks that jutted violently up from the deep water.

"This is the ocean resting home," my father said, barely whispering. Even in his steadiness on the water, I could see that this unnatural act we were about to perform was getting to him too.

"It would have been nice if your mother had come," my dad said in a feeble tone.

His words rang embarrassingly false and we both knew it. I could not imagine my mother stomaching any part of this ocean burial; this was one more thing he and I were protecting her from, letting her sit inside, safe and comfortable, while we combed her life to keep it free of any distress, any messy thing.

Dad tried a second time: "I hope she's said enough of a goodbye."

We postponed it for as long as we reasonably could—but the sun was rising and soon it would be hot and we had a body we needed to let go. So together we picked up Nana and slid her small bony body out of the blue shroud. I was embarrassed for her modesty, having never seen her naked, but still I watched, trying not to blink, and I kept my eyes open from the moment we set her floating on her back in the water until she began to sink, first through the clear shallows and then into the murky depths, and finally out of sight. Then at last I blinked.

For the first time in my life and to my complete surprise, my father began to cry. While he wept in silence, looking back toward the rocks, I rowed us gently home.

Around sunset that second night after Nana died, a swarm of people from town showed up at her house. A hundred uninvited strangers flooded in with potluck dishes and bottles of wine and home-brewed beer. One stranger leered at me and kissed my forehead before saying in a singsong voice, "You city people say 'from dust to dust,' but here we know that life lasts from water to water."

What kind of place is this? I wanted to ask my mother, for she would have known about these strange Dragon Island death customs, and she could explain them to me. But I knew that she would offer no straight answers, and any answer she gave would be pointed toward getting us home. I thought of our old apartment, sitting empty, all those dry goods in all those jars, how either I would learn to cook them or we would throw them all away. Beans and rice last for years. *Evergreen, evergreen.* The only job we had here was to clean up Nana's house to sell it—we could go home, after that.

But until then we were stuck here, squatters in a haunted place, hosts to a hundred well-wishing islanders and their food.

Marella was not in the least bit happy about any of it. At first, she refused to come downstairs and it appeared that my dad and I would have to make excuses for her, but eventually she recognized that her mother's memorial party was not an effective time for a pout, so she combed her hair, put on a black dress, and came down Nana's staircase and waded into the party.

People turned to stare at her. They always did. With her waist-length black hair and tiny nose and ever-mournful eyes, my mother is the sort of beauty who people stop in shops and ask if they can photograph.

While Dad was nodding in conversation with a dozen somber strangers, I walked over to join my mother. Then I noticed a silvery-haired woman who was threading her way toward us like a spinner dolphin.

This woman was small-framed and dressed in a shift that looked homemade, with silver bangles snaking up her tiny arms. She had long hair, almost as long as my mother's, and she came right up to where my mother and I stood.

"Beautiful Marella," the silvery-haired woman said, clearly enunciating her words as if they were foreign to her. "Now you've buried both a son and a mother. But at least you still have a girl."

My mother snapped her neck upward like an eel. This woman had punctured her sac of secrets, had brought death into death, the stale death of the very young into the fresh death of the very old—this woman had spilled seeds that I somehow knew would sprout.

Before my mother could speak, the woman spoke again. "But with death comes new life. Maybe newer than you think."

Marella stared. "Ilya," she said viciously. "You were not invited."

But it was too late. I knew, I knew, *I knew*. I knew that other people besides Nana knew about Adam, knew the secret underpinnings of my mother's past and present grief. I knew, somehow, that I could find my anchor with this woman, that I would no longer be adrift among my family's secrets. I had a wild instinctive feeling that if I found the right questions to ask, this woman Ilya would tell me.

Ilya smiled and retreated, the funeral party roared on, I bobbed from well-wisher to well-wisher, having my hands held and condolences whispered at me. My dad, as he occasionally did, got drunk, which brought out his opinions, and my parents got into a loud and public argument that started with my mother saying, "I know what you are going to say. If I never hear it again it will be too soon. How this island is uncivilized, full of these *savage* rituals, so *deathly*...being as you are such a good well-*behaved* animal who buries his ancestors in *reasonable* dirt..."

I excused myself from the conversation I had been having and hurried over to them. They were standing next to the boat-sized dining table. If I hadn't anticipated a blowup, it might have been interesting to hear Marella half-defend this island. It seemed to be like family to her—she could complain about Dragon Island all she wanted but could not bear to hear anyone else complain.

Beyond them, small lizards scrambled up and down the backyard screen. *Keep busy, lizards. No need for this kind of talk.*

My dad was scratching his beard as he does when my mother makes him nervous. "But surely you don't think littering the ocean with human bodies is a good idea. And not having a place to honor her memory. Think of Sage. Where will she go to remember...?"

"She'll go where all of her ancestors have gone," my mother said in her haughty voice, her posture straight as a queen's and her frantic hands full of her hair. "She'll go to the ocean."

My father took a breath. "Right. And you've certainly set her a good example for going near the ocean."

My mother slapped my father. Right there on the face, while all the guests watched.

Humiliated, I stood between them. "Don't do this here. Come on. Come *on*."

But neither of my parents cared what the world saw or thought. And on Dragon Island, it seemed that people didn't care much, either. The guests shrugged and went back to their conversations and their beer. Nobody ran to either of my parents' sides, the way people would have done on our home island, where social conventions mattered and you could get your child taken away for hitting a spouse in public.

As I walked away through the film of people, I caught sight of Ilya with the silvery hair. She was watching me intensely. It made me uncomfortable but I looked back in case she was trying to tell me something. Then my mother grabbed my arm and said, "Let's go," and I kept looking back at Ilya while following my mother upstairs. Marella held my arm while we ascended and then as soon as we were out of sight, she let go and vanished without a word into Nana's bedroom.

The guests continued on—I could hear them for hours. The

house smelled of Nana, and it felt sad and crowded and empty all at once. Upstairs in one of the guest bedrooms, my thoughts calcified into a plan, as certain as a wishbone: I would find this woman Ilya and ask her questions about my mother.

3

Ilya

All right, Girl, here is the story I want you to hear. It is as real as the wood on this deck.

My story, like yours, is a story that only a daughter could tell. You think I am distant and old, but in truth I am just like you.

My family is native to this island. One of my ancestors gave Dragon Island its name. From where we sit, we can see why. See the black head and shoulders rising from the ocean? The green hips, the trees that bristle like spikes on the tail? My mother's lineage has lived and died here since before the first flood. You can find all of my ancestors' names and birthdates in the record books at Town Hall. Except my name and my son's. Soon you will see why.

My father died of the island flu when I was six and as a consequence my mother was as lonely as a woman can be. There was a heavy sadness about her, and she did not like raising children. She opened her legs to many men who came asking, and each time my sisters and I were left to sleep outside, to see if this effort at happiness would catch. Always the next day she screamed my father's name out to the ocean, frightening the other children. People in our village called her the howling woman. Some claimed she caused the great tsunami that nearly drowned the whole island. But she was not a witch and that could not be true. Many said she stole women's husbands after nightfall. I would not argue against that charge.

I think she is why I turned out the way I did, not needing men at all.

When you live here a long time, you hear stories. And if you are curious, as I was at your age, you scratch at those stories to see what is true. I learned from somebody who learned from somebody else that in the rocks underneath a certain point of ocean, there is an entrance to the Underworld—*Take that look off your face, Girl.* Believe me, I am telling you the truth. There is no reason why a person would make this story up.

As you know, it is nearly impossible for a girl to grow up with a grieving mother and not wish to rescue her. I decided that in order to bring peace to my mother, I would go to the Underworld and bring back my father's ghost. It was said that such things could be done. Why not by me? I would fix everything.

I began to read widely—anything I could that dealt with mythology and the dead. I knew most of it was fiction, but still I scratched at it in order to find some fact that I could use. And then something happened that I never could have expected: I got pregnant. I was fourteen. The boy was an island boy. Nobody had ever talked with me about contraception. When I had my first monthly bleed, I thought I had cut myself on a shell. When the bleeds stopped and the nausea started, I thought I was sick, until an aunt noticed and explained.

I was in trouble then. What could I do with the baby? It did not seem possible to take an infant on such a journey. But my mother was suffering, my sisters were suffering as a consequence, and I had to do something. So I fought through the first three months' nausea and kept on with my preparations. I hid the pregnancy from my mother for as long as I could.

Do not think, Girl, that I faulted my mother. She had three daughters and that was too many for her. I knew that when it was my turn I would want to have as many children as I could, six, eight, and that number would still not be enough. We are always different from our mothers. I had thought I would name my baby, boy or girl, Ola. For it means life. My plan was to name all the others that followed "Life" in all the languages I could learn. But when the baby was born at the hospital in Middle, I came out of anesthesia and learned I could have no more children. So I thought of a better name for my first and only son: Adam. I had read all the origin myths from the west and it felt fitting, as he was the only man I could make.

I held Adam in my arms and read over his head, constantly. I don't know how I thrived so well on so little sleep. I suppose that is the prerogative of the teenage mother. She has a strong supply of energy and can focus it anywhere she wants. And I only had two points of focus in my life then: take care of my son and take care of my mother. I told no one of my plans—if I vanished into the Underworld, at least I had tried.

I learned in my reading that the dead are eternally thirsty, so I packed a bottle of wine, stolen. I also learned that the dead have blue nails: a cobalt blue. It is a very beautiful color. Their fingernails and toenails are where all of their blood goes when they die. It's how they recognize each other as dead.

I learned too that the spirits would be likelier to let me return home if I had a baby with me. The dead respect babies. They don't like to see them unaccompanied.

I knew from swimming with him that my baby instinctively held his breath when I put him in the water. One of many ways infants are built to endure. This reflex would be necessary for our swim beneath the rocks. We would need to go soon.

I practiced holding my breath.

I had no money, so I traded my body for one night to a cloth-worker so that he would make me a sturdy sling from hemp fiber, waxed with linseed oil, so Adam could ride on my back. *Don't look shocked, Girl.* I had been sullied once. What was one more time?

My final job was to paint Adam's tiny fingernails and toenails—as well as my own—blue. In those days, things like nail polish could not be found on Dragon Island; there were no drug stores, only medicine women. You think one generation can't change everything? I went to the general store, where I found a suitable shade of blue furniture paint and slipped the bottle inside my dress.

At home, my mother saw me sitting on the bathroom counter, varnishing my nails while Adam slept on my back in his sling.

"Vain girl," my mother said. "When I was your age, I didn't have time for such vanities. I was busy helping my mother."

And she left it at that. So did I.

4

Charon

My name is Charon and I am a boat woman. I row souls across the river between life and death. I live in the upturned C of my boat and name: a sliver moon, a curved spine, a partially aborted O.

Souls offer me coins.

I have so many coins.

5

Sage

AUGUST — SEPTEMBER

"So are we selling this house or what?" I blurted to my father over breakfast, a week after the ocean burial. He was hunched over the table reading a complicated-looking chart about the tides.

He looked up absently, scratched his beard, looked at my mother. "Marella?"

With us as tenants, Nana's house was falling into disarray. The rose bush next to her front door crisped into a spindly sculpture of dead brown petals and fierce thorns like tiny flames. It had a deathly glamour to it. Water-rings appeared on the wooden furniture, for my mother never used coasters. One of the wall-ladders broke when my dad was trying to study how it was built, but he got busy with other things and forgot to repair it. And our life atrophied, too. Laundry only happened when I did it. We stopped eating vegetables and ate only fish, the single thing my father knew how to prepare. And instead of a sparkling load of fresh dishes to unload each morning, as we had when Nana lived with us, we scrubbed our own plates and forks before meals. For that first week, I tried to clean up after us all, under the illusion that we were working together to prepare Nana's house for sale. But it wasn't working. My parents' apathy was contagious.

My mother sat curled onto the purple chair, her eyes half-closed, an unread book of poems on her lap. "Who would want this absurd house? We can't sell it. There's too much work to do."

"But I thought you didn't want to stay here any longer," I said to her. "I thought you hated it here."

She shrugged. "What we hate doesn't matter."

My dad frowned. Making decisions was not his forte. "Either of you have a reason to go back home just yet?"

Nobody spoke, because everybody knew the answer. I had no job and no school. High school had ended just four months earlier; college fall semester was starting this week, but not for me. That ship, for now, had sailed. There was work here that needed to be done, and a mystery that needed solving. If I were living another life, if I were somebody else's daughter, I would have gone looking for an apartment of my own. But fishing season was about to start, and I was Nana's girl, a second-generation caretaker, and somebody needed to take care of my mother.

My dad made a few calls. One of our more industrious neighbors from home cleaned out our apartment, put our stuff in a storage unit, and had the apartment rented by the next day.

"That was easy," Dad said. "Stay here a spell, see what we can make of it."

That night I had trouble getting to sleep. Each time I closed my eyes, I pictured earthquakes on the sea floor, the uneasy knowing that even though life looks smooth on top, deep down it is quaking. I stayed awake long after midnight, listening to the ocean, caught up in the unanswerable questions that stay buried when everybody stays alive. We were heathens. No one in my family believed in an afterlife, but still this whole messy business prompted me to wonder what else there could be. I spent hours wondering where Nana was, where my brother Adam was (was he my big brother or my baby brother? Both? Either way he was my dead brother) and wondering if they were somehow together or if ghosts of different ages go to separate places.

I awoke with a tired face and an achy jaw and a fear of the long empty day ahead, a day when my dad would go to the fish market and my mother would sit despondently in the purple armchair with its back to the ocean, half reading, half making lists on a series of yellow sticky notes that then would migrate all over Nana's house. She had done this sort of thing at home, but here in the glare of the ocean and her past, her note-taking, it seemed, had grown malignant and metastasized.

When I went into the kitchen to make some attempt at breakfast, these slips of paper poked out like neon islands over the dark cabinet wood, each one scratched over with my mother's handwritten codes to herself: "Brother – Mortalis – Dream?" or "Bargain – River – Reincarnation." It was as if a paper volcano had erupted in Nana's kitchen. And in the midst of all the paper sat my mother, stoic and sad, looking like a figure made from origami.

I knew this place would drive me crazy if I let it. I unpacked my suitcase into Nana's wooden drawers, made my mother toast and wrapped her a sandwich for lunch, and left the house for a long walk around Dragon Island. If this was to be my home for the fall and spring, I might as well get to know it.

I walked at first around the bay, beneath the jagged green mountains that rose up into the low bright lavendering clouds.

I curved along the shoreline, walking past the endless blues and greens. I walked up into the hills past the empty mansions with "For Lease" signs in front, where the tourists lived during the summers—I knew about the uphill tourists from hearing Nana talk about them, those outsiders who liked to visit and stay far up from the ocean where you could see the water but not touch it. I walked past strange trees with pinkish bark and warty trunks, trees filled with wild cats with matted furs who climbed up and hid in the branches, their suspicious eyes shimmering like water. It seemed anywhere you went on this island you could still see the ocean, even in the eyes of cats.

I walked down into the island flats past the smaller houses where the native Dragon Islanders lived with their backyard piers and their messy, gardened, practical yards. From the neighborhoods I walked toward downtown, where the supermarket was, along with a few schools and the floating fish market where the day before my father had rented a stall to sell tuna and marlin. I walked past a bookstore called The Page-Turner, past the acid-pink souvenir shop that sold cheap coral necklaces and t-shirts with jagged red-rimmed holes in the side to look like shark bites. Past the florist with wild purple orchids bursting out of the doorway, past the surf shop that was open all year, "even Christmas," it said on the door. Past a diner called "Spam-a-Lot" that sold potted meat cooked eleven different ways. It had a sign that said, "Hiring."

I knew if I kept on walking past our little downtown and into Middle, the next town over, there would be the hospital, where I hoped never to go again. There would also be the community college and the movie theater, the mall and several dour office buildings where the people worked who didn't make their living off the sea.

Thinking of Middle made me feel guilty, for why had Nana spent her final years raising me, if not so that I would have the freedom to get an education, to have a non-sea job? Eventually I would have to sign up for some classes at the community college. I would need a job, too. Not at Spam-a-Lot. Somewhere. My mom had never done these things—her college was interrupted, she always said, by having me. She had never, to my knowledge, worked. And I knew how much energy it took to support a person who wouldn't help herself.

Not ready to walk home, and feeling like an island vagabond, I decided to make a stop at the floating fish market, a ramshackle operation built onto what looked like an industrial Styrofoam floor that bobbed and rolled with the waves. The market had a dozen stalls, like at a fairground, though each stall had a wooden front counter that was part of the dock, and everything smelled of dead fish. When I approached, my dad was deep in talk with the other fishermen who were all firing ideas at him for a temporary business partner. *Try Lance,* the crab guy said, and all of the other fisherman nodded, *yes, Lance, Lance*. And I shrugged next to my father, having no idea who Lance was. The fishermen then began talking about a boat accident that must've just happened; somebody they called "Maroon" capsized in shark waters and survived. They retold the coordinates of the story several times, each fisherman filling in the blanks he knew, and in between facts it seemed they were speaking a slang of the island, peppered with the phrase, "Good luck, thank her."

I left after a few minutes. I could feel in the other fishermen's stares how unnecessary both my father and I were, how inconvenient. However far I tried to walk to escape it, I had no purpose on this island and never would.

At twilight I finished my walk. From outside Nana's house as the sky darkened, you could see my mother's silhouette in the bright living room window, her hair twisted into a heavy bun, her chin bowed toward some book she was not really reading, her tea long cold beside her. Even if you did not know her as I did, you could sense that she was a hurting, angry, childlike, motherless mother.

"How was your day?" I asked her as I took off my shoes by the backdoor, trying not to track in sand. She looked up dubiously, smelling a rat in the false brightness of my voice. She did not ask me how my day had been, and I did not press on hers. Instead she folded up her book and walked up the staircase to bed. Soon my father would join her. One benefit of living in a huge house was that I could not so easily hear his snoring.

It was obvious she hadn't left the house. I could see the dishes in the sink—she had eaten my meals. I promised myself another walk tomorrow, and then by October, a job. This felt doable. It would work.

It was only a few days later, near the first of September, that I decided to walk to Sliver Moon Park, a grassy crescent built on top of a wall of rocks leading down to the ocean at Dragon Island's northernmost tip. Below the wall of rocks, beautiful boys my age surf. On the park above, parents fly kites with their children, crowded families eat picnic dinners, and musicians with ukuleles are always singing island songs. Here, adolescence and childhood seem like magical places.

And I saw a dark-haired boy who interested me. He was standing near a railing separating the park from the ocean while he stretched, as if preparing for some athletic feat. He curled his body into a ball, then unfurled it as if he were saluting the sea. He was tall and slender, and when he breathed deeply his chest puffed out like a blowfish. He then perched up on the railing, and all of a sudden he turned around and smiled at me just before his feet left the edge and his body flung upward like a fishing hook and then slipped without a splash into the green-black water.

I panicked at seeing this boy go under; my mind felt salt-washed. I had sudden visions of my own body falling into the deep dark sea where bus-sized mammals swim and the bottom is untouchable. I felt myself losing air just thinking about it.

I didn't know I was holding my breath until I passed out on the concrete slab in the park and woke to find the boy standing over me, his broad shoulders blocking the sun. His hair fell around his face, but I could see that he had the dark complexion and small features of a born-and-bred Dragon Islander. His dark eyes blinked, wide and solicitous. He had a bright, lopsided smile. My first oxygenless thought was that my brother might've had such a face if he had lived.

"Can you open your hand?" he asked, his voice echoing as if from far off. My hand uncurled. Into it he placed a small sea snail. "For you."

I took the snail, not quite sure what to do with it. It had a solid, pearly black shell from which the thick muscle of the snail's body was starting to poke out, like a tongue.

He then asked if I was okay and gave me a sip from his water bottle. He told me that newcomers faint often, probably it is the sun, or the salt, and in any case he would walk me home. Then he said that his name was Pupuka. "It's Hawaiian," he said. "My parents met in college there before I was born."

I asked what it meant.

"Ugly," he answered. "It's not my real name. It's just the name my parents called me as a baby so the spirits wouldn't steal me."

I blinked back at him. He was not ugly.

I asked his real name.

"I can't tell you," Pupuka said, smiling with bright drops of water around his eyes. "You might be a spirit."

Then he offered me his pocket to keep my snail in until I could put it in a terrarium, which he must've assumed I owned. He looked at me carefully and I felt like I was being scrutinized by a biologist. I suspected he was wondering why I fainted, whether I was weak in constitution or just ocean-frightened or else some sort of dumbbell who forgot to breathe. I began asking him prophylactic questions so that he would not yet ask about me.

He told me that Dragon Island formed after an ancient volcano exploded and crumbled over millennia into the sea, forming a coral reef around the volcano's footprint, and gradually the center filled in. Then he told me about his younger twin brothers and his parents who together had started the local radio station. I learned that he studied snails and slugs and mollusks and wished to be a malacologist once he could go to college, after he saved enough money from tending the aquarium animals in Dragon Island's elementary school. Until he told me this, I did not know that there was such a thing as malacology.

"I've been calling schools on different islands and introducing myself. None of the programs can offer me scholarships. That's why I'm living at home and saving my money. All my friends went on to college."

"So did mine," I told him.

He looked at me curiously.

There was a silence.

Then Pupuka embarked on a new story about Dragon Island: about the Great Whale Shark who chased around a young fisherman for a decade until the fisherman made a vow to stop fishing. And a drought that lasted a full year, and then the year it rained every afternoon at 2:12. He told me that his cousin's head grew into a bucket—"just the shape of it can hold water!" And another cousin got chased by the Great Whale

Shark...but that was because he brought a banana on a boat.

Each time Pupuka arrived at an exciting part of a story, he picked up my hand and squeezed it, as if the story's full significance could not enter me through my ears alone.

Only one of his stories did I recognize, and it's a story you can't take one step on Dragon Island without hearing some reference to. It was the one and only Dragon Island story that Nana told me when I was a child—usually myths were my mother's realm, if they were anyone's at all—and when my mother found out that I knew it, she went into a rage. Marella said it was just like the backward Islanders to believe such things and to perpetuate them through stories told to children, though afterward Nana whispered grimly: *It is a terrible story, and your mother has every right to hate it, but only through this story will you know Dragon Island.*

The story tells of the Shrieking Lady, a beautiful young Dragon Island woman who married an intriguing foreigner—a "Maroon," as Pupuka called him. "Means outsider. It's not a bad thing," he added delicately. "It just means that a person got marooned here, you know, like abandoned by a boat."

"Anyway," he continued after interrupting himself, "she got angry with her husband for something, and to punish him she drowned their only son. Just hiked up the mountain, stood on the edge of the rocks at Lizard Head Point, dropped the kid in the ocean and went home. Of course she regretted it and threw herself in after him. Later that same evening, Dragon Island had its first and only tsunami of the century and it wiped the whole island out, tearing down the fancy hotels and fisherman's piers. People survived on rafts and in their boats, and not a single person drowned. This became proof that our island is both enchanted and haunted."

"I know this story," I said when Pupuka finished. "Don't they attribute the fact that all the islanders survived to the

Shrieking Lady, for she gave up both herself and her son?"

He dropped my hand in excitement.

"You know it!" Pupuka said, smiling widely and then picking up my hand again. "Means you are less of a Maroon than you think. Have you ever heard anyone say, 'no rain today, thank her?'"

"No."

"You will," he said simply. "That's who they're talking about."

He went on to tell me how people see her ghost all around town: at the beach in the early morning, at the clubhouse after hours, loitering in the alleyway behind a store called Ilya's Herbs.

Pupuka then asked, "What do you think of all this, Sage?"

I think superstition is a boat you build when you spend too much time around water.

But instead I asked if he would take me to Ilya's Herbs.

"Of course," Pupuka said, squeezing my hand. His hand felt warm and comforting, and I could not tell whether he meant it romantically or just as if he were somebody's brother. And he kept on talking while we walked downtown.

We lived several months together in the hour that followed. I learned that banana slugs have genitals near their heads and that when they mate, they sit in a yellow yin-yang for hours.

"It's beautiful," Pupuka said. "Can you imagine if we mated that way?"

I said nothing at first, wondering how to appropriately respond. Then I realized from the neutrality of his face that by "we" he meant humans in general, not specifically the two of us.

"No," I said at last. "I can't imagine having genitals on my head."

He laughed and then asked, "Do you want to keep talking about this or have you heard enough about slugs?"

I liked his directness. I found him intriguing too, even a

little bizarre, because of all the magic he seemed to believe. I said I was happy to talk about anything.

"Okay, then," he said. "Your turn. I didn't want to ask right off, because Maroons—sorry—don't always like to talk as much as we do, but why are you here?"

I told him briefly about Nana's death and our move. Then in an extreme act of logorrhea, the story of Adam rushed out of me. I was shocked to hear it come out of my mouth. I didn't know anything yet, so it wasn't yet my story to tell.

Pupuka listened but did not say anything in response. I suppose living on this island, he had heard enough stories about children drowning. He squeezed my hand, and simply said, "How sad."

I let the story sink from our conversation and asked him to tell me more about snails.

We kept walking toward the tourist-blotted crossroads of shaved ice stands staffed by high school girls in bikini tops and cut-offs, pretty girls with Pupuka's coloring who chewed gum and wore silver bangle bracelets. We passed the bookstore, a short block of restaurants. We passed the places I knew.

"This is the front part of town," Pupuka told me. "Now we'll go into the back part." Still holding hands, we ducked into an alleyway. It felt at first like the color had been shut off. The streets were unpaved, and gray concrete walls went on for many blocks behind the bright downtown façade. Suddenly the color all came back, brighter. The Dragon Island artists had certainly discovered this alleyway, for graffiti bathed the walls. Among the spray-painted flowers and fish there was a giant purple squid that spanned an entire two stories and about half a city block. Its eyes were red, white, and blue Pepsi signs, and its tentacles disappeared above and below the building as if it might uproot it at any time. A sprayed-on tag above the squid said, "Squid Ink Alley."

We walked in silence. The occasional windows were mostly broken, and different rancid smells wafted out from the back-ends of restaurants. At the far end of the branching alleyway, shops started again, but these storefronts were shabby and it was evident that they were the underbelly stores, the places where Dragon Islanders visited but uphill tourists did not know: the daycare, the pet groomer, the Lubbock Twins Accounting Services, and Ilya's Herbs.

"Here we are," said Pupuka.

I peered through the dusty front window and could see all sorts of witchy things, powders and crystals and herbs and books with moons and green-robed long-haired wild women floating around the covers. On the store window was a handwritten note that said, "Open mornings and by appointment."

"I've never seen that store open," Pupuka said, and I felt severely disappointed. It had to be the same Ilya. And she would be the type of woman to run a magic store that would sell both answers and questions. Then Pupuka went on: "I've heard that the owner had to close the store because she got caught selling abortion herbs."

The word *abortion* shimmered in the air between us and disappeared. It was not a polite word, I had been taught, or a word for use in casual conversation. It was surprising to hear a boy say it as just another neutral fact.

"I think Ilya knows about my brother Adam," I said. I knocked on the store's window.

Pupuka let go of my hand and looked closely at me. I noticed he had tiny freckles on his nose. "How do you think she will be able to help you?"

And then before I could answer, the door to Ilya's Herbs cracked open and a man with the face of a baby stuck his head out.

"Do you want to come in?" he asked. I could tell by his voice that something had happened to his brain.

"Yes," I said immediately, and Pupuka followed me in.

The man closed the door behind us. He pointed in the direction of the merchandise. His thick bush of dark hair was trimmed in a child's bowl cut. He walked as a toddler walks, jerkily and on his tiptoes. But his shoulders sagged and his eyes looked ancient and tired.

Inside we found baskets of quartz crystals with the dirt still clinging to them, bunches of dried herbs, and a small pail of finger-sized witch dolls made out of cloth and magnets and cinnamon sticks, with a label that read, *Un-curse your refrigerator!* Next to the witch dolls sat a blue bucket of almond-sized rubber babies and a sign that read, "Drown for good weather." Pupuka pointed to it and mouthed "Shrieking Lady," and mimicked throwing one. I did not respond; I did not see how this could ever possibly be seen as funny or something to sell. At the back of the store a spiral staircase vanished up through the ceiling, and underneath it was a nook with a black curtain and a sign that said, *For spells and prayers.* A wall-sized bookcase held a thousand brown bottles with various substances inside. A skylight brought in some sky, but it had grown so dusty that the blue light took on a gray hue.

The man with the face of a baby had a vacant and secretive smile, as if he were seeing something that the rest of us could not see. "I am Adam," he said. "Who are you?"

The name startled me and I jerked my head up to look at him again. Pupuka began to introduce himself but this man named Adam looked straight at me.

"You look—" He appeared to be searching for something. I could see him struggle as he scratched the air for the right words. He tried again. "I know you. We used to be—known. You and I." He kept smiling at me as if he wanted me to understand.

"Is Ilya here today?" Pupuka asked.

"Mom is in the houseboat, waiting for the women," Adam answered enigmatically. Then he bowed his head. "Good day," he said, and I knew he was ready for us to leave.

"Why do you think he recognized you?" Pupuka asked as we left the store.

I said I had no idea.

Pupuka frowned. He was working something out, appraising this encounter as if it were a many-faceted gem, or a new breed of snail. After a few moments, he shrugged and turned to a different topic. "People say he had an accident when he was a student at Dragon Island High. He was this brilliant guy, bound for an exceptional future, but then something happened. Apparently, the Shrieking Lady didn't work for him."

I told him that I'd had enough Shrieking Lady stories for now.

"Okay," he said. Then he took up my hand again and led me on.

My mind was churning to connect these fragments: this person named Adam who seemed to know me, this Adam being Ilya's son. Adam's drowning, Ilya's abortion herbs. Ilya knowing my mother. My brother being named Adam. Nana knowing these secrets but not telling me until her last moments alive.

Pupuka and I sat on a park bench next to a dingy fenced-in daycare, where dozens of Islander children monkeyed up and down a pair of slides and a jungle gym. One of them, a little spiky-haired girl, stood at the chain fence and stuck out her tongue at Pupuka, who laughed and stuck out his tongue back.

"Well, where else do you want to go?" Pupuka asked as we stood, stretching our legs.

I shot my last question into the air, promising myself that after this, I would put aside my chase and try to act like a normal person. "Do you know where Ilya lives?"

"Sure," he said.

He began walking us toward the ocean, all the while

explaining to me that in the Dragon Island dialect, there are not cardinal directions, only "toward-town" and "toward-water."

We turned a few side-streets, crossed what Dragon Islanders call "the highway," even though it has only two lanes, and stopped. The house we faced tilted against the edge of the rocky shoreline like a boat.

"Here," Pupuka said.

I paused to get a good look. The house was a stacked-up series of wooden planks and roofing bits and windows askew, all with colored glass like a green and blue church window. The water splashed up behind it. The wooden steps leading up to the house were crooked. It had a chimney that looked crooked too. The whole house teetered.

"All right," Pupuka said. He looked closely at me and squeezed my hand. "Where now?"

It was my turn to lead. I took him to the only other place I knew: The Floating Harbor Fish Market at the east end of Dragon Bay.

Entering the fish market felt like getting onto a boat. I walked Pupuka past the stall-fronts that rooted the floating market to land. Islanders swayed like fronds around the market, inspecting the day's catch and paying for fish with mora, the heavy copper Dragon Island coins. In Blue Island, we didn't use mora; we copied North America and had our own inflated dollar. Seeing all the swaying made me a little seasick, but I could tell it was nothing to Pupuka.

I saw the Big Mouth Fishing Company banner at a stall between the crab guy and the shark guy. My dad was the only hairy bearded man among a dozen smooth-faced Islanders, except for a blond guy standing next to him.

"Hey there, Seabird!" Dad called, unfolding from his seat behind the counter, wiping his slimy hands on his overalls and sweeping me into a hug. His beard smelled metallic and his sleeves were streaked with fish blood. He leaned back and lifted me, and my feet left the undulating floor.

"Good morning, sunshine!" said the blond guy, who stood watching us in cowboy stance with his arms crossed and his legs planted wide.

"Morning is over, and who are you calling sunshine?" my dad responded, easing me down to make introductions. "Sage, this is Lance, who will be helping me with the business during fishing season. Lance, my daughter Sage."

Lance was younger than my father, tall, tanned, and built like a surfer, with light eyes and fine hair so pale it gleamed white in the sun. He was good looking in a way that was almost unreal, nearly scary. If his face could be molded in plastic, without question he'd revolutionize the toy industry. While Pupuka looked like a demigod of the ocean, my father's new fishing partner looked like a full-fledged god of the sun.

"This is Pupuka," I told my dad.

"Oh, good," said Dad.

"Ugly?" asked Lance.

"Correct!" said Pupuka.

They all began talking very fast about fishing and water and boats. When their conversation lulled I asked Lance politely how he was surviving working with my dad.

My dad answered for him. "Are you kidding? Lance loves it! He's opted out of marriage and darling kids like you." He rumpled my hair. "I'd bet the market he'll make our company grow. Equally at home on land and on a boat."

My first thought was that if Lance were equally comfortable on land and sea, he'd be one step more versatile than my dad, who even with so darling a kid, vastly preferred boats. I wasn't sure how to respond without sounding snarky, so I just smiled. Lance smiled back.

Then he said, "Your dad heads off this weekend to the Northern Pacific, nearly up to the Bering Strait. Six months gone." Lance whistled. "There'll be lots of halibut. It'll feed you and your mom and half this island all summer. I'll watch the market shop, selling the fish he froze last season. Stop by if you like, set a few lobsters free, you know, make some trouble."

"I will," I said. Then, feeling a little mischievous, I added: "It'll be a nice break from Marella. She's hardly taken off her pajamas since July." It was not a kind thing to say and I wasn't quite sure why I said it.

My dad waved a prickly tuna spine between us. "Seabird, go easy on your mom. You are a great source of strength to her. You might not see it now, but she depends on you. Remember, she's a shell-woman, she processes all that stuff inside. You're like me—we both wear it all on the outside, and that makes everything easier."

Pupuka looked back and forth between us, and I was imagining what my dad's "you-are-this, she-is-that" distinctions sounded like to him.

My father beheaded a swordfish and continued: "Oh, and Lance."

"Yessir?"

"You can help Sage while I'm gone. Do your best to keep Marella company." Then he turned and began whooping at the crab-man, telling him to back off his sales pitches so he himself might sell some tuna.

Pupuka was excited as we left. "I like your father," he said several times, in a very serious voice. "Now I want to meet your mother."

"My mother is...different," I told him. But we had gotten this far already. And so we walked down the seaside road, past Sliver Moon Park, toward Nana's house at the base of the hills. We passed the humble island flats. Pupuka said that this was his neighborhood and gestured toward a flat-roofed blue house with a cracking concrete patio and a yard full of plastic flamingos. Above a picnic table spread an umbrella with a plump cat sleeping warily on top of it, one eye open toward passersby.

"So your mother grew up here," Pupuka was saying, propelling us forward. "Does she like being home or is it strange for her?"

"Well..." I began. We were walking straight in the direction of Nana's house, and I was contemplating next steps. In her current state there was no way I would invite Pupuka inside to meet my mother, but I didn't want our conversation to end. I compromised by inviting him to sit out on the backyard pier. We sat on the edge, our legs dangling a few feet above the water.

Mostly Pupuka talked. While we sat, Dad and Lance came home in Dad's gray beater of a van that read "Big Mouth for YOUR Mouth!" on the side, surrounded by loopy fish-scales, with yellow fish eyes painted around the headlights. He had driven that van all my life, so it was no surprise that he had it shipped as soon as it was clear we would stay. The men nodded at us and stood by the edge of the water, talking what looked like business. It was a still, idle moment, the four of us lingering on the beach at sunset. But then I heard a fierce shrill cry gathering up in the air behind me.

It was Marella, her hair wild around her face, her bathrobe still on but gaping open, as she charged toward us.

Even as the moment was happening, the image of my howling mother curled into burnt edges—it was so ugly, so inhuman, that I almost could not look at it straight, and I primitively did not want to remember it. Marella raised her hands as if to tear us apart, unfurling her fury to where we sat so innocuously on the pier. She hovered above us and yelled too close to our faces, "Who are you and what are you doing here on this pier where people drown! Bird, you idiot, who is he?" She kicked in the direction of Pupuka as if he were a dog.

I scurried up and stood between them, but Pupuka took my hand, looking preternaturally calm. He stood still and looked at me gravely and asked, "Are you okay?"

I said, "It's fine, go home, it's just my mother, I'll handle her."

But he would not go. She kicked at him once more, barely missing his shin. Her bathrobe was falling off her shoulders so that she looked not only crazy but nearly naked. Still Pupuka would not move, nor would he acknowledge my mother. He just kept on looking at me with deep concern, as if she could kick him all day if she wanted, but he would not leave me there. Finally I yelled at him, "GO!" and at last Pupuka jumped off the pier and into the water, landing as neatly as a drop of rain plinking back to its puddle.

I faced my mother, who was trembling, looking monstrous and terrified and flushed. "Marella!" I said, trying to keep my voice level. "Marella! Calm. Down."

But she would not hear me and she raged on, shrieking at me, *You idiot!* and yelling at Pupuka, *I hope you drown!*

Pupuka was underwater and couldn't hear, and at that moment I hated her. With everything in me I hated the fact that she only had two modes, grief and fury. I hated her inability to control her inner dragon.

Now my father was lumbering over while Lance looked on. Even with my dad's best intentions, he was too slow, leaving my mother's women—Nana, me—to be her handlers when she went beast. My father took my mother's arm, said something in a whisper to her, and she collapsed sobbing on the pier, while the dot in the ocean that was Pupuka grew smaller and smaller.

Lance vanished from the scene and my father scooped up Marella and carried her into the house. I followed while he put her into bed with a cup of chamomile-hibiscus tea, whiskey-shot-through. The island remedy, Nana used to say.

When my dad came back downstairs I tried to speak but couldn't. I searched inside for my voice and found it, miniscule and weak, under a moon-shell in the corner of my mind. "Dad," I whispered. "What happened to her?"

"Seabird," he began. My father looked lost. I felt a swell of disdain for him, at how long it had been since he had called me by my real name, but I dammed it up—he was my only ally in our dwindled blood-pool of relations. "Did Pupuka get home safely?" my dad asked, stalling.

"How would I know?" I retorted in my coldest voice.

We sat next to each other on the tall stools in Nana's kitchen, sitting in silence like comrades after a skirmish. I broke the calm meniscus of our silence. "Dad, you can't just leave without answering. What makes her just go crazy like that?"

Dad looked at his hands. "It isn't something she can control like turning on and off a switch. Seeing you out there, so close to the water, on a pier that holds for her terrible memories, set something off. You didn't do anything wrong and she knows that. But still it touched a broken thing inside her that she is trying to fix."

I thought of my mother upstairs in bed, whiskey-drunk and tea-warmed and probably asleep. Why was I hearing this sallow explanation from my dad instead of from my mother herself? And why did my dad have to smooth things over without addressing the roiling beneath—to pick her up and carry her off the pier and make her tea and catch her fish that she did not eat and buffer her from the world, keeping the conversation mild and far away from water?

"Seabird," he said to me. "Your mother didn't want to come back here."

"None of us did."

"Sure. But you and I can handle it."

I thought of Marella sitting in the purple chair, her back

always to the ocean—so delicate, so afraid of so many things. All the years my father had lived on and near boats, my mother had kept her back to the waves, hiding inside while my father and I roughhoused in the shallow water. It was hard to believe Marella could be anybody's mother. She was nobody's line of protection. She was fragile china, a magnolia blossom that fingertips would surely ruin, pages inside a book so frail that nobody dare touch it. She had needed Nana for protection. Needed me, needed my dad. Afraid of water. Afraid of everything, always.

My dad, thinking he was off the hook, flipped idly through a fishing industry magazine that was several years expired. "Seabird," he said, "it's hard for your mom to be here. There are certain things that are impossible for her to forget."

"Like what?" I asked, hopeful that I might gain some new information. "Adam?"

"Things she'll tell you when she's ready. It's all the past. It doesn't matter anymore. You know, Seabird, how your mom's a shell woman. She keeps things inside longer than most people do. And she's spent her whole adulthood avoiding being near water, and now here she is, right back at its edge. Can you see how fear could make a person lose their mind a little?"

I begrudged him and said that I could. Then he reminded me that he needed to pack. "Surely you and your mom will go back to being old pals without me around."

Old pals? At times my father's clueless optimism reached oceanic proportions. Yet my dread of having him gone felt stronger than my desire to argue.

I simply nodded and said I was tired. I creaked across Nana's floor to my bedroom beneath the grand staircase. Of all of the things upsetting me, one was how much I had liked Pupuka. I was not looking forward to facing him after what he had seen of my mother, and it irritated me to think how other girls' mothers didn't erupt right in the middle of their lives—but a single thought cheered me, and it was a thought about my brother: I knew that even if I never saw Pupuka again, at least he had told me how to find Ilya.

But the night was not over yet. Just before I went to bed, I stepped out on the back porch to have one more look at the ocean, so surprising in its nearness, and I found two banana slugs on a leaf.

Their beauty startled me and made me laugh. Their yellow hue had a touch of black-brown brindling and their muscles were longer than my thumb. They gleamed in the moonlight. They curled up against each other, slimily nestled in their corner near the hibiscus. I touched them and their slime stayed on my hands for the rest of the night, no matter how hard I scrubbed.

"Those aren't native," said my dad. "They must have escaped from some kid's terrarium."

But I knew better. I knew they were a gift. I knew that with these slugs Pupuka was saying, *You are all right just how you are, don't worry about your mother.*

6

Marella

So many things I would like to tell you: stories that belong to you but that I have guarded, jealously, the way a dragon guards treasure.

That summer you were conceived, we slept in a wooden house that rose around us like an ark. Our lives layered inside like sticky leaves after rain. We were married, we were two. Then we were three; then two. You made us three again. All in this house.

But the right number is four, and I cannot seem to get there.

I am writing this to help you understand. To tell you stories about your mother. To better make us.

But first: *us*. Us is such a big word, so circus-tent inclusive. All it takes to puncture *us* is for one person to stand up and step away, whispering "me." Which I see you, nearly an adult, starting to do.

And then *us* billows and waves, its clownish flags falling.

If I fill this notebook with my failures of being *us*, I will be tempted to toss it into the sea.

I am tired of the fecundity that changes a woman into too many people. I wish to lower myself into a quiet place and wait out the winter. But here, no winter comes. I would rather think about earth, water, rocks, sand, whales that are heavy and light at once, things that live and die without having anything to do with us: there are plenty of such things on this island, but none feel familiar to me. To us.

Even if all signs point toward it, you will have to believe that your mother is not a terrible person. Even if she never has any peace and goes about everything terribly. Even if the only *us* you really ever have is me, your wicked stepmother minus the step. Even if they call me the Shrieking Lady and talk of the trouble I've caused. Even with so many disgusting stories these Islanders like to tell, I am still your mother, which makes me your fact and not anyone else's fiction. I am here, now, writing to you. Everybody has one story that is hardest to tell. This is mine. You might call it a ghost story, or maybe a seduction story, but it is not what you'd expect.

Just like any story, it's true and not true. It is a fairy tale, broken.

Broken over and over by the grammar of the ocean.

The stones of my memory lead back to an unassailable cliff: my father brought my brother back to life.

I was seven that day. I was digging in the sand with my brother Kai who was two. We were trusted to play by the ocean. I told him to stop splashing. I told him to catch us a crab. I found a starfish and looked up to show it to him and he was not there. Had it been a minute since I saw him? Had it been two? My brother had fallen into the water while I was not watching. Nothing sinks like the body of a toddler boy; they are all meat and muscle and soggy dumb shoes.

Dad! I screeched, tossing the starfish into the sand.

My father burst out of the house throwing open the glass

door so violently that the glass slammed and shattered onto the living room carpet: so violently that for months to come, we would find splinters of glass in the callouses of our feet. He plunged into the water and pulled from the dregs of seaweed a bluish, heavy boy, the weight and hue of a dead mermaid.

How can I describe the my faultness, my faultness, my faultness?

My father set Kai on his back in the sand and began pumping water out of his body, pumppumppump, then breathing air in, breathebreathebreathe and within a minute, just like magic, my brother gasped.

This is the truest fact of my childhood: My brother died on my watch and came back to life.

Nobody spoke about it again—it was just an interruption, like any other childhood interruption. Lucky my dad was there and he was a doctor who knew these things. Fixed.

Nobody scolded me—then or ever.

As my brother breathed, I noticed somebody watching. A blurry somebody.

It was, perhaps, just my own confusion. But after my brother was hauled alive into the house, I kept looking out toward the waterline, near the pier. There *was* someone.

It was a he. The narrowness of the hips told me that. And he was light-skinned and light-haired like the surfer men who come here from other parts of the world to bleach themselves out on our beaches. Yet there was something different, more formal, about him.

He was watching me.

I looked back toward the house quickly, but still he caught me looking. He laughed a little. He walked up to me and said, *Close one, vestal. How about a kiss to toast the living?*

I stood there silent and unkissing—what did vestal mean, anyway?—but still he brushed his lips against my cheek and dropped a card at my feet. A business card, like the ones my father gave to his patients. In the sun and sand, it was hard to read the smaller letters but on the card's center there was written the word MORTALIS.

This man, so blond and so pale, did not belong here. But it was as if he could read my mind, and he gave a little laugh and said, *If I don't belong here, then neither do you. Do you remember that you used to belong to me?*

Now this spooked me. Unsure of what was real, but sure I didn't want anything more to do with this stranger, I looked back to the house. Kai was standing now, waving at me to come in. I turned back to Mortalis and leaned over to pick up his card. But both the man and the card were gone.

Could there be an actual man who appears at precisely the moment someone is supposed to die?

I did not know if the man I had met existed or not, and if so, whether he had come to harm or comfort me. I didn't think I should tell anyone, for who would believe me? I thought perhaps I was slightly crazy. Crazy or not, that day haunted me. I had seen two things that could not exist.

I became obsessed with the ocean after that day. Kai's drowning/not-drowning left me miracle-hungry, and the ocean seemed its own form of miracle, a force strong enough to give life and take life away. I learned deep-diving, scuba, the names of all the fish, all the Dragon Island ocean mythologies, which seemed to change constantly. I won all the school awards for swimming fastest, diving deepest, staying underwater longest. My bedroom walls filled with pictures of seascapes, photographs of fabulous creatures of the deep. I became the youngest lifeguard on the summer squad. I could sail anybody's boat. All my teachers predicted that surely, surely, with my skill at swimming and love of ocean stories,

I'd have a career in underwater movie-making. I loved the attention. I loved feeling that I could stay alive in somebody else's realm. And myths began abounding on our island: *That girl can hold her breath for an hour, that girl is half-spinner dolphin, that girl once met the Great Whale Shark who offered her his single magic tooth if she would stay underwater and be his wife.*

Then a new boy moved to town. Adam.

He *was* interesting.

He had a strange mother who was different from all the other mothers; she had a young face but her hair was silver. It was as if she were suspended between girl and grandmother. Her name was Ilya and she enjoyed talking with kids. She asked us questions about what we thought, what we played, and she listened closely to our answers. She did not seem to have a job or a husband.

Adam and his mother lived in a tiny cabin that floated at the edge of the sea. They didn't seem to have any other family members. When he got sick, his mother treated him with teas and herbs and homemade stinky ointments and by sticking tiny needles into his hands and feet and head. There were no rules at Adam's house, no behavior charts or curfews. But it didn't matter. All Adam wanted to do was read. He wanted to learn as many languages as he could so one day he could travel all over the world and speak to everyone he met.

I began going over to Adam's house instead of going home after school. Better to sit in trees with Adam, showing off the facts we knew, and creating sign languages of our own. It was not romantic. We were twelve years old. We trusted each other completely. He told me a story about his mother travelling to the land of the dead when he was a baby, and I believed him. I told him how my brother died and came back to life, and how some surfer-ghost who was maybe named

Mortalis showed up afterward, said I belonged to him and wanted to kiss me. Adam promised not to tell.

Eighth grade arrived. Twice my parents made me switch swim teams because some boy on the team tried to kiss me or stashed in my swim-bag some gross, graphic love note. Adam was safe, according to my parents; all other boys were off-limits. I mostly didn't care. Boys didn't interest me except as swimming companions. They were like slightly slower fish.

But then our island swelled in high school; outsider kids were arriving, their families drawn to Dragon Island by the climate and the ease of living. Adam and I stuck together at first. But then, the year we turned sixteen, there appeared on our island a boy-man whose name was Zach. Zach, who was shaggy-haired, blond, sure of his power. I had a crush on Zach—as did every other girl in school. There were so many reasons to choose Zach. He even had a house of his own, ostensibly owned by his mother, but everyone knew he lived there alone. There you could be an adult, you could pretend to be husband and wife. It was said that his mother lived across the ocean with her new boyfriend and she left her house in Zach's care. It had a hot tub that was rumored to have once gotten jammed with a girl's earring.

I was invited to a party there. Adam was not invited.

I felt disloyal going; I went.

The house had two bedrooms with a balcony coming out of one, and Zach spied me in the crowd and took my hand and led me up the staircase and through the bedroom and onto the balcony where he kissed and kissed and kissed me. I never learned what the rest of the house looked like. I knew only the balcony where we kissed until the sky went blue and black like a bruise and the clouds disappeared and the moon glowed, perfect and uncracked, right in front of our faces.

I went home dizzy, hoping my parents could not read the

language of my face.

On Monday, when the science teacher asked me the weight per ounce of water, I was still on the moonlit balcony and did not hear, and Adam kicked me under the table and whispered the answer.

"Twenty-nine point five-seven grams," I blurted, not knowing the question.

I had dressed for school with Zach in mind, dabbed my mother's perfume on my green blouse and white skirt. His class schedule formed a map in my head, Math-Language-History-Lunch-Science-Art-Soccer. I looked for Zach on the soccer field after school but found only Adam, standing there with his heavy backpack of Russian and Turkish dictionaries, looking at me sadly and saying, "I've waited for you."

My present-self and my future-self faced off, glaring at one another.

My future-self said: *Adam is the best man you'll ever know.*

My present-self said: *I want to kiss Zach again.* No doubt Zach would lose interest in me before the end of high school, I reasoned. There was still time to choose Adam.

Adam took his loss gracefully. He and I continued to climb trees and talk about books. I still went over to his house after school. This was mostly because my parents feared Zach and trusted Adam.

One afternoon Adam, Zach, and I got permission to take my parents' sailboat and explore the jagged rocks that grew like glass shards straight up from the water about a mile off the coast of Dragon Island. These were the rocks that Adam swore were haunted. Zach laughed at him for thinking that. I lay in the sun and felt a clean simple happiness at being the girl on the boat with these two boys who were trying to be friends for my sake.

Zach didn't like Adam; he had no interest in Adam's love of knowledge, the fact that he had memorized many of the world's greatest stories and could recite them in their own languages. All Zach knew was that I was *his* girl and who was this sissy boy who followed me around like a dog? Adam didn't seem to care much about Zach after the initial jealousy. He was my best friend again, as he had always been. And he was kind to Zach, for he was kind to everyone. We didn't have enough life jackets, so Adam offered his jacket to Zach.

When we got near the rocks, the water turned rough. Zach moved the boom fast and it hit Adam in the head, casting him off the boat and ricocheting him against the jagged lower rocks. Adam fell into the water and floated face-down, and for a sickening moment Zach and I did nothing. Then I jumped in after Adam. I was a fast enough swimmer to reach him quickly. But I wasn't strong enough to pull him back onto our boat.

"Zach!" I called. "Help us!"

But Zach just sat there on the boat, looking away.

"Zach!" I yelled louder.

He ignored me. And slowly, slowly, he shifted the tiller and began to steer the boat toward shore. I could not believe what was happening. Was this Zach, or was this some creature that had become Zach? I would not know and could not consider it any further, for here was Adam face down in the water and I needed to rescue him.

The wind was in my favor: it held the sailboat near the rocks, so dragging Adam I was able to reach the leeward side. Zach seemed to have a change of conscience. He grabbed Adam by the shirt and hauled him back on deck. I climbed on after him and stared at Zach, the coward. Then I tried to do CPR on Adam, as I had learned in my lifeguard training.

It was the last time either boy spoke to me.

The doctors never knew exactly what caused the damage, whether it was the hit to his head or the protracted loss of oxygen. While Adam's body lived through the accident, his brain did not. He would never become the learned traveler he was supposed to be.

As a result of our accident, Zach was expelled from school for failure to assist during a boating accident, Adam started a new life in a group home for brain-damaged young adults, and I left Dragon Island for college at age seventeen.

But I didn't stay in college long. My father died of a heart attack during my first year away. It was sudden and sad, and it set my family reeling. I returned to Dragon Island for what was supposed to be a short visit: I had outgrown the place. I worried that people still talked about me, speculating about what was and was not my fault. I had gone once to visit Adam in his group home, but it was too sad. He didn't recognize me and couldn't talk. As I left I promised, "I'll come again soon." But I knew I would not.

I arranged to spend two weeks with my mother and brother, and then go find a summer job. I spent my evenings at the Salty Dog Bar and Billiard, a depressing place, but at least a place where I didn't know anyone.

Playing pool came easily, the way that swimming once had. The balls were symbols the colors of fish, and you did not have to talk. It had rules that could be played and won with an airtight precision, if you were any good. It was not murky like the intricate world of men and women.

During those weeks I met a man who was visiting the island. His name was George Brouge, he was tall and smart and kind like Adam had been, he was a graduate student studying whales, he had moved here to be near the ocean, and he was from Long Island, the most distant and unknown place I could imagine. He came to the Salty Dog late one night and told the room his life story. Then he looked straight at me.

I thought, I know how this will go, trying to love a man who loves the ocean. I know what the ocean can do and it is more than me or you. When I looked at him I saw jealousy ahead, years of vying against a ferocious and unalterable first love. I saw myself reaching into his depths to scoop out his passion-seeds for something not me, something that would best me. Looking at him, I felt drained-out, exhausted, old.

He told me later what he saw: a storied woman who had seen the secrets of the deep and who looked back at them, unflinching. He also admired my skill at pool.

His first night in town George informed the bartender, as well as anyone listening at the bar, that he was going to marry me.

"Good luck," they all said and went back to their drinks.

I set for myself a test, like any girl in any fairy tale. I had no father to set it so I set it for myself. I said I wouldn't go on a date with him unless he could beat me at pool.

George was a brave man. He was also a man who had never played a game of pool before in his life. "Give me a week to practice," he said.

During that week, George spent all day and all night at the Salty Dog, asking help from anyone who would give it. On the seventh day, he was ready for me. We matched each other the whole game, but when it came time to hit the 8-ball into the pocket, I missed.

7

Charon

Souls offer me coins. I have so many coins. My job is to keep ferrying: keep the souls calm as they go On. I myself have never been On, but still it is my job to tell them that death is nothing: no pain, no loss, just me, and I harm no one. I have seen every ending, every life story, and I know all stories end the same. On the far side of the river, where trees grow bare and the air smells like just-burnt sage, I tell each soul: *Here I leave you. You are safe, so like any husk I fall away. You can forget me now for I am just a myth.* Being alive so long is lonely beyond words and water.

8

Sage

SEPTEMBER

Just like that, Dad was gone—into his boat and gone. He left us a freezer full of fish and instructions on how to cook it. But I knew that before his fish would run out, the hard stone fact would descend that my mother and I were alone together.

That first week I missed Nana urgently. I missed talking about books with her, watching her bustle industriously around every room, and knowing she loved me. The rare daytime moments my mind quieted its grief, I thought about Pupuka and wondered at his gift of slugs. At the day's corners, the sea-murmur hours before bed and the bird-song hours before sunrise, I sat in my too-big room with the ladder and the loft and I worried about my mother.

For it was increasingly certain that Marella was a woman whose past was a haunted country to which I would never be granted passage. I could not trust her to act in rational ways because the ghosts that colonized her secret life might erupt at any moment. So I watched her as if she were a wild animal or a small child. I spent the first week of fishing season sitting outside on the wide wooden steps of our back deck, waiting for something to happen. But my mother stayed quiet and Pupuka did not visit.

The one who did visit was Lance. It was early, just after sunrise; Dad had been gone five days. I was barely awake, and at first I thought it was just a trick of light, instead of Lance wheeling his bike along the sand past our house. It was strange to see him so early and out of context. He had a surfboard tied to the back of his bike so that it poked up like an antenna. Lance couldn't have been older than thirty. He looked exactly in the middle between my own age and my mother's.

I waved to him and he walked over. He leaned his bike against the back steps and sat next to me.

"George asked me to come around in case you and your mother needed anything," he said in a somewhat apologetic voice as he raked his fingers through his perfect hair. Then he told me I could reach him on my dad's cell phone. Then he said, "Sage is a seriously serious name for a young person."

"I'm eighteen. That's not so young."

"Trust me, you're young. Do you have any nicknames?"

I shrugged. For as long as I could remember, nobody in my family had called me by my actual name. My dad was still stuck on Seabird, Nana had called me sweet things like Lovey and Sugar, and my mother hardly ever called me anything.

"What is it about your mother that makes your dad think she needs such…protection?" Lance asked.

"My mother is—" I didn't know quite how to say it. "Marella is delicate."

This seemed the most tactful way to say a true thing. Things hurt her deeply. For some reason it never occurred to me to worry about my dad. He was strong and sturdy, from the meaty palms of his hands to his fierce, wiry beard. Dad could stay afloat. It was my mother, with her fragility and grieving face, who I worried about going under. There was always the sense that we, Dad and Nana and I, were sending her off into the great alarming world. Patting her on the back, handing Marella her lunch, and then poof! Anything might happen. Each time she went grocery shopping or got her hair trimmed or had a meeting about the poetry book she'd been trying to write for over a decade or did anything outside of the house—always it seemed to us that these events might swallow her. Swallow her right up, my poor beautiful frightened mother.

Lance watched me as I moved through these thoughts, and I decided to change the subject and ask where he lived before coming here.

"Montana…for adventure…no…I don't know…" he said with an inside-joke gleam in his eyes.

"What?"

He then explained that he had given me the answers to the four most frequently asked small-talk questions: Where are you from / Why did you move to Dragon Island / Did you always know you wanted to work as a fisherman / Will you stay here for good?

"It makes the small questions efficient so that it's easier to move onto the big ones," he added.

I considered asking which big ones he was after; then I let the thought go. Above us the sun was rising like a lollipop on the spiked tail of Dragon Mountain, and across the sky the moon was a thinning marble. I stood as if to leave, and Lance gave me a little salute.

I watched him disappear into the half-dark. Something about Lance made me want to behave badly. Lance seemed at sea—like my mother, who I was tired of behaving well for. Before I could go inside and start making us breakfast, I heard a crash from the house.

"Marella?" I called. I ran upstairs to Nana's room, where she and my dad now slept; the bed was unmade and she was nowhere. Then I heard a shriek from downstairs and a sound like water running. *The downstairs shower*.

I raced back down and heard the sound of glass breaking: my poor Nana's porcelain shell collection was strewn, shattered, all over the downstairs guest bathroom. Marella was inside the shower, pounding against the shower door.

"What's wrong?" I called. "Are you stuck?"

The steam outside the shower and inside ran together, a world of angry wet. My mother stared at me with terrified eyes. "Mortalis," she whispered with urgency.

"Is everything okay?" I heard Lance's voice coming from outside, like the relief of gravel thrown against a window when you've been waiting inside a long time.

Through the green glass of the door, I saw Marella raise her hands over her head like a furious child about to hit something. "You do not let him in here," she hissed at me.

The automatic back porch light turned on, signaling an intruder.

"You okay in there, girls?" Lance called. "The backdoor's locked but I can break a window."

Marella opened the shower door and water flooded onto Nana's wooden floor, all over the broken shells. I grabbed a towel and pushed the shells aside and wiped as much as I could—the soft fibers soaked in my hand.

Lance knocked again, and Marella screamed.

"Send him away!" she ordered in a furious whisper. "That man is *not* our rescuer, he is not to come in here. You don't know who he is and *I do*. He is here to do you harm."

"Marella, calm down!"

"I've got the deck chair," hollered Lance through the walls, "and I can use it to push open the window..."

I found my fingers turning the sticky old knob that led from the guest bath to the porch—no doubt it had sat locked for years. Marella glared at me, but something in her eyes, some child-look of hope for rescue, seemed to surrender.

"Well, this is just like breaking into a museum, isn't it?" said Lance, once I wrenched the door open. He stepped gingerly onto the steamy, flooded, bathroom floor. It was a hazard of broken shells.

"Hardly," whispered Marella. "It is like breaking into a seashell that can never be repaired." But then her voice fell and she slid naked and sobbing onto the wet marble tiles, her wet hair spinning around her like syrup.

Lance knelt on the floor and covered her with a towel. "Tell me how to help," he said quietly, lowering his voice to match hers.

"Mortalis," whispered my mother, raising her head in a feeble attempt to look fiercely at Lance, "you may take me to the hospital but you must leave her here."

"What are you going on about?" Lance drawled, patting her gently through the towel. "No mortal wounds here, just a scratch from some seashells. Nothing to worry anyone."

I tried to read my mother's face, but she had closed her eyes.

We both helped my mother into the car. When Lance opened the door for me to get into the back seat, she said: "Leave her!" as sharply as telling a beast to drop a bone.

"Pardon?" Lance said.

Marella stared him down, now speaking in her ordinary voice, calm with undertones of menace. "Keep away from her." Then she said to me, "You stay."

I looked at Lance to override this, as I would've looked at my dad. As soon as I caught myself, I felt foolish and hot-cheeked. Now we were back to normal.

Marella laughed, and I felt profoundly the trap of our fairy tale, with her as triumphant queen and me as the dull skill-less girl. "I don't want you coming. They will just pronounce me panicked and send me home." She paused and looked away from me. "Please. Just go…inside…or away."

"Easy, girl." Lance skipped his eyes from my mother to me. "She's just having a day."

"Get out of the car," Marella said lightly, knowing full well that I'd obey.

I obeyed. And I went back into the house to wait and to clean up the mess my mother had made.

The bathroom didn't take long to mop. Afterward I went up to Nana's room to try to shed my anger. It was my first time alone there since the night we cleaned house. It was a comforting room, full of sweetly curated furniture and objects: a weird table with different feet for each leg: a bird's claw, a fish's fin, a padded mammal foot, a high-heeled shoe. On top of it rested a collection of sea-glass, now dusty. I felt the kindness of my grandmother's possessions, and it made me feel a slight softening toward Marella for not getting rid of them all—my mother prided herself on not being attached to material things. But Nana, it appeared, had been so attached to so many: a lifesaver from somebody's lifeguard days, a relic that she kept above the toilet, which I could see through the open bathroom door. Her bedside table made of driftwood, on top of which rested her collection of coasters with hermit crabs etched in red and silver onto the white ceramic. So many ocean objects. I rested in the room—hours passed, but I don't know how many—until I heard the garage door open.

I came downstairs just as Lance was settling Marella in her soft purple chair where she belonged. Lance acted like it was not a big deal, just your garden-variety weekday rescue. He said, "Just a few stitches where she got cut and a prescription for the anxiety, nothing more." Then he gallantly made us both lunch while we watched. Once we were settled at the table eating, Lance took a long look around our kitchen at the grandeur of Nana's cabinetry and at the magnetic poetry pieces Marella kept on the refrigerator in an attempt to inspire herself. Though the pieces were hers, all of the poems were mine. He read one of my poems aloud:

Persevere
my melancholy mother.
Learn the tides
and chase water.

Lance laughed and laughed, showing his perfect ivory teeth. He looked like a flourishing member of some endangered species. He swept his eyes around the kitchen, from the hanging pots to the nook where the phone book was kept. Then he turned to Marella, and I saw in his face that he was preparing to cut directly to the real questions, to brave the actual fizzing material of our lives.

He began with me. "Do you have any friends here yet, besides your mother?"

I had one, but my mother scared him off. "No," I said. "Not yet."

He turned to Marella. "George tells me you are writing a book," he said. "What kind?"

"Poetry," she said shortly. "But these days I don't have time. I'm a full-time person! It takes all of my time to parent Sage, get the chores done around the house, pay bills. That's job enough."

I am sure I made a face, but Lance simply responded, "A full-time person. I like that." Then he asked for a tour of the house. That sounded like fun, and I could see that my mother liked the idea, too. We started in the kitchen and showed him the ladder in the pantry that led into a hidden larder, as well as the ship-inspired portholes in the formal dining room.

I showed him my bedroom with its sparse décor and ocean-view. "Just like a ship's cabin," he said. "Nothing more needed."

Upstairs we looked into each bedroom, at the ladders on the walls leading up to the lookout lofts.

"Wow," Lance said, and he whistled when he saw the bathtub in Nana's room, large enough to fit a baby dolphin. "I wish I had grown up in this house. This is a great place for a kid to play."

Marella got a funny look on her face when he said this, and to break the tension, in an effort to make a joke, I said the least appropriate thing that I could have ever said to my mother: "Maybe you should have another one."

"Bird!"

One look from Marella told me exactly what I already knew. "My reproductive life is none of your business. If you want a baby, have one yourself."

Lance just laughed. It was a sincere hearty laugh, not the nervous laughter that most people would've responded with. You could see that he was enjoying being around us, and it made me feel more like family to have him there. At the very least, Marella was talking. Lance went to look around a walk-in closet that contained a length of decorative fishing net. My mother cast me another dirty look and peered out the window. Then Lance smiled at me across the room and it made me a little dizzy.

He walked over to the window and stood next to my mother. We were still in my parents' bedroom, Nana's huge white bed looming like a lifeboat in the center of the room.

"It sure is beautiful here," said Lance in a quiet voice.

"It is."

"Growing up here, do you ever get used to it?" he asked her.

"No. Never. But I don't trust it the way I used to."

All three of us fell quiet. Outside, the sun had begun its

descent, bathing the grass and water in a fearful brightness full of heavy tropical reds and soft yellows and an exuberant green glinting off the palms. Beyond stretched the inescapable blues of sky and ocean.

Lance excused himself to use the bathroom and I followed my mother back down into the kitchen.

"Lance is too old for you," my mother observed as I washed the lunch dishes.

"He's too young for you!" I retorted.

She turned her dark eyes on me reproachfully. "I am a married woman. Lance does not interest me."

His sudden reappearance in the doorway silenced us.

"So Marella," he said. "You know there are rumors about you on this island."

"Oh? What kind of rumors?"

"Rumors that you used to lay on the beach covered in nothing but palm leaves. And that you could out-play anybody at pool."

Marella's shoulders rose like spikes. Then, to my surprise, she giggled and in a voice like cocoa-butter she asked, "Who told you that?"

"I'm not telling," Lance said, in a voice like bait. "Is it true?"

Looking at my mother as she basked in Lance's attention like a fish swimming slow circles in a warm patch of water, I saw something I had not seen in quite some time: her charm. While her beauty is obvious—how bright and polished her skin is, the special quality of her rare smiles—her charm lurks so deep that I sometimes think of it only as a myth.

"They might be true and they might not be," Marella teased.

"Who can I ask? Would George know?" Lance persisted.

"No," Marella answered slowly. "He came into my life too late. And there are things he could never know because even though he loves water, George is an earth-man."

Lance squinted at my mother. I felt like they were speaking in code.

Then he said slowly, "Yes, I know what you mean."

And my mother went on, "And though I prefer dry land, I am a water-woman."

"Yes. I see that too."

Lance waited. I waited. "You," she said to him. "You are made of water."

Lance nodded. "And Sage..."

They both stared abruptly at me.

"Sage is something else," she said, spooling out these pronouncements like one of the Fates deciding life's length. "She is not quite land, but not quite water either."

It was spooky to hear my mother talk like this. I wondered if the safety my mother felt with my father was because perhaps as an "earth-man," he would not try to follow her into the hollows of her shell. And I knew at once that Lance would.

I had a sudden picture of my mother as a sleeping beauty in her ocean-side tower, waiting for somebody, some hero, to wake her. Maybe it would be Lance. I feared with increasing certainty that it was not going to be my father. Up until that point, I had been feeling that the day was magic. Marella was happy, we were making a friend.

But the day was stretching into night. It didn't take a genius to see that my mother found him attractive. Who wouldn't? They looked like deities from some other world—whereas my dad and I, with our messy hair and rough hands, were simply mortal.

Now they were sitting together on the sofa, and she was pulling out her notebook and saying that she would read him some of her poems. I understood that I should leave. They did not want me here; I did not belong, and anything that happened between them was out of my control. I excused myself and sat on the porch and willed myself to think of other things.

I watched the geckos on the window screen as they breathed, pushing out their pink bellies until they turned translucent.

Night had fallen and the night-surf roared invisibly. I thought of the smells of the house, and went through each of the people I knew on the island, breaking them down into their smells:

My father smelled like the sea, like the bad breath from seashells that have gotten clogged by seaweed and left on the beach to rot. It was a fishy, salty, body-decay smell. Very mineral.

My mother smelled red. Like hibiscus flowers and cinnamon and fresh tomatoes on the vine, and like blood. She had its edge, its metal.

Pupuka smelled like clean laundry, hot pavement, dirt and exertion, like sweat and boy.

Lance smelled the best of all, of tobacco and citrus. He smelled like an orange on fire.

Our house smelled like seawater and garden flowers and a bit of exhaust from the road nearby. It came on in gusts.

And my grandmother—I thought hard. I could not remember exactly how she smelled.

I had no idea how late it was, but the inside lights were dark and the sounds of animals were beginning to come up around the house. I heard to my left a strange and sudden noise, the panic-shrill of a bird getting caught by a mammal. "Marella?" I called nervously into the altered air.

Nothing. I began to feel frightened. It seemed that I was alone in the giant house, which was alone on the tiny island, which was alone on the giant ocean.

I slipped back inside and the scene in the living room caught me off guard. There they were, sitting on the sofa, my mother's notebook open on the table. They were naked and wrapped in an afghan blanket, two beauties bathed in the starlight, with their arms around each other. There was my mother, but different, lighter, sleek as a satisfied cat, her eyes low and sleepy. There was Lance, his shirt on the floor, next to his discarded shorts. In that moment they felt as unfamiliar to me as if I had just opened a hotel room door and found strangers sitting there. She was kissing him, her hair draped around his shoulders like it used to drape, when I was a child, around mine. She looked way too old for him, like she would ruin him just like she could ruin the life of any child.

Questions swarmed in my mind like schools of fish. When they noticed me at last, Marella didn't do anything that I would have expected. Nobody jumped up or looked guilty. They just sat there with their moist eyes, like two sleepy seals.

"Are you all right?" my mother asked. "Do you need anything?"

"No. I was just—going to bed."

"Sit down," said Lance, with his cowboy grin. "Sorry to give you a surprise. It's just that I am in the middle of falling hopelessly in love with your beautiful mother..."

"Will you tell George?" I asked.

Lance laughed. "Sorry, I can't help it. I love that you call your dad George. You are at once so old, and so very young."

"We're going to tell George when he returns," Marella added, a pulsing note in her voice as she spoke.

"I love her," Lance said simply. "Sure, I get that she doesn't belong to me, all that coveting your neighbor's ass crap. I know. And I'm sorry it had to happen. But she thinks I can provide something for her. I think maybe I can."

I felt as old as the world, listening to Lance explain himself. It made a person feel powerful to be reasoned with, and apologized to, in this way. But not exactly a "good" kind of powerful.

"You don't worry one bit," Lance went on. "We're handling this like adults."

"Good night," I said, going into my bedroom.

It seemed a bizarre moment for them both to pretend to be rational adults. As I cast one look back at them, I saw that they were looking down at a conch shell that had been filled with caramels on Nana's coffee table. They had eaten all the caramels and were examining the conch. She was touching his hand, and it looked weirdly innocent: just two grownups, two nerdy science geeks, playing with a piece of the ocean.

I sat on my bed, behind my closed door, thinking. Feelings swarmed; I tried to identify each one. I felt sad for my dad. This was the biggest feeling, and at least it felt like a sincere and noble one. He deserved better than my mom.

I also felt sort of grossed out, the way I used to feel as a kid when I read stories about Beauty and the Beast, though when I thought more about it, I couldn't decide ultimately who was the beauty and who the beast. It seemed both were both.

And the final sadness I felt was for myself, and it was mostly just embarrassment. Marella was like a gorgeous slinky tiger, whereas I was just...me. Not ugly, but not beautiful either. Not extraordinary in any way. This feeling left me hollow and overall sort of bummed. I mean—if this is the fairy tale my mother and I were stuck in, wasn't the handsome prince character supposed to notice me, not her? Even if I didn't care—which I didn't, really—still it felt sad to think that a man right in the middle of our ages, with both of us opening up our house and lives to him, would choose my mother instead of me. Even if I wouldn't choose him.

I had just turned out the light next to my bed when I heard them again.

"Lance—" My mother's voice came through the dark hallway, as delicate as fish scales. "Would you please bring me some water?"

I heard a creak as Lance rose and tiptoed to the kitchen.

I could hear the sound of bare feet. I did not know but I suspected that he was still naked. I almost wanted to look out my loft peephole to see if he was, but I held myself down.

Suddenly a pang of longing hit me hard in the stomach. I thought of Pupuka, wondering if he would come back. I wanted somebody like Lance, somebody who found me as alluring as Lance found my mother—I wanted somebody to bring me water in the night.

I stayed awake for a while longer, even though I knew I would be tired in the morning. Somewhere in the early hours before dawn the roar of the high morning tide quieted my mind and I finally slept.

The next morning Marella carried a new sort of exuberance. She polished her nails, washed and combed her hair, and dressed in her brightest clothes. She even made dinner. Her sticky notes disappeared. Lance came around a lot that week and the next. I felt like their chaperone. They giggled and kissed and once I caught them in their underwear in the kitchen in the middle of the night, making chocolate chip cookies. They wanted to be together every moment, and when they were apart she grew listless.

At least Lance rode his bike to and from Nana's house, instead of driving the Big Mouth Fishing van, which would've been betrayal beyond what I could stomach; I could accept that my mother was her own beast and anything could happen, but my dad's company was *his*—Lance was just a temporary employee. I wondered if I should try to radio my dad to tell him what was going on.

I did nothing. I let the train keep racing off track. And every night Lance visited.

When Lance left each morning, Marella lingered near our kitchen phone, picking it up every few hours, as if testing the dial tone. She dusted. She pulled things out of drawers, stacked them, and put them back in. She complained about my father.

I crab-walked around her with tentative questions. "Are you okay?" and "Any news from Dad?" She mostly ignored me. I finally asked, "Are you going to write today, Marella?" knowing that question, if nothing else, would get a response. I learned that rousing trick from watching my dad. He used to come home with hand-wrung exuberance and ask her, "Did you write? Did you write?" for writing was her only activity other than pouting. Finally Marella put an end to that question by writing "DON'T NAG ME" on a square of paper and wearing it like a nametag until Dad cowered and begged, "Please take it off. I'll stop, I'll stop."

She avoided my eyes. "My writing is none of your business. Here, look inside this cabinet," she said. "Look. Look at how many coffee mugs your grandmother kept. Your dad refuses to let me throw them away. I am surrounded by pack rats!"

This was not true—well, the dad part of it was not. My dad lived on a boat half of the year, metering out exactly what he needed; extra mugs were not part of his definition of need. A mug, a plastic coffee filter and reusable linen bag, two days' clothes, his net, his poles, a sharp new set of hooks. The only bait he carried was a single gullet, quartered: he used his first catch as his next bait, and this pattern sustained him through months at sea. Catch, kill, gut, lure. Catch. My grandmother's belongings were another story—it did seem that taxidermied hermit crabs were probably the stuff of pack rats. But I also felt it wasn't my mother's business, for she was squatting, as was I, in Nana's house.

But I knew better than to tell my mother this. She dusted the counters then emptied the drawers and added items from her purse to each as she refilled them, and I knew she would have a devil of a time finding her checkbook.

"Your father!" she burst out. She caught herself, straightened up, composed her face. "Your father uses creatures too hard. Remember when the dog died under his watch—were you old enough to remember? He let our dog follow his boat all the way out to the Tomorrow Atoll, and the dog drowned on the way back. He wouldn't let it in the boat. He said boats are hard enough to clean as is, without bringing dog hair into the equation. Goddamn selfish man."

I had heard my mom curse plenty, but never at my dad.

"And your brother—If your father had been home...if he actually taught his son to swim, instead of just teaching him to love the water...if he hadn't been off in his boat, doing god knows what, you would have a living older brother."

This was what I had hoped for.

Even my breathing grew silent as I waited for more. I contemplated egging her on by adding my own father-complaints to her list, but a stray bit of loyalty held me back. Instead I pulled two frozen halibut filets out of our now spotless freezer and prepared to follow Dad's cooking instructions. Usually one filet would feed my mother and me for dinner, but that was before we were also feeding Lance.

My mother hoisted herself to sit on Nana's counter while I gathered spices, mostly at random, to make something like a marinade. She kicked her feet lightly against the cabinet and watched me. Something about work being done that she herself wasn't doing opened Marella up. Sure enough, she kept talking. I wished she would have said something more about Adam, but instead she continued her litany of complaints about my dad. I had never once heard him complain about her. But then, my father moved on from sadness much faster than my mother did.

"Marella, what is going on with Lance?"

She stopped talking suddenly. I offered her a taste of

my marinade just to give her something to reject—her "no" would at least be a word—and I watched as her sad eyes gold-panned the sea outside our windows, as if looking for someone to help her answer my question.

She slowly said, "I have been only one person to your father for so many years, and now with Lance I can be anyone. You don't understand yet, you're too young. But one day you may know what it feels like to be stuck in a rut so deep that you don't recognize yourself, let alone *like* yourself. Lance thinks I'm so…exotic." She spat out the word.

"And he is a relief to be around. He's new here. He doesn't just think of me as some mourning mother, or worse, some Shrieking Lady superstition. He takes me back to a time when I was someone else…"

That was all she said. We set the table quietly and waited for Lance to come and turn her night into fireworks and magic lanterns. I expected their giddy routine to continue unchecked for the entirety of fishing season.

But the next morning Marella woke up nauseous. I saw her kiss Lance goodbye before he left for work and then vomit twice into the azalea bushes in our back yard.

"Bird," she called, her voice weak and sickly. "Bring me a wet rag." She was sitting on the back steps and she wound the cool cloth around her forehead and stuck her head between her knees.

I ran downtown, hoping to find something to calm her stomach. My mother was never sick, and I was frightened.

I tried the pharmacy. *Closed Sundays*, the sign cheerfully read. I tried the small market on the edge of Squid Ink Alley. *Come back again*. I ran into the alley past Ilya's Herbs. Its dusty windows were dark.

I kept running—there had to be someplace, someone…

Then I caught sight of another person trolling these

streets. I could tell by the way the person moved that she was a woman. She had straight posture and long silver hair and flowing clothes that blew around her in the slightest wind.

Ilya.

She was walking toward me—and without thinking I ran in her direction.

"My mother," I said, when we came near each other. My voice was gasping from having run so hard. "She's sick. She woke up sick and she's been throwing up."

Ilya did not look concerned in the least. "Well, of course," she said. Her words surfaced like driftwood in the quiet air. Her voice sounded like something that was half-song, but rubbed in the silt of the ocean bottom. It was a weird bare-coral-sort-of-voice, as mysterious and silvery as her hair, and as foreign as the deep. Her voice didn't have kindness in it, but it didn't have cruelty either. Ilya opened her shoulder bag and took out a vial. "Tell her to chew this six times a day."

"What is it?"

"A spicy ginger that I grew myself and made into gum. Midwives use it to still the seasickness that comes at the beginning. Now a question for you, Girl—do you know how to swim?"

"No," I said. I had never gone into water above my waist.

"Learn," she said simply. "And come visit me when the ginger runs out. Your mother is pregnant and will come to see me soon. And I will need your help."

She walked away, toward-water, as Pupuka would say. I thought, what a strange encounter. I thought of my mother and how shocking it would be for her to have a baby, if indeed Ilya was right. And then I thought of Ilya's curious instructions and it occurred to me who could teach me to swim.

I brought the ginger home and gave it to Marella, where she sat hunched, clutching a glass of water, at Nana's counter.

"Chew this six times a day," I told her.

She opened the bag and then stared at me as if I had just slid out of the ocean on my belly and arrived, muddy and dripping in her living room. Then she hurled the glass of water against the wall next to me. She looked pained with regret as soon as she did it. But I didn't stick around to talk or to clean up the glass shards.

"Pupuka!" I called. I had come to Sliver Moon Park, where I first met him, on a hunch that he would be here again. I was wearing my bathing suit beneath my clothes. Once again he was shirtless, wet from a swim. He was lying on the stone boundary wall, inches from the far drop to the ocean, with his face to the sun and his head on a rolled-up towel.

His face broke into a crooked smile. "Did you ever find Ilya?" he asked.

"I did," I said. "And I have a favor to ask: will you teach me to swim and dive the way that you do?"

"Today?" he asked.

"Yes. If you don't mind."

"I'm happy to. But first, is your mother doing any better?"

Yes. No. Who knows.

"She has been this way for years," I said. "The difference is that now I'm stuck with her on an island where I don't have any friends or other family."

Pupuka grinned and took my hand. "I'll be your friend. This island will become your home."

I didn't answer. I didn't want to tell him that I had plans beyond this place. But I held his hand as he led me through a short maze of roads to the shallow water at Kite Beach, where the beginning surfers go, and he gave me my first swimming lesson: the frog-stroke. It felt the most natural. *Bend, open, together, bend, open, together.* I did this until it became easy.

Then he had me practice holding my breath.

"Turns out you're a natural," Pupuka said. "Now, diving."

This was the part that worried me. I feared touching the bottom under any water. I didn't want to know what lurked down there. I had always been fine standing in the shallows, as well as comfortable on boats that skimmed the surface, but all my life I had harbored a fear of the deep. An inherited fear, something that came to me just like my mother's brown eyes and toes that grow into each other like ill-tended beans.

But here I was in the water, with Pupuka asking me, "Are you ready now to dive?" *No. Never. But Ilya had asked me to learn and I did not want to fail.*

I closed my eyes, held my breath, and dove in headfirst. I kept my eyes wrenched closed, but after a few seconds I opened them. The water was surprisingly clear, and I could see everything. Yellow fish swam past, goggling curiously at me. Then I saw the bottom. I was almost there, and I still had plenty of breath. I kept going.

I wanted to bring something back, something to show Pupuka that I had done it, I had touched the bottom. I grabbed the first thing I saw when I reached the ocean floor: an algae-covered rock. Careful not to touch anything else on the bottom, I turned around and kicked my way back to the surface. Halfway up I began feeling that I was running out of air, and the words from the medical dictionary came back in pieces: *bradycardia...heart-rate slows...blood reroutes... thoracic cavity stays intact...either way the victim inhales...*

I knew if I had kicked off the ocean bottom I would be at the surface already, and that it was my own small fear of touching the ocean floor that kept me from doing it. I told myself, *Don't panic.* I said, *You're almost there.* And I kicked harder, bursting into the sunlight with a splash, gulping air gratefully, holding my rock out for Pupuka to see. Around us the surfers were reaching shore and carrying their boards back home.

"How was it?" he asked.

"Fine," I lied.

But I was shaken at how close I came to running out of air. Without anyone down there to teach it to me, I learned a lesson underwater. It is our fear that gets us into trouble.

"Didn't look fine," Pupuka said. "What made you dive so deep so soon?"

I stared at him. He had met her; he knew the answer; was he just waiting for me to say it? "I need to shed an inherited fear."

It felt dumb, the having to say it. But Pupuka just sat there waiting patiently, so I kept talking. "A…fear of the deep. My mother hates water. She always has. My greatest fear is to grow up and become exactly like her."

"I see." He stretched and shook off, water droplets flying. "Do you have to go home?" he asked. "Or should we do this again?"

Over the next two weeks, I went swimming every day with Pupuka. Below the surface we saw porpoises at play, yellow tangs darting inside boughs of coral, and drifting sea-turtles like gentle grandfathers. I felt frightened at the thought that I might see a shark but Pupuka advised me not to worry; they are shy, he said, and not hungry for me.

Each time we saw a new animal, Pupuka gestured his arms toward me, and I knew the bubbles coming out of his mouth were asking: *Do you like it?* After my first day of being afraid underwater, it turned out I liked everything. I could not believe how much I had missed by listening to my mother. And I was happy to be around Pupuka again. I loved how secure he felt on the earth and in the ocean. I loved our long and lazy afternoons. But I knew also that I had learned to swim for a reason, even if Ilya had not explained it yet.

9

Ilya

My son Adam was three months old when I made my descent. Here is how I went down—*Girl, listen hard*. You swim out from the shore toward the rocks that rise like jagged tulips. And you tread water, looking until you see a mark on the rock in the shape of a boat. A simple boat, like a canoe. This sounds crazy, I know.

When you see that boat, you've found the entrance, and what you need to do is hold your breath and go under—not so deep as you'd think, but deep enough to cut under the rock. You only hold your breath for a few seconds. It's frightening only because you can't help fearing that there won't be air on the other side. But once you come up, you are inside a cave, treading water in a two-foot swath of air beneath a floor of black volcanic ash, hardened by the centuries. Each breath smells like just-dampened fire.

But that's just the first part. Next you need to get onto that floor of black rock, or else you'll be stuck inside the cave but outside the Underworld—a wet dark limbo. You cannot imagine, Girl, how dark it is under those rocks, cut off from the sun. You must feel around above you for the tiny entrance and hoist your body up into it. My books said that a full-grown man, with broad shoulders, could not fit through.

Again luck was on my side. I was a child, and a small one at that. I had to put Adam through first, as I could not fit through with him on my back. I took great care to detach him from my sling without dropping him into the ocean. It is not easy to transition through, but others have done it, so I knew I could. And then, once you are inside, to your left is a long, deep stone staircase that takes you far down—you walk and walk, as if in a trance. At the bottom of the stairs, you seem to have arrived outside again, but above you is lavender light instead of the ordinary blue sky. You arrive in a grove of evergreen trees whose needles turn to coins when they touch the ground, and the first thing you see in front of you is a great river.

At a dock jutting into the dark waters, a woman waits by a boat.

From my reading I knew who this woman was: Charon. And I thought I knew what she wanted: coins. Either coins from earth, or from the evergreens that grow along the river. But it turned out I was wrong. She didn't want coins. She didn't want coins at all.

I approached Charon slowly the way I had prepared to do. It was clear that she was a god, for her skin shimmered as if she had swallowed a sunset. And she was tall. Perfectly proportioned, but at least three feet taller than any other person I had ever seen. Facing her stood what looked like a whole village of people, maybe four or five hundred, waiting in a switch-backed line. Only their stillness gave away the fact that they were not alive. She was singing to these souls in a hollowed-out voice.

I was prepared to wait in that line for days. But first, I took Adam out of his sling, sat down at the bottom of a tree, took him into my arms, and began to nurse him.

At that instant, Charon paused her song and looked straight at me. She began to walk my way. No souls looked up. No one seemed to notice that their ferrywoman had left her post.

Her face looked wise beyond all ages, calm and patient, and she stopped just in front of me. "You know who I am," she said. "But who are you?"

"I am Ilya," I said. "My baby is Adam. And I have coins for you—once he is finished..."

"Keep them," Charon said. "I do not need your coins. They give me coins. I have plenty of coins. You have brought something into the Underworld that marks you as still living: your milk. A single drop of it is all I ask."

That was easy. But it was also unexpected. I pulled Adam off. Milk spat out and I caught a drop on my palm. Charon, with an eerie and unexpected look of hunger, leaned down and licked it off. And then she re-composed her face again to look calm.

"It is fine to give me milk. Souls bring me gifts all the time, though milk is one I have never seen. But remember this: the souls on the other side of my river are going to smell and want your milk. Do not give it to them."

"I brought wine for them," I said, feeling as I spoke that wine was irrelevant. My books, it seems, had been wrong.

"They will accept wine. But wine makes them restless. Rebellious, the Auctioneer says. Milk lulls them. And more than anything, these souls want to be lulled. When you come into their realm, smelling of white milk and holding that baby, you will be in great danger."

"Why milk?" Adam began to whimper and root for more milk. I gave it.

"Give me your attention!" Charon said this with such ferocity that for a moment I was afraid of her. Her voice quieted and she said: "You have braved much in order to come down here, and with one so young. I will not ask you why you come, for that is your business. But I will tell you what I know so that it may help you. The reason for milk is this: whenever a person dies, they come here looking for their mother. You think everyone would be unique. Nobody is. My job is to act as that mother for each soul as they cross this final river. But of course, I am only temporary."

She came close to my face as she spoke and—*you must believe me, Girl*—her breath smelled of milk. Like puppy or baby breath. That is how she calmed that line of ghosts. It didn't matter what song she sang. She breathed milk into their faces and they all fell calm. This sounds crazy. I know. I know.

Charon settled down with her back against the tree and shaped a pillow out of bluish earthy mulch for me to sit on, and a second pillow for me to lay down Adam. I accepted my own pillow but did not let Adam go.

Charon stretched out, barefoot; her long lavender legs stemmed out from beneath her skirts. It was impossible to guess her age. She might have been thirty, or three thousand years old. "I am surprised to see you," she said, examining my face. "Though the entrance is in plain sight, it is rare to see one like you here. Do you come on an errand for yourself?"

"No. For my mother."

Charon arched her back and laughed a sudden, wild laugh. "How could a girl be of any help to her mother by coming down here?"

I glanced back at the frozen souls to see if her laugh had awakened them. None moved. But her laugh had agitated Adam, who had begun mewing the way babies do. I said to her, "I want to bring back my father's ghost—for as long as I can—because it seems she cannot live without him."

Charon rested her chin on her beautiful hands. "This is not an errand you can do for someone else. You cannot rescue your mother."

My cheeks burned. I had dreaded hearing this. But I knew deep in my chest and belly that it was true.

Then Charon knelt down right next to me and began to whisper fast words into my ear: "But if you must try, I'll have you know that you are here in time for The Ghost Auction. If your father is in the Underworld now, he will likely be at the auction." Then the ferrywoman produced a tiny vial out of air and asked: "Can you fill this with milk?"

I could and I did. I offered it back to her.

"Keep it," she said. "This is your bartering tool. If you give these ghosts your milk, just as you without hesitation gave it to me, you will ruin the industry of the land of the dead. When you arrive at the other side you will see factories. Each factory makes the same thing: milk. Synthetic milk from the plants that grow in the soil of the dead, the leafy plants that the ghosts call blue sage. You will see that their milk is blue, not white. The dead do not see this. If the ghosts taste the real they will refuse the imitation. The ghosts do not want to be here, they want to be up there in the sun, a place they only faintly remember. Milk gives them the ability to forget the sun, to forget their lives before, to accept this place as their home. The Auctioneer has tried other things: water, wine, spirits. None of them work. But cows, goats, ruminants of any sort cannot survive underground. Their milk disintegrates, like everything else that lives. It is imitation milk that keeps the ghosts quiet for all eternity. That is the reason why milk is made in such quantity, at such a cost, in this land of darkness. There are new factories being built even now. The manufactured milk subdues the Auctioneer's slaves, so they can work to manufacture more milk.

"You will offer your vial of milk to the Auctioneer—the Auctioneer only—in exchange for your ghost. Don't think that by helping you I am sanctioning this as a good idea. Don't tell anybody what you have in that vial—the dead will not recognize it because of its color, and the Auctioneer will know immediately. State your terms, tell him how long you want that soul to come above ground with you. Show him the vial. Make sure that none of the other souls get hold of it. It would be detrimental in ways that you cannot know. Trust me. You do not want to meddle with the ways of the dead."

"How do I get back?" I asked. In all my reading, I had never once come across an Auctioneer. "Will I cross the river again?"

"You will not. You will go behind the stage into the Auctioneer's office and you will see a tree that cuts through his ceiling. This is the World Tree, and it links our world to yours. If you can climb it, and it is easy enough to climb, it will take you back to the top of the stone staircase, at which point you can slip back down the hole and safely into the ocean."

"Thank you—" I started to say, but Charon shushed me.

"There is more. The way they identify souls here is through the blue of the fingernails. I can see that you have worked through that disguise. Be careful not to touch any Underworld water for it will strip off your paint and leave you undisguised. Notice the blue dirt on the unpaved roads across my river. Be very careful not to get any under your fingernails. That is the other way this world traps mortals who try to slip through."

Something was nagging at me as she spoke. One thing I could never find in all my reading was how Charon had become Charon. Was there only one Charon, or did different souls take turns? She seemed resigned to her post. Yet the wildness of her laughter and something else, something animal—I recognized something in her, from what I knew of women, that made me believe Charon was unhappy.

So I asked: "Charon, were you human ever? Before?" She

watched me quietly for a moment and I worried that my question was impolite.

But then she answered, "Yes, we all were human once. Every person is born. How is it, then, that we don't think of birth as having to do with us? How do we all forget?"

"I don't know," I said. "But Charon—how long have you been here?"

Charon squinted toward the river. "I was summoned for this job and I obeyed. Some days I believe I am new to this job. Other days I feel it has been a long time. Either way, there has been one of me here for many thousands of years."

While she spoke, she opened her palms and I saw creases of blue dirt on them. She reached a hand toward Adam, but I held him back and covered his head. Charon's hands twitched, then dropped. We were finished.

"Goodbye, young mother," she said, standing up. "Do not come back here alive. But when you come to me at the end, I will know you. Take your ghost and leave quickly."

"Thank you," I said, "for your help."

"I will always help my young when they ask."

"I wish I could give you something in return."

"There is one thing," she answered, her voice thinning as she beckoned me to lean close. Charon whispered in my ear—*Girl, one day I'll tell you what, but not now*—and then she asked: "Do you promise?"

I promised. I was young. I couldn't have known all the ways that my promise to the ferrywoman would set the course of my whole life. But I did and it has.

"Until we meet again," she said. She bowed to me before retreating back to her frozen line of spirits. "One day."

Two

10

Ilya

I followed from a distance and stood with Adam at the end of the line waiting to be ferried across the river. The line moved briskly. I watched Charon sing to the souls, putting them all at ease.

On the boat ride over I sat among the rows of spirits, graying away from their original colors. They got on the boat looking like ordinary people, and by the time we reached the other shore, they were nearly translucent. I sat near the edge of the boat, looking down at the inky river with dark shapes moving slowly under the surface.

The turbulence of the boat ride seemed to upset my baby's stomach, for he burped up on his shirt. I cleaned it with my handkerchief, flicked it over the edge of the boat. As the milk flecks touched water, the entire river came alive and flashed green, with living algae, and all of the dark shapes became fish, huge fish of electric orange and red and purple—and then the river turned back to its dead-hued black. I glanced at Charon, and she winked at me as if to say, *I told you so.*

After a few minutes, the boat bumped against land and we disembarked. I looked back toward Charon to say goodbye, but her eyes were turned down.

I slipped into the quiet line of souls as they walked down a thin dirt road. Each soul faced ahead and it all felt eerie and automated. No souls spoke or looked at one another, and none appeared to notice me. Aside from the quietness and lavender light, the Underworld seemed just like our world, with towns and mountains and water.

The path widened and rock formations rose on either side. One of the less-translucent souls tripped suddenly over a rock, casting up a blue smoke of dust. I walked carefully around him, turning so that my body stood between Adam in his sling and this dust. In my world I would've stopped to help. Not here. None of the other souls stopped, either. The isolation that this world seemed to breed felt cruel and unaware.

Soon the road ended in a clearing. A village squatted in the center of it, similar in size to my own town on Dragon Island. All the other souls tripped on toward the village, disappearing between the houses. In the silvery light, the peaks of the houses and the blue-hued pathways seemed patient and old. It was peaceful and quiet in a way I had not imagined. I stood and looked, and I thought: *The land of the dead is beautiful.*

But this was before I looked up, around the clearing, at the mountains that opened into a circle, rising back like rows of shark-teeth beyond my sight, and for the first time I truly understood that my son and I could be snapped up at any moment by some force of this world. We could be left here among the dead, never to see the ocean or the sun again. My son could never grow up. The picturesque village sat in the sharp trap of the mountains. I felt how quickly this world would become small.

And at the base of the mountains, I could see cranes and trucks and bulldozers. I could see the morning workers trickling in, coming to dig up the innocent blue hills to build a milk factory. Gray-walled and steel-doored and industrial. None of this was hell, but it certainly wasn't death as I had imagined. Was it paradise? Paradise had to be back there, in the sunlight, beyond Charon's river.

I kept going forward, for that was the only way to go. I saw just beyond the village a clearing that held a giant tent. The tent was striped yellow and dirty white, not so different from what you see in the country, where you expect provincial people—*like Dragon Islanders, let's not fool ourselves, Girl*—to go to purchase their salvation from some quack of a minister. It was staked to the blue dirt of this world. Inside the tent were thousands of small folding chairs, all facing a wooden pulpit. It was empty, except for about fifty stone-faced spirits sitting in the back rows. They did not seem to notice me.

The Ghost Auction, whatever it was, had not begun.

To my right, something shimmered. It was a small pond between the tent and a purple pine forest—and splashing in the pond, there were children. They flashed in bright bolts of color. The more I looked, the more children came into my view. They seemed to wriggle out of the blue dirt, rise out of the water, descend from the trees.

Oh, they were happy, Girl. They were also all naked, even the teenagers who looked my age—your age now. But you almost didn't notice for they had streaked their bodies in animal patterns with the blue dirt, the way earth-children do with face-paint. Tattoos of fur, stripes, spots; several children had drawn feathers onto their arms, making wings; one had drawn a tail curling around his leg like ivy. The world of the children, all but invisible from the tent or the town, spooled out forever. Dead children have forests, wild lands, ponds, lakes—an entire world to explore. When they get tired, they nap in safety on any plot of dirt. Then wake and join the game again. There is no fear for them, no edges for them to fall off, no drowning, no dying—they can play unfettered. The adult ghosts mostly fall into face-ahead lines, but in the Underworld there are herds and herds of wild children. Seeing them brought comfort: any mother's worst fear is to outlive her child, and I knew if Adam were to die before me, at least he would have children to play with.

One adult sat in the dirt by the pond. One familiar frame, a rake-thin man. His face different, more distinct, than the stone-faced adults sitting in rows at the back of the tent. There he was, just as I remembered him, sitting among the children.

"Dada," I said, in a low voice, lacing through the children so as not to interrupt their game.

At first he did not recognize me. I did not look like a baby anymore. "Kalia?" he whispered. My mother's name.

"No," I said. "Ilya."

Then at once he held his arms out to me and he began to cry, big child's tears, nothing like the unmovable face of the adult I once knew. He sank into me, and it felt like hugging a man made of moss and fog. I do not know how long we remained in this position, my father sobbing into my arms. Adam woke and began to make sympathetic sounds, but my father cried on.

At last he blinked a few times and said, "Tell me, honey, how you died."

I said, "I didn't die. I came to bring you home."

He looked confused. "But how did you fool Charon?"

"I didn't fool her. I told her what I was doing and she let me onto her ferry."

"She let you—?" He appraised me with a slight shake of his head. "Strange."

We sat in silence for a moment, which I then tried to break by turning the sling around and pulling Adam out of it to meet his grandfather.

"That's a solid-looking sling," he said. "What do you use it for?"

"Not the sling, Dada," I said. "The baby."

"A living baby? Try showing me again."

I held Adam up, and my father looked from one of my upraised arms to the other, shaking his head, patting the air, but it was no use. He could not see or feel Adam. Charon could, but it seemed the ghosts could not. Or perhaps just my father. It seemed a brilliant loophole—one more way babies exist somewhere between the dead and the living.

At last my father gave up, and we sat once more on the edge of the great children's game. My father looked anxious now. "Are you hungry, honey?" he asked.

I told him no, that I had brought myself food and drink.

"Good. You don't want to drink the Auctioneer's milk, or the berries from any of these trees. Down here the children don't eat. They're too busy playing. The adults drink that crazy blue milk, and they do whatever the Auctioneer tells them, and they spend an eternity paying penance for it."

"What do you mean, penance?" I asked. "Charon said the milk lulls them."

"It lulls them into following his instructions and getting trapped in his auction game. Think about it, honey. Someone feeds us milk, we attach to them. The Auctioneer wants to play this role. But the children don't drink it—see how they have no problems?"

"I gave Charon milk."

My father sat silent for a long time. "I don't know about that," he said. "There's deep magic there, but I don't know it. But it wouldn't surprise me if that gift makes you responsible for her, somehow. Not now, but—well, I don't know.

"What I know for sure is how the Auctioneer uses milk. He greets each soul with it and they drink it and want more, and he is the only source. Then every day he puts on that auction of his, and the ghosts bid for bodies in order to return to earth. The price they pay to live another life is years of work in the Auctioneer's factories. But after death in that body, you belong to the Auctioneer. If you don't do his work exactly as he demands it, the Auctioneer can send you anywhere he wants, into any living body. He can make you a piece of coral, or a leaf of poison ivy. And worse, he can pull you back at any time, and lock you into one of his factories, keep you chained to one of his machines, indentured to him for eternity."

Adam squirmed and gave a small cry while my father talked. One of the children, a stocky toddler with fish gills drawn on each cheek and shingled scales drawn down her arms, looked up sharply, as if she had heard. I shifted Adam's position, and my father went on:

"It used to be that souls just floated through, simple reincarnation, then moved into bodies before they were born. But the Auctioneer changed all that when he arrived. He didn't want to be a ruler of a second-class city, a suburb where all of the citizens keep looking toward town. So he started his experimenting, to devise his so-called milk. The Auctioneer got tired of the souls going back and forth, only to introduce themselves and leave again. He made this system so that they would be forced to stay. He needs souls, strong ones, to form an army of builders. You will see high bidding for the most desirable bodies: many years of slavery to him promised after the earth-body has run its course."

"Why are people so scared of the Auctioneer?" I asked.

"You'll see when you meet him."

"But what gave him such power?"

My father scratched absently at his forehead and his finger skimmed barely beneath the outline of his skin as if dipped into a pool of cloudy water. "He came into our world with power, furious that his power hadn't granted him immortality. Those who enter here in that particular fury often retain it. He was a king on the other side, and a terrible, violent one at that. He has been here longer than I have, longer than most spirits can remember. But there was a time before the Auctioneer. I have heard the oldest spirits tell stories of such a time."

"Does it go on forever—this leaving and coming back?" I asked.

"Only until the souls cease their hunger. When that happens, they go dormant. Air and water, dust and plankton, they all are bits of soul, like sea-salt, that rest for millions of years. But if they ever wanted, they could come back in an instant. They don't want to, honey. The souls in human form are the ones who are still agitated and want to live."

"You seem peaceful enough," I said. "Where are the other souls like you?"

He chuckled. "My peace is an illusion, honey. You can't see peaceful souls. They're gone. The souls you see here are ready to go back to life, and if they have worked hard for the Auctioneer, they get to. I keep away from him and pass my days here, with the children. It's not a bad way."

"But—how did you get around having to work?"

"Anyone can. But you have to give up hope of going back up. I did the ghost auction once, to send a child back up in my stead—oh you can do that, honey, you can pay for other people to live again. I sent a little girl back to earth as a queen in exchange for a thousand years work for the Auctioneer. Why not? I have time. But then I sort of just...stopped. The system was too awful, honey. I couldn't do it. I stopped drinking the milk, stopped working for the Auctioneer, and consequently I've racked up a lot of debt. I wouldn't dare go to auction, or else he'd turn me into a lick of fire, or worse. But it's okay. I don't mind this. And when I am ready I will just...dissolve."

"But—you have to come to auction. The whole reason I came here was to bring you home."

"Then you have to purchase me."

"I know. And I have payment. Charon helped me get it. I'll pay for you."

"Honey, what do you have to pay with?"

"Milk," I answered. "Not blue."

He looked grave. "The Auctioneer will want that—only so no other spirit finds it first and calls his bluff on the horrid blue stuff. But honey, if you give the Auctioneer your milk, and if he drinks it, you will be linked to him. It may not be a problem for you in this life, but it could mean that he sees you as an opportunity: you, Ilya, as a raft to his rebirth. There was a time before the Auctioneer," my father repeated. "He has been in other worlds. It's not inconceivable that he could follow you up to yours."

We both thought about this for a long time. All of this was theoretical, of course, for we were in the realm of uncharted waters, of myth and ghosts—but so far everything had come some form of true. When I looked at my life and where it was most vulnerable, of course it was Adam who I saw. I could not imagine what the Auctioneer could do to hurt me unless it was to hurt him. But I had come this far, and I didn't see another way. My milk was the only bartering tool I had.

"Do you have a preference for which body to return in?" I asked my father.

He drummed both palms lightly against his knees, making no sound as he did. "No. Just pick one that has a long life."

We agreed that he would wait in the bushes near the pond and I would go to the Ghost Auction. With Adam once more asleep in his sling, I went back to the tent to find a chair.

Finding a chair in the tent was not so easy, for it now held several thousand ghosts. The only empty seats were close to the stage area at the front. *Girl, you may be wondering if I was afraid.* Yes. Yes. I was facing the unknown, and I could not estimate the Auctioneer's power. But I had already made the journey and met the guides—Charon, my father. I had accepted the sharp teeth of death. I had come to barter, after all, and the Auctioneer would have to see my face. I sat in the front row.

All the ghosts were facing forward, rapt and waiting.

At the front of the tent, about ten feet from me, on a wooden pulpit, with a campfire burning beside him, and a voice that carried itself like amplified magic, the Auctioneer appeared.

11

Sage

OCTOBER — DECEMBER

After two weeks of swims with Pupuka, two weeks of coaxing healthy meals into a grouchy, nauseous Marella, I felt it was time. I woke early on the first rainy day of the season and walked to Ilya's house. I remembered where it was from my first walk with Pupuka. It seemed a strange place to live, in a tiny bobbing houseboat with a slanted metal roof, chained to shore and surrounded by water, perhaps neck-deep. Deep enough for fish to swim. Deep enough for sharks.

The gnarled front door looked carved from driftwood. An upside-down horseshoe was nailed above it. When I knocked, a voice called, "It's unlocked!" and I opened the door.

Ilya wore a burlap tunic and had her long silver hair in a braid. She was standing at the side of a young woman who was lying on a tall cot inside the living room, which also seemed to be the kitchen and the entire downstairs. Ilya did not look surprised to see me, and she only said, "Hello, Girl," and to the woman on the table, "Do you mind if Sage helps? She is learning."

"Fine with me," the young woman answered.

"Sage, Penny," Ilya said, nodding to each of us in turn, and then, satisfied with introductions, went back to her job.

"Should I—should I come back?" I asked. I was not sure why Ilya had let me in when she was obviously in the middle of something.

"Stay," Ilya told me. "I will need your help." She then began to speak to the woman Penny: "Twelve weeks old. Your baby's fingers are starting to open and close. Soon the mouth can suck. Your baby is beginning to flower."

Ilya asked questions about the woman's appetite. She gave her ginger gum. The woman reached for her purse but Ilya shook her head. "No payment. A favor."

The house rocked beneath our feet, we three women filling up the entire downstairs. It was a witch's house, a house that belonged on stilted chicken-legs, or alone in the moonlit woods. Brass pots hanging from the ceiling, an herb garden sprouting along the windowsill; behind the cot where the woman lay, a big bathroom with a claw-footed bathtub and a clean modern toilet.

And then Ilya said to me, "All right, Girl, your turn." She asked Penny to pull up her shirt. Then Ilya took my hands and warmed them between hers and lay them over the woman's belly.

I saw Nana's hands in Ilya's—so papery and brown. She instructed me, "First you find the pubic bone. Here. Then we are feeling for the fundus, the uterus top. We measure how it grows. Can you feel it? Without a baby it is the size of a walnut. Now it is more of a lime. Soon it will be the size of a coconut, then a pineapple."

Ilya moved my hands around. I could feel something hard but I couldn't tell what it was. I was feeling self-conscious; surely Penny could feel my nervousness in my hands. But we went on with the examination, which felt long but according to Ilya's wall clock, took only a few minutes. It seemed I did okay, for at the end Penny thanked us both with what sounded like sincerity. "See you in a few weeks," she said, smiling.

After Penny left, Ilya peered at me with strange gray eyes. She wore around her neck a wisp of a leather necklace.

I waited for her to speak. What she finally said was: "You look like your mother."

Nobody ever told me this. Most people looked in hopeless confusion from my mother to my father. But as it was a compliment, I bowed my head and said, "Thank you."

Ilya watched me and I felt it was my turn to say something. So I asked, "Penny didn't pay?"

"No," said Ilya. "She has no money. The women here pay me any way they can. Some trade for my skills with lotions, wines, homespun clothing and handmade shoes, husbands lent out to fix my roof or build a new cot for my birthing mothers. Others bring money. I pay for things I need with my own skills, too—I have vegetables and fruit delivered each week from a farm whose four daughters all came to me. I needed produce. They needed my hands. We both gave and got accordingly."

"Now Girl," she said, turning the conversation. "Have you learned how to swim?"

I felt, suddenly, brave. Perhaps I had something to trade. "Yes," I said. Then I lay down my wish before hesitation could stop me. "Will you tell me, please, what you know about my brother—about what happened in my family before I was born?"

Ilya didn't respond right away. Instead she walked over to the counter and began picking the leaves off a spiky plant. Then she said: "Your brother was named after my son."

A shiver of excitement spun through me. This was news, and I waited for more.

But instead she said, "Please get me a jar from the cabinet to put the juice in." She nodded toward the area below the counter to the left of the kitchen sink.

I half-expected frogs and bats to fly out when I opened her cupboard. Instead, hundreds of empty glass jars gleamed at me.

"I knew you would come here. Your mother has shown up in my dreams, and each time she has been pregnant. I knew her life would merge again with mine—it is natural that it would be in the form of you. It is true that these days I could use some help. Listen, Girl. Do you remember your birth?"

"Of course not," I said automatically.

Ilya frowned. She used a hand-press to juice the leaves from the spiky plant into the jar, then screwed the top on the jar and put it into a small refrigerator. Then she reached for a big jar filled with dry leaves. "Help me crush this raspberry leaf," she said, and I joined her at the kitchen counter. We stood together facing the window, the sunlight in our faces, pummeling raspberry leaf into crushed dust and then filling jars with it.

"You do remember your birth," she said finally. "You just don't *remember* that you do. You were born in the caul. That means the sac was unbroken so you came out surrounded by water."

I could tell that this was something she wanted me to find significance in.

Ilya gestured wildly with her hands, drawing pictures in the air. "The caul, the caul, Girl! Do you know what the caul is?"

No, no, I did not—I had no idea what she meant. Ilya sighed and looked around the room. There was too much to teach me, no doubt she was thinking, and she was probably regretting letting me come in.

"Sit down, Girl," she said at last. "I will explain. All mammal babies form inside an amniotic sac. It is a mother-made ecosystem that meets the baby's every need. Some call it the bag of waters. In most cases it breaks when the baby is ready to be born, so most babies are born into air. A baby in the caul is born in her or his own water. Babies born in the caul are said to have special powers—to find underground water sources, know how weather will change, when fish will become plentiful. They are said to see spirits because they are of two worlds: the living and the dead, the born and the unborn, the ocean and the earth. They know things.

"You, Sage, are a caul baby. You are marked to change your world. You were born with a promise that you will be safe in water. That should mean something to you. Born in the caul, you will rescue at least one person from drowning. Perhaps you will rescue many."

"Who?" I asked.

Ilya raised her eyebrows. "How would I know? I am not a prophet. But it is there, written clearly on your birth. This is one reason why you must become a good swimmer."

"But what about caul babies who aren't born on islands?"

Ilya coughed impatiently. "Everything is an island if you just look for the water. And you know what else." She leaned close to me. "If you ever want your caul, I have kept it for you. Perhaps it does not seem a sensible thing to inherit. You could sell it to a sailor. You could also forget this conversation and stay landlocked like so many women. Or you could keep your caul. See what luck it brings."

My face must have relayed how dumbfounded I felt by the turn this conversation had taken, because Ilya said sharply, "Take that look off your face, Girl. I am telling you the truth."

I tried to compose my face to neutral. Ilya seemed satisfied enough.

"And so," she finished, "I have long known that you would enter my life. But I must tell you this: I will die before the end of your story. Try not to lose time in grief. Just float in it. Be in it. That's all. The real work is helping these women. They will need someone else after I go—someone with your powers."

I couldn't hold a neutral face any longer. I hardly knew Ilya and here she was hatching real plans for what might happen after her death, plans that involved my "powers." Out of nerves and uncertainty, I began to laugh.

Ilya looked surprised at first, then she shook her head. "You think it is strange for me to talk so frankly about my death? Well, why not? It is life that is frightening. Life batters us in all directions. But not death. Death is the stillness at the bottom of the ocean."

When Ilya said this, an image flashed through my mind of Nana's poor dead body falling through the water. Her ocean burial still seemed more frightful than any fact of Nana's life. But I could not dwell on this thought, or any thought, because Ilya kept talking.

"And so, Girl. Come here mornings and I will teach you the wisdom that women know."

Then she asked sharply, "Do you have a boyfriend?"

"No—but a boy, Pupuka, is teaching me to swim."

Ilya looked at me with her stern gray eyes. "Get his help with swimming. Do not become his wife."

I must have looked startled once again.

She went on: "A midwife is married to her practice. Her first loyalty is to the women who need her. Birth is not a nine-to-five job. You never know when babies will be born. You can never predict anything. A man would have trouble understanding this. Including yours."

This stung. I could stomach the caul, the swimming, the witchy jars. But of the few people I knew on Dragon Island—including my parents—Pupuka felt the most nurturing by far. I could not imagine him doing anything but good in my life, and besides, his attitude toward me felt decidedly brotherly: it was not as if he were clamoring to marry me or even trying to kiss me. But Ilya had a point. This was not a time when I needed to make myself vulnerable to one more person.

Then she said: "Why should I tell you about your brother? What good will it do?"

"Because...I asked? And my mother won't tell me? And I want to know."

Ilya nodded. "I will teach you things. And I will tell you stories: not the stories you seek, but the stories you must know. Here is the first: my son Adam had a boating accident when he was with your mother and now cannot say but a few words. Your mother's son Adam walked into the ocean when he was eighteen months old. That's all."

I was about to press for more, but Ilya went on: "Listen, Girl. Here is what I can do—I can teach you the skills to become a useful adult woman. If your mother decides to trust you, you will hear these stories from her. What you must do is work for me for one year. In a year you will learn all that you need to help your mother and yourself."

"I'm not here to help myself."

Ilya gave me a look as if I were a fraud and said, "You had better be. I am investing in you." And then she turned her back to me, leaving me feeling like an inconvenient mouse in her tidy kitchen.

"But first," she went on, facing me again, "before anything else, there is work. Only from work can you learn your value." And she told me to wash my hands again.

Then she scattered a handful of slender dried leaves on the kitchen counter and said, "I will teach you how to make a tincture. But first, look." She knelt and opened the cabinet doors and began pointing to different small bottles lined up in rows: "Raspberry leaf will tone the uterus to push. Red clover will help it recover. Fenugreek is for the milk, honey for any bother, kombucha for the mother's throat when swallowing tastes too sweet. The tincture in the smallest blue bottle is illegal and we don't speak its name, but it will help her relax and trust her body. For that is the mother's real work. Our work is to help her find her power. In life there is only the work. All of the herbs and their uses are listed in the big leather book over the stove."

Her fingers branched out when she spoke and she raked them upward, as if she were trying to raise the world from its roots. It was a decidedly witchy gesture. After she finished speaking she dropped her hands to her sides and peered at me to see if I was listening. Satisfied, she nodded.

"Time to start," she said.

We worked alongside each other, crushing dry leaves into powder, measuring powder into bottles and filling them with alcohol, until the day grew dark. It was the moonlight that woke us from our chores. We had been working together in silence since noon. But before I could excuse myself to go home, Ilya said, "It is full-moon night. We must swim."

There, in the middle of the kitchen, Ilya pulled her tunic over her head.

She wore nothing under it, no underclothes; I looked away so I wouldn't have to see her naked. Then she walked outside and the wooden door fell back to its frame with a gentle slap. I followed her outside and watched from the deck as she slid into the dark water, rippling the moonlit surface and going under until I could see no trace of her. She surfaced and for a few minutes floated on her back, her tiny brown breasts slipping out of the water. All of Ilya was lit up by the moon.

"You must use these full moons," her voice commanded me from the water. "Go in the water. Get filled up. Glow."

All of this felt unreal. None of her rituals or logic touched anything familiar from my life before Dragon Island, but here I was, I had found her and she seemed to believe I could help her. I knew I needed to meet Ilya in her world if either of us were to get our wishes. So I undressed on her deck and joined her in the water, wishing I had my bathing suit, but suspecting Ilya would have some argument against my wearing it.

The water felt good, but I didn't stay in long. Just as suddenly as she summoned me in, Ilya rose out of the water, gripping the deck's edge with her thin arms and levering her body up as nimbly as a child playing leap-frog. She stood on the deck in the moonlight, dripping onto the wood and appraising me in a similar way to how Pupuka sometimes did. Then Ilya said, "Goodbye. Come back tomorrow."

It was an abrupt dismissal, but a relief at the same time. I shook myself dry and put on my clothes. I walked damply away from her house. Even once I reached the road, I swear I could feel her long wolf stare.

As promised, I returned the next day—and the next, and next, until I was showing up at Ilya's houseboat after breakfast each day. Often when I arrived I found Ilya bathing in the ocean, her long hair knotted on top of her head, her shoulders bare and so thin you'd think she was made of coral.

Right away she had me making salves, washing sheets from births that had taken place during the night, pulping ginger into a gum for women who came in complaining about nausea. One woman vomited into a metal tub during her appointment. I must have looked panicked, because Ilya turned to me and said: "No worry—she just has seasickness in reverse. It will go away when the baby grows."

On our fourth day working together, Ilya handed me a metal bowl with a bloody organ inside. She instructed me to "slice this up for encapsulation."

I was so grossed out that I set the bowl down on the kitchen counter, wanting the thing away from me, and Ilya said, "Watch and get used to this," and she picked up the organ with her bare hand, placed it on a wooden board, sliced it as if it were a loaf of bread, then placed the pieces on a baking sheet that she slid into her oven. "Dehydrate on low," she said. "Tomorrow we will grind and put the powder in these." She shook a jar of empty pill husks. "Then—one placenta encapsulated."

When the women came to the house, Ilya put me to work with the beginning tasks, such as giving them cups to test their urine for protein, and she showed me how to read the paper sticks: green is bad, yellow good. If the stick went green, I stood at the side of the bed while Ilya told the woman to eat more protein. "Fish, beans, nuts," she advised. "We don't want you to get preeclampsia."

After the first mention of it, I asked Ilya what it meant. "Look it up," she said, nodding toward her stove. Above her little stove was a shelf and on it sat a doorstopper of a book, heavy and leather-bound, entitled *Book of New Life, Herbs, and Mammals*. I had to stand on a wooden stool to get it down. I found both a definition and a series of preventatives, along with Ilya's handwritten notes in the margin. "A condition in pregnancy characterized by high blood pressure." Then in Ilya's hand, "Protein prevents it. Daily 80g. Birth is the only cure."

That day—and each day afterward—Ilya sent me home with reading, complicated books describing weird medical problems, offering simple solutions. They talked about making yarrow tincture and motherwort tea. They talked about harvesting herbs in certain seasons. They showed pictures of women groaning in the pain of childbirth and diagrams of positions a midwife can help these women into.

My days settled into a triptych: mornings working with Ilya, doing herbal work and prenatal visits. Always in the afternoons, I found Pupuka at Sliver Moon Park and we practiced swimming together. Often this included trips to the elementary school to meet his twin younger brothers; we would walk with them to a café by the water and sit at a big window table while the afternoon rains came and finished, leaving the air thick and salty with a few juicy mosquitoes and some fallen palm fronds, listening to Pupuka's brothers tag-team-tell stories about the kids in their fifth-grade class. Their names were Enuhe (Caterpillar) and Hanai (Adopted)—but neither brother was either of those things, and Pupuka was unwilling to tell me their real names. I always spent evenings in the house with my mother, but the fullness of my days extended my homecomings later and later.

For I loved spending these hours in the house where Ilya lived. It felt, for the first time since I had arrived here, like a place where I belonged, where my efforts were welcome.

Everything in Ilya's house was tiny, ship-shape, warm and wooden. It reminded me of the boat where my father lived during fishing-season. It was two-story: to get to the upper level, the loft where Ilya slept under a slanted ceiling, you had to climb a ladder that was bolted to a built-in bookcase holding hundreds of books about herbs and childbirth and myth and water. *It is good for laboring women to move up and down the ladder,* Ilya said often. *It stretches them out, forces them to move.* The lower level held only the bathroom and the kitchen, and in the center of the kitchen stood a cot that could be folded up but rarely was. The herb garden flourished outside the kitchen window, and if you looked beyond it you could see the ocean. I loved the mystery of Ilya's glass-bottled things, tonics, tinctures, dried herbs. When the sun came through the windows, it lit up her tiny space in blue and green and gleaming brown.

We worked through the wet season: October, November. Life felt better now that there was something else in my small world besides my mother. Unsurprisingly, the heft of the information I was learning kept my grief for Nana at bay. For the first time in months, I woke each morning with energy—an abundant green energy that ferried me through my morning rinse in the outdoor shower, through the drying off amid the fragrant flowers growing wild in our yard, through the houseboat mornings and the ocean-swim afternoons. The days in these months flashed together in a way that made me wish for them to continue forever, though in the back of my mind, I knew life would change. I would be pulled back by the invisible cord linking me to my mother.

Marella was quiet now, maintaining herself with relative ease, and when I came home at night I found her either cuddled on the sofa with Lance or seated alone in her purple chair, watching the sea darkly as if it were a predator she was tracking.

The days stacked behind me—I had been on Dragon Island longer now, one month, two, three, enough time that I was no longer purely a visitor. Thanks to Pupuka, I knew all the streets and the secret ways to get across town. Often after swimming, after walking by his house to drop off his brothers, we went for walks to see the art evolve in Squid Ink Alley. There was a new half-finished work of graffiti, a green and purple shark. So far it was just teeth and tail.

One afternoon Pupuka and I were sitting in the grass beneath a guava tree, and Pupuka picked a guava and pulled from his pocket a small knife and cut the fruit open. He scraped the fruit clean and cut it into pieces for us to share. It was the color of sunrise and tasted like it would be rotten if it got any riper.

"Pupuka," I asked, my mouth sweet and sticky. "Will you ever tell me your real name?"

He wiped his knife clean. "Maybe," he said. "I'd have to know you really well. Not today, though. Today I am vulnerable. I keep writing to malacologists at universities all over these islands, trying to get a scholarship and a job so I can study. But they keep saying no."

"I'm sorry," I said. "Their loss."

He shook his head, shrugged lightly. "Enough," he said. "Let's swim."

I thought of trying to say more, but it was clear he didn't want me to. Perhaps, like his name, his hopes for his future were too close to his heart for him to share. But looking at his closed face, I saw that there was something there that needed to be brought out, like the rock I brought him from the shallow ocean bottom. So I asked: "What does going away to college mean to you?"

He smiled at last and answered immediately. "My wish to shed an inherited fear."

Now he was being sarcastic. "Oh," I said, cocking an eyebrow. Swimming had nothing to do with college.

He saw my expression, "Oh yes. From my parents."

I did his trick. I sat silent so he would have to talk. But before talking, he gave a dry laugh. "Men are also born from women, you know. You can't have the monopoly on inheriting things from your mother!"

"Well you're just repeating what I said when I was learning to swim."

"Because it's true. Look, Sage. Both of my parents never finished college. As soon as they met each other, they came back home, back to the island traditions they grew up with. Don't get me wrong: I admire their life and their love. They've given me and my brothers everything. But I want to go farther than they did, learn new things, then bring back home something I can share."

He paused, took another guava, and sliced it open. "There are a lot of different deeps to be afraid of."

So he too came from fear of the deep. But a different kind of deep. It occurred to me that perhaps we all come from this, in one way or another.

It occurred to me also that perhaps Ilya was wrong. Maybe right about some men, but wrong about this one.

I took his hand, the way he always took mine. I gave him a smile, which he returned. Both our hands were ridiculously sticky from all the guava. Still, we held them tight.

That day, we swam into the coral reef. Pupuka loved the reef, loved how it was the outline of an old volcano, the ghost of the older earth. A swath of yellow tangs rang past me and a long-nosed cleaner fish skulked along the coral, looking for something to eat. I saw an eel poke its head out of the rocks like a shy dog, a blowfish filling its round balloon-cheeks, and clouds of fish in every color.

I had learned by this point to control and deepen my breath, and we went out deeper and deeper. Once in late November we borrowed scuba tanks and saw a whale shark. It was the single largest living fish in the world, a dinosaur-sized fish. *It was a fish, how could it possibly be a fish, when it is longer than my dad's fishing boat?* It swam past us, curious. It tickled Pupuka's feet with its vacuum mouth, and then glided past him, sucking in plankton.

We went down deep together, again and again. And always the next day I would return to Ilya who began asking me to dive down and get kelp and wakame and other seaweeds. "You've gotten good," she said near the end of the wet season.

I nodded, catching my breath. I had been under for a long time, perhaps two or three minutes. Ilya had said that in her strongest form she could go down for six. I didn't know if I would ever get there. But I would try. That time I had seen a school of clown-fish, a manta ray, and—from a distance—a tiger shark. I was not afraid anymore.

I was learning, however, that Ilya had a fear: doctors. They frightened her and brought out her defenses, and so I added hospitals to the invisible list of taboos that I knew not to bring up. Around my mother the thing not to mention, of course, was Adam or the ocean, or anything sad or frightening. Around my dad, when he radioed us as he occasionally did, the taboo was trying to pin him back to shore; I could hear the land-trapped unease in his voice whenever I asked too many questions about coming home. Around Pupuka, it seemed that all topics were fair game, and that was one of the reasons why I liked him.

I learned about Ilya's fear when I asked her, one day in the middle of the wet season, if she had given birth with midwives. Her answer surprised me.

"No," she said abruptly. And then she began scolding me: "You cannot waste time in anger, Girl. You have to wish them all well, even those who have hurt you. Forgive them and then peace will come out from you like moonlight."

I waited. She was going somewhere with this, but I wasn't sure where.

"I was angry once," Ilya continued, "when my son was born. I had a long labor, over ten hours, and although the baby was fine, the doctor was tired, and finally he cut me open and took Adam from me. But the doctor was no hand at sutures, and people get infections in hospitals, and I got an infection that raged and raged until finally I had to have a hysterectomy if I wanted to survive."

She paused. Her face looked pinched and I saw her trying to work her expression back to calm. "The knife can be useful," she said. "In the old days, if a baby was in distress and could not come out, the only way to save the mother was to insert scissors and cut up the baby so that it would come out in pieces. We must be grateful for caesareans. But the human race has survived because birth is an action a woman can perform on her own."

I was still dwelling with horror on the scissors. But Ilya would not give me time to dwell.

"I became a midwife to give women the birth I wanted. The birth I should have had. For many years I hated the doctors. I hated them for killing my body's hope to have more children. But I saw how badly the anger harmed me and distracted me from my real work. And work," she said with extra sternness, as if I were about to argue, "is what preserves us. I saw that those doctors couldn't help who they became, for they are experts at surgery, not at birth. All I could do was forgive them and teach them, once I learned myself, how birth should be. I have never been angry since. Not even at your mother. She didn't know that she was leading my son into danger. She was doing her best in her own broken way. She could not help the soul she was born with nor the parents she was born to nor the things that happened to shape her. She was seventeen and thought she had seen already the worst that life can give. The story of Adam is a story wrapped up in other stories, and for me to tell you one means I have to tell you the story that birthed it, too. Stories come like women, one inside the next."

Then she changed the subject, as she often did, to the question of whether I had made any progress in remembering my birth. *Who can remember that?* I answered each time, but Ilya was not the type to change her views just because one teenage girl was unable to remember how her life began.

My mother had still not seen a doctor or midwife for her pregnancy, and as we moved into December, I got to work on persuading her.

"I'm not ready," she said. "Besides there is too much history for me to see Ilya."

But I think it was her own denial at having another child coming, more than it was discomfort with Ilya, that was keeping her at home and unwilling to seek care. I started placing articles about the risks of inadequate prenatal care on the refrigerator, and finally one day just before the new year, my mother agreed to come with me to Ilya's.

Walking with Marella to Ilya's house reminded me of the earliest days of my childhood when I still believed that my mother, with her long hair that could cover me like a tent, could be my protector. That of course had never happened, and here I was now, an adult, always the protective one, ushering my mother into a place that she feared.

We arrived at Ilya's house, and as had become my custom, I knocked once and then let myself in. My mother watched me questioningly but said nothing.

The two long-haired women faced each other like mirror-copies, an age bracket apart.

"Hello, Marella," said Ilya in her quiet voice. "You look the same as you did when you were pregnant with Sage. Now look how beautifully she's grown."

"Yes, she has. She is going on nineteen years old," my mother said.

"Almost a woman," said Ilya, nodding.

"Very close."

"I am grateful to have her as my apprentice, assisting me in my work."

Marella looked uncomfortable.

"What do you wish to tell me?" Ilya asked with uncharacteristic gentleness in her voice.

My mother twisted her hair and crossed her arms. "Look, Ilya. I've done this twice before and the pain nearly broke me. I plan to go to a hospital. I want a doctor to deliver the baby."

Ilya's next words flickered like a snake's tongue, the faintest of interruptions. "You will deliver the baby. Delivery is the mother's job."

Marella looked taken aback. She stood in the center of Ilya's kitchen and twisted and twisted and twisted her hair, tying it into a knot and then twisting the knot some more.

Then Ilya spoke to my mother in the gentlest voice I had ever heard her use. She said, "Hospitals won't cure you. There is still too much of Adam and it is poisoning you the way afterbirth poisons a woman when it is not expelled with the child. You could have this baby with doctors, surrounded by artificial lights and knives that stay sharp and machines that pump a woman so full of pain relief that she falls asleep and wakes up with a baby. But it won't help you. I will help. Sage will help, too."

Marella's hands flew instinctively to her belly. Ilya continued on, as if all of the information were written in a book in front of her. "You want to be pulled, and a doctor could do that, throw you a rope and pull you through the currents. But you have seen everything already. You know birth, love, and death. We all have gunk under our fingernails and it is not just dirt."

"But. I don't want it to hurt..." My mother was whispering now.

She and I both stared into Ilya's stern, sympathetic face, waiting to see her solution.

"Well, of course," said Ilya, as if this were the most obvious thing in the world. "Of course, it will hurt terribly. Just like having your heart broken, or swimming in cold water. You are opening like the earth to let out a new creature. It is violent. But it is a privilege. Men do nothing this grand. There is nothing so grand to be done."

My mother let go of her knot of hair and it spilled like liquid around her shoulders. She bit her lip then turned to me, and said, forcing a smile for the first time, "Well, then. Well—okay."

"When will he be born?" I asked. Nobody corrected my use of "he."

"Depends on when he was conceived—and you are the only one who can know for sure." Ilya looked soberly at Marella. "Do you know the date of your last menstrual period?"

Marella shook her head. She didn't pay attention to details like that.

"Well," Ilya said briskly, "I can estimate from your size that he will come between mid-May and mid-June. If you permit me to measure the fundal height and palpate, we can confirm that range. But if we don't know the conception date—and because babies come when they're ready—the day will be anyone's guess. For normal pregnancies—and yours *will* be normal," Ilya said in a voice that was almost too firm to be reassuring, "gestational lengths can vary up to five weeks."

I could see in her eyes that Marella was frightened. But she agreed to the measurements, which confirmed Ilya's best guess. Marella scowled and kept silent the whole time, masking her fright, as usual. But I could have burst for joy at the thought of getting to help my mother prepare for her new baby. And I knew it would be a boy. I don't know how. But I would have bet Nana's house on it.

As we left Ilya's house, my mother said, "Bird, you inherited the role of secret-keeper. It was my mother, but now it's you. Nana loved Adam, but she loved you longer. Yet she still kept the secret of Adam until the day she died."

It felt like my mother had cast a heavy net of fish up on the deck so I could see them—and I wasn't sure what to do, where to look, with all of these wriggling family truths casting their blue-veined underbellies where I could see. I didn't know what to do with this information.

"What secret am I to keep now?" I asked, at once knowing and dreading the answer.

"None," she said simply. "You don't have to. You can set them free. You can tell your father about Lance—I will tell him, anyhow. I am tired of the burden of these secrets. They nauseate me."

This was news. I looked at her face, trying to gauge her honesty. My mother had always seemed a cauldron of secrets, and disturbing their hidden places seemed the worst of crimes. She set her face sternly, glanced at me once, and then twisted up her hair.

For once I believed her.

12

Marella

It was a short courtship, a floral island wedding with waves wetting the bottom of my dress, and it came quickly to a pregnancy.

"It is a boy," everybody said, looking at the angle of my stomach.

"It is a boy," a nurse said, feeling the stronger pulse in my left wrist.

"It is a boy," said my mother, with a hopeful patriarchal smile.

"Yes, it will be a boy," agreed my husband, proud to have done it right the first time.

I gave birth at Dragon Island Hospital at age nineteen. The boy slid out, the doctor cut his purple cord and let him come to life breathing fast, like a train engine, on my chest. George stroked my hair and we stayed in bed all afternoon. I named him Adam: my dearest friend and my worst mistake.

George abandoned his research with whales. There was no money in it and he was getting hints from my mother, who believed men should have regular jobs with income. George bought a small boat and began a fishing business, which became a great success, as you know, supplying all of the Charon Islands with tuna and marlin.

It did not concern me that my old classmates had careers. Even Zach, after being expelled from high school, went to college and was now working in the mayor's office; people said he was likely to become mayor himself one day. Two girls from my swim team had found success abroad, one a chiropractor who worked on professional athletes, the other a journalist who covered politics and wrote a weekly column. They had become famous in the eyes of our island. Even my baby brother Kai had gone off to a boarding school where he was being trained to go to law school. He remembered to send cards for my birthday, but they were ocean monster cards, for the swimmer-girl I used to be. Our families always remember us that way, stuck in the amber of who we once were. Everyone in my world moved on while I stayed behind. This was fine with me.

After Adam, for the first time in my life, I felt like an ordinary woman, just getting pregnant and having a baby, as women do. It was so lovely, so simple. Nothing else required. I wanted nothing in the world except to watch him grow, to listen as he learned to talk, to feel him fall asleep each night in my arms, his tufted dark hair silky on my chin.

A year passed, a year and a half, five hundred quiet days exactly like each other. Long days, lovely days. We lived with my mother, who had all that house to herself. We could not afford anything else, and it felt like old wisdom to have children in a big house full of the generations.

Then this day.

This day was the one—

I could not stop this day from happening.

It was noon, the sun was so dazzlingly orange it made me dizzy, the bright sand was hot on my feet, there were no clouds, there were no other adults, the warm ocean water was at low tide. I was watching Adam.

There were no other adults.

Where were the adults? George was fishing. Mother—she could have been inside, doing chores. Or maybe she had gone for a walk on the beach. Either way, she was not there, watching Adam, watching me watch Adam.

Adam was one and a half. I was nearly twenty-one and pregnant with his sister. I seemed adult enough in my own mother's eyes and my husband's, and in the eyes of the invasive-species men who touristed on the island—one of whom I had married. I was lying on a towel, half-reading a book. It was one of those awful parenting books, how to raise your baby well enough so you can say goodbye to him one day. Maybe the heat made me sleepy. Did I nap? Did I just look away? Adam walked back and forth in front of me, holding his plastic bucket and shovel, making villages in the sand and then squatting, waiting for the waves to destroy them. Build-destroy, build-destroy. He was fine, busy, occupied, alive.

And then he wasn't.

I looked up and he was gone. There was the sun, the sand, the low tide, the no-cloud sky, the no-adult beach, everything in the picture was unchanged except the little boy was gone. Even Adam's sand castles had not yet been washed away. He never screamed "Mama!"

There was no sound. Only the ocean.

My mother found me when I was splashing through the waves, knee-deep and deeper, frantically looking for my son. She began to cry and one of the tourist men, out for a jog, put down his headphones and helped us comb the waves. The tourist jogger found him. He came to shore with his head bowed and Adam in his arms.

His face and hands were blue. I remember how heavy he looked as the tourist jogger lay him on the sand.

Immediately I thought, I will solve this problem. Nothing is irreversible, not yet. I thought this and other hopeful things as my son's body lay there in the sun, heavy and the wrong color and impossibly still.

The tourist jogger put his arm around my sobbing mother. I think he thought Adam was her son, not mine. I was not reacting yet. *React, Marella,* I told myself. *React. Feel something. What do you feel?* My mind raced to find a solution, while my heart was beginning to believe that no CPR would save him, no pumping water from his veins and lungs and stomach, no magic trick, no father-doctor present, no sun to dry him back to one-and-a-half-year-old normal.

All I could think was that it had happened again, but this time it would not reverse. Water did this. Water, again.

Finally, I began to cry.

The tourist jogger came home with us. He sat with me while Mother called the fishing company phone who radioed a motorboat to go find George and bring him back to shore. Adam lay on the deck of the house. From the window I could see his blue puffed-up stomach. I didn't want my husband home; I didn't want to face his questions about how it happened, who was watching, how long he was underwater, or to face the answer that it was I, I was watching, I was the adult mother who looked away.

The tourist jogger set the teakettle to boil and found blankets that he put around Mother and me both, as if we needed protection. He closed the windows that faced the sea. He mothered us.

Before George came home and the police arrived and the funeral conversations started and the teakettle whistled, the tourist jogger, whose name I don't remember, said to us softly in a Mainlander voice, "You two are going to be okay. Nothing will be worse than today, and every day afterward will get easier. You are still alive and you need to keep living."

For the weeks that followed, George hung around the house in his salt-thinned guayabera shirts, pulling at his beard, his shoelaces, his shirt buttons, watching me, telling me I should probably take a shower, eat something for the baby's sake. He initiated lovemaking once but I started to cry so he stopped. At last he went back to work and his days at sea grew longer.

As for me, I was swarming with visions of tactile objects: the cloth diapers with snaps around Adam's bottom. The bibs, the amber teething necklaces, the stuffed seahorse, his wooden boats, the plastic cereal bowl I taught him to carry to the table. I was the one who taught him to smell flowers and not blow out candles at other children's birthdays. I taught him all the things I thought would be useful. Except swimming: George had wanted to teach him that, had asked me to wait for him, but he was always away and never found the time.

Where did all that knowledge go? So much energy went into Adam. It had to have gone somewhere. Where?

There was a small funeral in a garden near Sliver Moon Park. Somewhere in those weeks, Adam's toys vanished. Someone (I suspect Mother) purged our house of Adam's toys, diapers, and bed, so that his room lay empty, just floor and windows. I found one of his wooden cars under the sofa when I was looking for my shoes, and it startled me.

My mother's house grew suddenly too big for us. I saw how the wooden floors were damp, bendy, about to sink, and the windows too wide, with too many views of the ocean. The eternal smell of salt in the rugs and curtains began to make me nauseous. There was too much water, and water meant death. We saw water everywhere.

And then the dreams began. The guilt. The constant thought of *my fault, I did it, he was mine to watch...*

And gradually I couldn't hear the normal sounds of the ocean anymore, all I could hear was it speaking to me, swelling into me, telling me that it had Adam. *I have him,* the ocean kept saying to me, over and over. *I have him.* It spoke with every tide.

I couldn't sleep. I couldn't eat. I didn't care that I was pregnant. The doctors agreed I would lose the baby so they took me into the hospital and hooked me up to machines that filled my veins with liquid that forced sleep. Even in the hospital where I delivered my daughter, I didn't notice the pain because all I heard was the ocean, who kept on saying to me, *I have him, I have him, I have him, he walked straight into me, and he is mine.*

When labor started, Ilya showed up at the hospital uninvited. She interfered with the doctors, making sure she would be the one to catch the baby; I didn't know why it mattered. But she pulled the sac away from the baby's face and body, and afterward she danced around the room like a tiny white-haired witch. She was chanting words that I hoped the doctors would ignore, words that made her sound crazy and provincial: *Your daughter is in the caul! She will feel at home in the sea, it will be her destiny to rescue people from drowning. Celebrate this daughter! This girl will be good luck in water.*

I thought, if I can get out of this bed, I just might kill Ilya with my hands.

When she danced within reach I grabbed her braid like a rope, I pulled her toward me, and I hissed into her ear, *Shut up, Ilya! Shut up and get out of this room. Good luck in water has come too late.*

13

Charon

Being alive so long is lonely beyond words and water. In the silence of my boat at night, the mind keeps ferrying. How did I become the woman who never lands, the deliverer of newly boiled pink souls who howl as they leave one life and enter another? All this rowing between land and land and I, always fighting nausea. By the door to the cabin below deck where I sleep is a red button that reads FOR EMERGENCY ONLY. I ignore it, mostly. I have never had an emergency. But I grow tired of this job, tired enough that I might do something wild, I might create an emergency. Something deep in me knows that if I press the button my boat will founder and I will be cast into the river. The fear of falling in water, the fear of drowning. This is the fear shared by all souls, the reason they come to me. It would be a hideous thing to go beneath. There must be a way to get through to the other side that does not involve water. I am told gods are immortal, but immortality is not something I understand. Water is. Mornings I wake in my cabin, rise from my mattress. I know it is morning because the first souls of the day are stomping their small pale feet on the dirt of my riverbank. In my world, there is no sun. No moon. Mine is a seasonless world. My world a lavender wood with trees bearing coins. My world a river. My world a wooden boat, solidly built. In the silence of my boat at night, I try to measure time; I hunger for chronology. Past and future are nothing to the immortals; they are just dirt at the bottom of a boat. Still, someone must have brought me here—there must have been a point in time when something happened. Will there be another point when someone comes to take me away? Time moves backward and forward, swaying despite my best efforts to anchor it.

14

Sage

JANUARY — MARCH

I remember every single thing that happened during the first birth I attended: the way the mother opened her mouth to let out the pain, and the way she could not stay still and kept plunging around the tiny house like a dolphin in a shallow-water panic, and the way Ilya said to her, *Good, you are doing fine, the movement will put your baby in just the right place.* How when the baby began to come, the mother squatted in the bathtub, pushing so hard she burst a capillary in her eye, and Ilya said *Relax your jaw, relax your jaw*, and once the mother relaxed there was a red halo between her legs and then a head and then a baby slithered out afterward, this bloody sea creature that Ilya caught and placed on her mother's chest. How they heaved together. How I tried to help by clamping the cord, but Ilya raised her voice and said, *No!*

And I remember my breathlessness when afterward Ilya told me that while the cord is bright-purple-alive and pulsing, the baby is still getting iron and oxygen from the mother. I saw what I had almost done by cutting it too soon. But Ilya was stern and she would not let me waste time on fear. She said, *Every new midwife learns the same lesson: try not to interfere.*

Then there was another birth. Then another, and after a dozen, all births looked alike to me: thin women, fat women, young and less-young women, scared women and brave women, all birthed the same way. *This is a good thing,* Ilya said. *It will help you be ready for the ones that go wrong.*

I saw women with twins, breach babies, big babies and small. I saw one woman who as soon as the pains came drank a pint of sugar cane rum and delivered her baby within the hour. *Each woman will go at it her own way,* Ilya said. I saw upward-facing babies who took all day to be born, and I watched Ilya rub those women's backs to soothe the back-labor. I gave remedies for nausea and I helped position women during stalled labor. I checked dilation. I listened through a carved wooden Pinard horn to the fast whirr of the fetal heartbeats, fluttering like hummingbirds. I checked mothers' pulses. I picked herbs. I dried herbs. I made tea. I planted seeds for new herbs. I made salves. I rubbed salves on the bellies of women who moaned in labor. I squeezed primrose oil into gelatin capsules and gave them to women whose babies were slow to come. I maintained the log of birth, weight, date, time. I lavished new mothers with attention and propped them up with pillows while Ilya supervised their first attempts at nursing. I saw women Ilya had caught as newborns come back asking Ilya to catch their own babies. I watched Ilya as she flicked tiny acupuncture needles into women's wrists and feet: wrists to hold the nausea at bay, and feet to tell the baby, *Come, come.*

Each time a birth ended, once the mother and newborn had spent a few hours resting together, we called a car to drive the family home, always from the same chauffeur service: *I helped his wife once,* Ilya remarked with satisfaction. Each time the house was empty after a birth, Ilya and I cleaned up: mopping the house from corner to corner, scrubbing the toilet and bathtub with vinegar, washing the bed sheets in the little washing machine under Ilya's bathroom sink, then lighting a bunch of sage and smoking out the smell of blood. Only then did I go home. And each time I left, Ilya sat up, perched on her stool, watching out the window and waiting.

We saw women like Lala who arrived unexpectedly, never having met Ilya before, and who squatted on Ilya's deck and delivered twins. "The doctor would've made me lie down," Lala said cheerfully as she pushed out the placenta, one newborn on each breast. We saw women we knew from town, such as Delia the baker whose wrists always had flour on them, and whose prenatal visits we did in the back room of the café where she worked: we measured her fundal height while Island Christmas carols crackled out of the overhead radio.

We tried to help one woman who showed up on Ilya's doorstep like a wounded mouse, shrouded in a gray pashmina. She looked prematurely old. "Even though he is a doctor, my husband doesn't know," she whispered. "The last time the doctors cut me up when I know they didn't have to. You have to help me get rid of this baby. I'm not doing that again." Ilya asked to feel her belly to find a timeline.

"I know exactly where I am. Eighteen weeks in. He doesn't know yet. I'm not going to tell him."

Ilya looked her over and sat on the cot, letting this woman stand, letting her be in control. "You've come to me for help, which I will gladly give. Are there others you can trust, Iolani?" she asked. Iolani looked taken aback that Ilya knew her name, for she had not introduced herself. It seemed Ilya knew the name of every woman on the island. Iolani pressed her lips together and looked away: a gesture I recognized from my mother. It meant: Do not ask me any questions.

Ilya gave this woman two options: "I can stop this baby from growing. But you should know that some women suffer afterward. Not in their bodies but in their dreams. They are haunted by this unfinished child. But there is another option. I can help you have this baby in secret, in a way that you won't need to be cut open again."

"How?" Her face told that she didn't want to rid her body of the baby.

"We will falsify your delivery date. I have a nurse friend who can help us. The hospital in Middle will trust her. And then your job is not to let them give you sonograms or any medications. This is the hard part. You must refuse them, and you must not let your husband talk you into it. That will give the whole secret away. Then you will continue to visit me throughout your pregnancy, and when you are still weeks away from your false date, but near your real date, I will induce the baby to begin stirring. There are ways midwives know. And there are ways to strengthen the uterus, teas you can drink, in order to push out the baby fast. You must come to me at first contraction, so your husband doesn't know."

Iolani looked at me, then again at Ilya. Her eyes filled with tears but her chest was puffed with pride, her strong shoulders back. She asked, "What if something goes wrong?"

"Sometimes it does," Ilya answered in a quiet breath, like a silver truth. "When it does, I transport the woman to the hospital in Middle. True emergencies need modern medicine. Most births are not emergencies. But in that case, yes, doctors would intervene. Either way, there will be a midwife to help you."

Iolani left and never came back.

Occasionally we helped women whose babies didn't make it out. Mina came to us at four months, weeping with cramps, then sat on Ilya's toilet and pushed out a bloody fetus. She came back into the room sobbing, incoherent and inconsolable, and I patted her back while Ilya tidied the bathroom, all the time talking in her soothing voice: "It is sad, certainly, because you were swelling out with love. But that is about you, not about the baby. The baby will flow back to the dark sea from which we all come. There will be another one who comes and you will belong to each other. Let this one go." When Ilya finished cleaning up the blood and the remains of what would have been a baby, she sat down next to us on the cot and I got up to make tea. While I blended Blue Cohosh with Cramp Bark so that her uterus would stop hurting and heal, Ilya asked her to lie down and checked her cervix. "You are sad," she said, "but your body is just fine. Heal your heart, use birth control, and next month you will be ready, and you will have love to transfer to the one who will live." Mina came back pregnant two months later, and this baby would live.

We also saw women who needed more help than we could give.

During one birth the baby's heart-rate was too low, the mother had been pushing for too long and was starting to hemorrhage, and Ilya said, "I know this is not your wish, but we need to take you to the hospital."

And the mother, who had been hurting like an animal for hours, spat on Ilya's face and screamed, "I won't! You can't make me! I will have my baby as nature intended!"

Ilya peered calmly into her face, as still and round as an ancient spool of thread, and said, "Nature intends for you to die."

Her baby was taken out of her by caesarean section, but both the mother and the daughter lived.

And there was Fara's baby, born on a full moon night with meconium, unborn baby feces, all over his face and nose, and even after Ilya suctioned his nasal cavity we called an ambulance and had to go straight to hospital, where Ilya and I waited all night with Fara for the doctors to assure us that the baby would be okay, and where every few minutes the doors to the labor and delivery rooms skewed half-open revealing mothers hooked up to tubes, lying flat in their white beds like pale sardines, not moving or making noise. It was the first time I had been to the hospital since Nana had died.

In the neonatal intensive care unit, where Fara's baby began his life, there were eight babies lined up in bassinettes, each wearing plastic bracelets on their ankles—"That's to make sure they don't mix them up," Ilya whispered—and nurses paced through the maze of bassinettes, giving the babies pacifiers or squeezing a bulbous tube into their noses and mouths. The mothers limped from recent labor and wore thin hospital gowns with slits at their breasts and repeated the same things to their babies, "I know, I know," and "Hiya, handsome." The mothers cried as the nurses instructed them on how to breast-feed their babies, and one of them said tearfully, "I'm doing everything you tell me to do, but it just won't work!" One baby was in what looked like a terrarium with a bright lamp shining on her. Her parents weren't there with her; only the nurses tended to her.

There were so many nurses. A new one came on every twelve hours. There were old nurses with gray hair, a deaf nurse with a hearing aid, brand-new nurses fresh from school, and even one male nurse. The male nurse seemed reluctant to give nursing advice and a few of the mothers looked relieved.

Nothing looked right to me. The babies seemed too far away from their mothers. They seemed too easy to mix up. The nurses didn't look like the nurses in Nana's wing of the hospital who wore white scrubs and white caps. Instead, these nurses had colorful animals all over their uniforms, which made me sad because it seemed for nobody's benefit—the newborns in the wing were too new to notice. Fara's baby lived, but we would not know yet if there would be effects in the brain from lack of oxygen.

Most of the births we saw during those months were just births. I was learning so fast that I feared my head could not hold it. We watched women birth in the bath tub, on Ilya's cot, on their own beds in their own houses, with husbands there or husbands away or no husbands or boyfriends anywhere in the world. Standing up leaning against the wall, squatting like a bear, bearing down on the birth-chair. Ilya and I, in those months, witnessed women birth under trees, in moonlight, in mid-afternoon, and once we helped a woman to give birth in a cave.

It was Pupuka's idea to explore another cave. There were a thousand reasons why not to go in, but our going changed everything.

I found a pearly snail on my porch one night, and at around midnight I heard my name whispered. It seemed not to be coming from outside the window, but underneath the house. Then there was a knock on my floor.

"Closet," said Pupuka's voice. I stepped into the giant closet—going in always felt like being swallowed by a square wooden mouth; I still could not get used to the size of this house—and got onto my hands and knees and felt around. There were three pairs of my shoes, a rug, and some old suitcases. I scraped off the rug and found a wooden trapdoor, simple and rustic. I wrenched the door upward. Below me, I saw dirt—the underside of the house. And there was Pupuka, in his bathing suit, smiling. He held out his hands.

"Bring your swimsuit," he whispered. I grabbed it from the hook next to the bed and swung my feet down into the hole. It took all my flexibility to fold myself into the two-foot crawlspace beneath the house; Pupuka held up a flashlight and guided me out. Then I emerged, and we stood facing each other in the white moonlight. "I borrowed a bicycle for you," he said. "Let's go for a full moon ride."

I thought of Ilya, doing her moon-worship swims. "How did you know about the trapdoor?" I asked.

He shrugged. "All these old houses have them. When you grow up here, you don't have much else to do except swim and explore."

We rode out into the moonlight, past the ice cream store, past the gardening nursery, Glinda's Day Care center, the one-room aquarium, the Fiddler Crab Night Club. ("It used to be the Salty Dog Billiard," Pupuka told me. "You should've seen *that* place!")

We rode off the main road with its bright streetlamps and onto a tributary road that ran closely along the beach. There were no cars. It was perfectly calm, and the night felt like something that we owned. The road ended suddenly in a thrush of forest. Then I saw a small pathway that led straight into the black rock of Dragon Mountain.

"This way," Pupuka said, and we took off on the path. The path had roots that were fierce to ride over, and rocks so big I feared a flat tire. Ledges of black rock hung over our heads. We curved around one of the rocks of the tail of Dragon Mountain and toward its enormous middle. Then we stopped.

"Rest your bike here," Pupuka said. "Let's go in."

"You want to go in there?" I asked. From the road where we parked our bicycles, it was just the underside of the volcanic rock—black and scaly, like its giant lizard namesake. We eased over to the edge. What I had thought was black dirt was actually water: a smooth, unmoving pool of it that started at the road and carried on, far, far back. I could not see the other side. The rock arched above us like the concave underside of a giant turtle's shell, rising and black and reticulated with rock patterns. Inside, water stretched from side to side and all the way back. Layers of rock swirled and swirled around. You could only enter this cave by water.

"I have always wanted to explore this place," Pupuka said.

We stood at the entrance to the cave. The tunnel of rock swelled. I could have pointed out that it would be better to wait until daylight. I could have said that the sign next to our bicycles read, "No swimming / Do not enter." I could have given a thousand excuses, yet I trusted Pupuka and I said yes.

I slid out of my clothes and into my bathing suit. Pupuka went first into the water, wearing a waterproof headlamp turned off. He swam easily, like a porpoise, barely making a splash. I tried to follow his strokes. The water was warm, *blood-warm,* I thought—then I chided myself for thinking it. We swam into the cave silently. In the faint moon-glow from the entrance to the cave, I could make out the black rock, the rising of the curved walls. This was the mountain and we were in its belly. I felt like we were intruding.

We passed through the antechamber, swimming through a narrow opening, and then the rest of the cave opened up darkly in front of us. Its shores to either side seemed very far off. The farther we swam, the harder it was to see. Pupuka stopped and began treading water. I knew he was looking for a beach or some sort of edge. He turned on his headlamp. He let out a low whistle. Even in the scant light, the blackness of the water and of the rock blended. We inched our way around this great underground pool until we reached the back of the cave where Pupuka found a climbable ledge. I scurried up the rock. Our voices, when we spoke, echoed.

Then off to the left I heard a splash. Then another. It was

the sound of something or somebody getting out of the water.

"Pupuka..." I trailed off. "Somebody else is in here."

"Let's go see who it is."

"Pupuka!" I hissed, not caring that my voice sounded like my mother's. "Where is your common sense?"

"Same place it always is. What reason would a human have to fear another human?"

I did not want to be in this cave with him, but it scared me more to try to leave the cave alone. Irrationally I followed Pupuka further into the darkness beyond the halo of his headlamp. The large cave sprouted into many tiny caves, like doorways. And there was a wet path left by a dripping person or animal going into one of them.

"Hello?" Pupuka called. "We are just exploring. May we come in?"

No answer but his echo. He bravely took a few more steps and suddenly he vanished into the darkness and I was left on the shore by myself.

Oh lord, I thought. *What had I done? Foolish, foolish girl,* I heard myself say in my mother's voice. *You've gone and followed a man and now look.* I knew I had to get out, and the only way out was through the water.

While I was summoning my courage to go back into the inky warm water by myself, I heard footsteps and the warm sound of Pupuka's voice.

"Here she is," he was saying to someone behind him as the headlamp brought back light. He reappeared with a group of women. One was pregnant and showing in a very big way. And I realized that I recognized her.

"Iolani?" I said.

She looked terrified.

"I'm Sage." My name registered nothing in her face. "How long have you been in here?"

She looked at the faces of the other women, as if searching for an answer, and she said, “Two weeks.”

Not knowing whether that was long or short in the scheme of cave-dwelling, I asked a practical question.

“What do you eat?”

She made a sound that was like a laugh but mirthless. It echoed against the rock walls. “We brought some food,” she answered. “We supplement it with whatever we find outside when we go out at night.”

“But you look as if the baby will come any day,” I said. “You need sunlight and plenty of food. Are you getting any eggs? Liver?”

Suddenly Iolani’s face changed from suspicious into soft. “You work with Ilya,” she said. “Now I remember.”

“You work with Ilya the midwife?” one of the other women asked. She had been silent up until now. “You look like a child.”

“I am eighteen and have attended over two dozen births,” I told her.

“Well perhaps you can help us…” said Iolani slowly.

And they told me the story that Iolani was too afraid to tell us during the visit to Ilya’s house when she came seeking an abortion. How Iolani’s husband, a prominent island doctor, but a drunk and an abusive husband, threatened her when he found out she was pregnant. It was from another man, she said, and her husband knew it because it had been over a year since they had shared a bed. She told us that she feared every night that he would kill her in her sleep. She told us how she arranged for her other children to live temporarily with an aunt, and then Iolani and her two sisters moved down into the cave.

“How do you know he will not find you here?” I asked.

For the first time, Iolani smiled. “Because he is frightened of the water.”

“That’s good,” I said, my mind racing ahead. “Well, let’s

get you safely to Ilya's house before the morning. That way..."

She interrupted me. "No," she said. "I would rather die in childbirth than go up where he could find me."

In the darkness next to me I heard Pupuka draw in a sharp breath.

"You won't die," I said crossly.

But inside I felt that she had brought a threat into the walls of the cave, one that I had hoped to consider only peripherally. Women did, on rare occasion, die in childbirth. It happened when birth went wrong and emergency medical intervention wasn't available. If ever there were a place where it would *not* be available, it was in this cave.

If something went wrong—the labor stalled, the baby shifted into the wrong position—what would we do? Force her into a kayak and paddle her across? A single contraction would tip a narrow boat. What if she had the baby in the water? Even if we did, by some miracle, get her safely across, neither Pupuka, Ilya, nor I have a car. Would we call Ilya's chauffeur, or an ambulance, to drive her to Middle? How long would it take for a driver to find us there, in the middle of Dragon Island, near no landmarks? And would a phone even get reception through these thousand feet of rock?

The threat that I did not want to look at straight was descending down my stomach like a stone. If ever there were a birth that had to go perfectly, it was this one.

Pupuka and I stayed all night in the cave formulating a plan. We would bring back a battery-operated sun lamp and fresh food. We would contact the aunt to purchase one-way tickets on a boat to Blue Island for Iolani and her children once the baby was born, and we would make calls beforehand to some relatives she had there to let them know she was coming. We would visit every night and when it was time for the baby to come, we would return with Ilya. It was not a perfect plan.

But it was better than leaving her here unassisted.

We left in the morning, as first light was spreading its circles through the water into the cave. Pupuka had to be at the school to care for the animals and I would go straight to Ilya's to tell her what we had discovered and where.

It took only two days before the birth began.

We worked fast. Ilya brought her birth bag and Pupuka paddled us across the underground lake in his little sea kayak and held up the light while Iolani tried to writhe out the baby on the blankets we had brought, alternating lying on them and on the hard cool rock. The headlight made her nauseous: "Turn it off!" she cried, and none of us knew what time it was or how long she was in labor.

Then the labor stalled and the threat became real. I wondered silently if the baby was stuck in an incompatible position, then at best she would end this adventure in the bright light of Dragon Island Hospital where her husband worked and anything might happen. And at worst…I could not go there. Instinctively I looked to Ilya but in the dark I could not see where she stood.

I felt panicked—both at the risk of the cave and because I could not see Ilya, and the whole situation transported me back to the day Nana died and I knew I would have to be the grownup from then on. But the thought flickered in my mind only for a few seconds, and then it smothered itself out—for there was work to do and I was the person who needed to do it.

So I did what I knew: I gave Iolani a tincture of Life Root on her tongue and I held down my fingers on the pressure points outside her smallest toes. Then I instructed the other women to help: *Hug her, touch her, talk to her. Make her oxytocin flow.* Time passed invisibly. Iolani lay still for a long time. And at last the contractions resumed.

Ilya stood silent the whole time. Because I could not see

or defer to her, I found myself doing the work, all of it, in complete and utter darkness. Pupuka flickered the light when I needed to find something, but my main tools were my hands. I checked Iolani's dilation but I hardly had to, as I knew by now that the sounds a woman makes would tell me how close she was. When it was time and Iolani was heaving and whimpering, I crawled up behind her and held my hands in the warmth under her birth canal, and she squatted like any mammal and heaved out that baby into my hands.

"Turn on the light!" one of her sisters squealed.

The baby, we saw, was perfect.

We waited with Iolani while she recovered, left her alone while she pushed out the placenta, and finally Ilya handed me the knife. I waited longer, until I was sure it was done pulsing, and then I cut the cord.

15

Charon

Time moves backward and forward, swaying despite my best efforts to anchor it: yet two points in time are fixed. Each point a gift. Each gift made from the body of a woman. The first gift came from a dead woman's dead baby. Each day women land among the dead like surprised tourists, clutching newborns like passports. When there are the babies squirming on the riverbank alone, the women pick them up. A pairing. The day was at first ordinary: the waiting souls were nearly all men. This happens when there is a war above. It seems this war has been going on a long time—or perhaps it just started and is stretching into the future. No matter. When the men forget coins, they shake and shake and shake the tree branches until silver coins fall. The women do not shake; they wait and barter. At the end of a line of a thousand men, I saw the woman and her baby, the baby's eyes wrinkled shut. This is not so surprising. Always some will die before they are born.

The surprising thing was a bluing thin film, like a water bubble, floating around the baby's head. A thing the color, nearly, of my world's dirt. A thing that does not belong here. Woman says, *I have no money. May I give you this instead?* I ask what this thing is. *It is a caul,* Woman says. *A sac to hold the baby before it is born, and usually it breaks in birth. But my baby was born dead and the caul stayed. A caul is good luck. Sailors keep them close. You can't drown if you have one. Do you want it?* She peels it off before I say yes and water splashes out, and then she gets on my boat. I put the thing away, in a secret place beneath my mattress, because you never know.

The second gift came from a living woman, a young mother with a living baby. She had come through to my world and needed my help. In return, she gave me milk. The existence of both gifts startled me. Here, bodies make nothing. Two gifts, two points in unbroken time, awakened in me an idea. Perhaps I could get to the above-world as somebody's baby. I could escape if only I could borrow a mother.

I waited. If nothing else, I am patient. I waited for a third point in time, another day that would be different. A day like a gift. One day—it could have been the next day, or a thousand boat trips later—no matter—there was a woman hiding in the tree shadows. I believe I had been waiting for her. She had long black hair glowing blue in the light and searching animal eyes. She hid in the trees so that I could not quite see her outline or the blue of her fingernails, to determine if she belonged here. On this day, a dead child waited in line. This boy could walk. He could wave as if hailing a ride, and he kept calling out, *Boat!* No woman picked him up—each time a woman tried, the long-haired shadow-figure scuttled out of the trees, scattering the would-be mothers. She was alive, then. She was alive and possessive. I took the boy onto my boat without a coin. He sat next to me the entire ride across, then back, then across, then back, and every ferry trip I made that day; all day he hummed songs that I could almost remember. This boy stayed on my boat until nightfall, and then he began to cry. Hunger forces them over. Souls get hungry, and I have nothing to feed them. I made a final trip across the river in late evening. The boy was crying but still I delivered him ashore.

This night I cannot sleep. I am waiting for the morning, waiting to see if the woman in the trees is still there, or if she has returned to earth where she belongs now that her boy is safe on the other side. I do not understand what has happened any more than I understand anything else, for all I have ever known are the three facts of my world: that I must keep rowing, that water is not safe, that souls need help crossing rivers.

In the morning, I cannot see her anywhere, and I think: this is as it should be. But then I see that my river is all wrong. The water has come alive, too bright for my eyes, and all of the dark shapes have formed into unknown fish like underwater giants swimming around something or someone who has fallen in. I see her hair, tangled like river-grass, below the surface of my river. I recognize her but cannot tell if she is still alive or whether her movement is only the current jerking her this way and that. I pull from beneath my bed my drowning shield, the smooth-as-a-sea-creature caul. I press it into my clothes. I push FOR EMERGENCY ONLY.

There is a rumble in my boat as if the river itself has been upturned. A tidal wave upturns my boat and I am slammed overboard, floundering in my river, cold and with no idea how to swim. I have never raised my voice, never once screamed, but a petrifying sound leaves my mouth. Then my mouth fills with water. *So this is drowning, then.* It is sinking in swirls of black and salt. It is past and future collapsing my air. It is kicking toward some vanished safety, toward what used to be my boat. It is going under, telling myself, *this happens to us all, it is no matter, no matter, no matter, but*—I am grabbed by the shoulders and pulled into air. I gasp. Am I alive or am I dead or both, forever? The animal-eyed woman is in the water with me, smaller than me by half, and her strength is ferocious. She drags me onto the riverbank, where I lie panting in the blue dirt.

16

Marella

There is no word for somebody who loses a child. If I lost George, I would be a widow. If George and I both died, our child would be an orphan. But for me, there was no word. I was nobody, not-a-mother. Without a word to describe them, people sink into invisibility, as into the ocean.

The ocean had words: *I have him…I have him…I have him…I have him…*

The ocean was not the only voice I heard after Adam died, in the months after Sage was born. The other voice was even stronger than the ocean and it took shape in a familiar form: a long-legged man who hung about the shadows and followed me everywhere. He was like a dog. Like a hopeful suitor. He dressed in a somewhat old-fashioned way; he carried a pocket-watch. His hair was pale blond with streaks of gold, shoulder-length; his skin taut and tan, his eyes blue with eddies of green, his bone structure perfect, as well as his lips. But his teeth, his teeth were not beautiful; they were sharp, like the tiny, layered teeth of a shark.

I knew who he was: the one who showed up and vanished on the beach when my brother nearly drowned. I had aged since then; he looked the same. He appeared again in the hospital room when my daughter was born, just after my mother and George left me alone in the room so that I could have a private moment with the baby. He materialized into the air, *wahoo*-ing like a surfer-boy. As if my after-birth was his safety raft and he was a refugee from some thrilling shipwreck. He stretched, found a plastic hospital chair to sit in, and crossed his legs. He watched as I surveyed the closed face of my baby. He looked hungry, like he wanted something.

I knew him. This man was Mortalis.

But nobody could see him except for me. I tried to point him out to George and to my mother. They thought I was losing my mind. I thought so, too. But then something happened to prove that my mind was still intact.

People brought meals those early weeks, as they had with Adam. Ilya came to see that I was healing—as she had with Adam. I undressed in the baby's room. While she examined me, Mortalis stepped silently through the closed door. It embarrassed me that he could see me naked. It embarrassed me that such a thing could embarrass me. I squirmed and Ilya looked up and straight at the intruder.

"What are you doing here?" Ilya asked him, her voice suddenly sharp.

"You can see him?" I asked. Nobody else had noticed, even though he had been in the house a long time.

"Yes," she said quietly, without taking her eyes off him. "I know that man. A long time ago he and I made a bargain."

"About what?" I whispered, trying not to wake the baby from her fragile nap.

"About you," said Ilya. Never one to coat anything in honey. "And—if I'm not mistaken—you've been down below those rocks before too. And you made a bargain about *her*," she said, with a tilt of her head toward the baby's crib.

I began to sweat. Mortalis knew that I was agitated. He grinned wider, showing those teeth.

"Shoo," Ilya said to him, like he was a stray. "Get out of here!"

When he didn't move, she grabbed a bottle of milk from the table near the crib, and she squirted him right on the face. He licked his face where the milk landed, and he disappeared. Had he used the door? I kept looking.

Ilya took my chin in her hands like a firm grandmother. She turned me to her and said, with a stern face, "As long as you cling to life, he's got you. As long as you're afraid."

"What does he want?" I asked Ilya after he had gone and the baby had begun to stir. But Ilya wouldn't say. She would only shake her head and look long at the baby.

When I healed and began slowly riding my bicycle to the market to buy fish and fruit, I saw him watching me, winking at me when I clipped on my helmet. I tried to go about my days but still he was everywhere. Each time he appeared I tried to avert my eyes, but he showed up whenever I had one of those imaginings that we all have, such as finding my bike's brakes stuck just before a busy intersection, or choking on salmon bones, chicken bones, too-big bites of meat. Getting slammed by a careless driver, thrown from the car, decapitated on a sharp edge of a road-sign. My deaths were always accidents, catastrophes, things that nobody could prevent. And I saw my daughter's death too, everywhere: drowning face-first in the dog's water bowl. Drowning in the bathtub, in the ocean, in any body of water. Falling off a railing on top of Dragon Mountain, sliding out of my arms and onto the rocks below. I hated imagining it. But I could hear the snap of her broken neck.

In the deep pockets of night when I woke to feed her, treading water in my exhaustion like a half-woman, half-shadow, the only question in my mind was *What will it be? How will she die?*

My awareness of loss spread everywhere, making my life leaky, permeable as frog-skin. My fears kept me awake in the night, curling into my belly and cramping my muscles like a phantom-child. If I could get an answer now, I was sure I would stop worrying. How would I know that she would be okay, that all of this love I was putting into her wouldn't be wasted?

I tried to leave my daughter with George and Mother, for it seemed that Mortalis wanted me, wanted me alone, and I felt she'd be safer if I kept myself away from her. Ilya's words about him felt noble but ultimately useless. Of course I was afraid. Isn't everyone?

I could not sleep, I could not eat, with the ocean always talking to me or with Mortalis lurking in corners and sponging me up with his eyes. At first I tempted myself, walking into the ocean, going as deep as I could go without getting caught by the undertow. I spent three weeks of nights in this way, while George and my mother watched from the lit porch, worrying. Neighbors watched too. Myths began about a ghost woman with long hair who hovered at the beach-line, looking for her lost son. *She will pull you into the water with her,* people whispered. People began to warn their sons about me. I hated living on Dragon Island, all of the eyes staring without reserve; I hated how much every stranger knew. I stopped leaving the house, except at night.

My mother paid for me to see a shrink who came to the house. He was the first of many. New myths circulated about me, and the myths were not flattering. I was the Shrieking Woman. I had caused the great tsunami.

"Get me out, get me out, get me out!" I wailed at George and Mother through the fog of those first months after the new baby came. I told them that I would not live by the ocean another day in my life. They made all sorts of protests but they could see I was slowly losing my mind and so when my daughter was only four months old, George and I said goodbye to my mother and left Dragon Island and moved to dry land for what I hoped would be forever.

When we moved into our high-rise apartment on Blue Island, a landmass so big it felt like a continent, I couldn't see the ocean from my windows. I couldn't see water from anywhere in our land-locked neighborhood. I felt safe, at last. I felt that I might move on.

George's days at sea lengthened and I was home alone with Sage. My sense of safety gave way to a horrible fact: even away from Dragon Island, Mortalis *still came around.* And I realized a pattern: Mortalis only came near me when I was alone or alone with the baby. I had escaped the ocean, but still he followed.

"Stay here," I begged George. "Get an inland job." And when he said he needed to keep working the fishing boats to make our living, I turned to my mother and implored her, please, *please* to come live with us whenever George was away. It tore at her heart to be away from Dragon Island, but she did. My daughter and I stayed safe that way for a long time.

Mortalis looked where I looked, and he placed value where I placed value. I learned to look everywhere except at Sage. I couldn't let him see how much I feared for her. Let him see the dog, Julep, or some lesser creature. Let him see me, just me. He can drown me in a heartbeat but don't take her. I dragged my eyes away from her, and kept them on myself, on my mother, on George, on any book I read or glinting thing that caught my eye.

Eighteen years passed this way. I could love her only when other people were chaperoning me. Otherwise when I looked at her I could only see how mortal she was.

Of course, those years were all you'd expect, with a daughter who couldn't get her mother to look her in the eye. Sure, I tried to get better but these islands are useless in matters of the heart. All the smarties moved to continental cities, but I could not imagine going there—they seemed too big, they would swallow me up just like the ocean. If you go there you'll drown dry.

So I moved from office to office and L.P.C. to Ph.D., and I shed fragments of my story all over town. Each office looked the same, so bare, so neutral: tan sofa, tan rugs, tan walls, the only color coming from the candy bowl where all of the salt-water taffies were stale. I brought my own food and kept talking. Telling my secrets to soft-toothed men in offices, each man as pink and hairless as a baby rat, men I could eat in a single bite if I lost control. But I couldn't lose control. All those office visits were so that I would *not...lose...control.* All those men felt like pale versions of my father, a true doctor and rescuer, though even he couldn't have rescued me. The men tried me on one antidepressant, then another, tinkering with my brain-magic, saying *perhaps this will work*, but—*disclaimer disclaimer*—there are possible side-effects, weight gain, hair-loss, hallucinations.

I took them. I did not care. I needed to get better fast, because she was always watching. Always. I know she watched her father too, could see the tired marks around his eyes, sunburn from too many hours outdoors and scars on his hands from being hooked too many times, all to support an island woman who doesn't wish to work, who just moons around the house like a sad work of art and eats the fish he brings home.

I followed one doctor's instructions to keep a diary and I told my daughter, *Hush, hush I'm writing, I'm thinking, I'm working on getting better.* Sage always wanted to know everything, like all the curious women in history: Pandora,

Eve, any nosy wife. When I grew tired of writing about myself, I read the old myths and wrote about them. Each word I wrote seemed a small and vacant island, at risk of drowning in the space at the edge of the page. I wrote less and less. Even so she always wanted to know what I was doing and so I gave her crumbs: *I'm making notes on Underworld myths, this one is about a ferryman but I've made him into a woman. No, you may not read it.* But she ate up the crumbs and wanted more. This hungry, hungry daughter. I knew from the start that she was clever, while Adam would have been kind. She was always hungry, even as a baby; her eel mouth struck out and demanded more all the time. While he took what I gave him. He rested. Maybe I gave him too much, I exhausted myself, and that was why I slept that day.

Sage watched all her childhood long, trying to decipher me. But I could never relax; I could never find the right distance away from her, far enough but still close. Maybe it is a daughter thing, seeing how you look through their eyes and how much bigger it is than you could ever be on your own. Your husband knows better—you've fallen off his pedestal enough times—but the daughter persists, she has to believe in a perfect whole woman. She rolls your faults into a picture that she loves and wants to hold up and show everybody, and the whole idea makes you sick and sad at once.

I remember when she came home from school with a picture she had drawn of me, and it was so beautiful, her lines and colors were just so *her*, and it was of me smoking a cigarette in the morning, something I sometimes liked to do…but all I could think was of the other mothers, none of whom were pasteled with their cigarettes. Do you think Mrs. Kamu was pictured anywhere except among her garden-award flowers? Or Mrs. Mull who shows up at school with her thousand hair bows and her Virgin Queen make-up, certainly her daughter didn't catch her in a private moment without her ready-face on. Mine did and I loved and hated her for it.

"I used all sixty pastels!" Sage said proudly.

The pictures had hung on the school bulletin board for a week: a week when all anyone would be able to remember was that Mrs. Brouge, Sage's sad/mad/bad mother, was caught on her porch with a cigarette.

I got worse every time George came home. One night, when she was maybe three or four years old, it got so bad that I had to run away. Go ahead and say it. Mothers don't run away. Well, I did. It was the time we stayed a night at the Sand Castle Motel because Julep the ancient one-eyed dog rolled in feces and then rolled all over the living room floor, delighted at herself for bringing such an extravagant scent home. It was George's job to bathe her, but George was out at sea.

I kept my temper all afternoon and into the evening when the fishing boats came home to roost. George came home tired and said, "Relax, call the groomer tomorrow," and I ticked silently and finally exploded and packed the car, and Sage and Julep and I slept in a little filthy hovel that night with silverfish on the shower grout between the tiles. I spread out a towel and Julep slept on the bathroom floor, whining all night because I would not let her in the bed. There were flies on the pastries in the continental breakfast buffet. George picked us up and said severely across the vastness of the car's front seat, "Your flights are a mad dash toward divorce. If that is what you want, just say so."

Was it after that that my daughter became a rescuer? How when I caught the shaved coconut for George's birthday cake on fire, George kept saying, *relax, relax,* and Sage, tiny even for a kindergartener, stood between us and stared at him with adult eyes and said, "Dad, never tell a woman to relax—you must see she has a *reason* for not relaxing!" Yes, it was rescuing that she did, telling George how to be gentle, trying to make friends for me by setting me up with her friends' mothers, one time as a teenager going so far as to sign me up to host a foreign exchange student, because she decided I needed another child to be happy. *Did you know that there are four thousand Chinese students who want to study abroad before college?* she asked. I called the program and told them my daughter had signed us up as a prank. I knew it wasn't a prank but still I needed to embarrass her a little, show her that she can't go meddling all the time, that a mother doesn't want to see her daughter play all those desperate Prince Charming tricks. The rescuing went on, the cliché of who-is-helping-whom, and thank-god-for-Nana-because-Mother-is-falling-apart.

There was the village they built, Sage and my mother, when Sage was twelve and too old for make-believe. How they found boxes in our building's trash room and made them into a town that looked like Dragon Island, a place I had refused to let Sage visit, even though my mother kept asking. It had a store that sold fishing tackle, two rival schools, a doctor's office, homes with family rooms, a marina full of boxy cardboard boats, and six flat boards painted blue for the ocean. They were in the middle of building a five-story hospital complete with surgery room when George returned from sea and my mother went back home and we threw out all the boxes.

Sage cried at the loss of her village. Did I read too much into it? Was Sage living in that cardboard world because she did not trust her parents' world? Because she saw that real adults in real houses inside real villages define their lives by real sadness?

But at times I felt hope, and those times I knew I could perhaps be a decent mother if I tried hard enough. When we were sitting at the kitchen table during an afternoon thunderstorm, Mother was with us, and Sage was laughing about a boy in her class who had too-long monkey arms and a goofy voice, and I stopped her and said, "Any time you feel like making fun of someone, remember that that person has a mother who loves them best of all. If you treat them badly, it is their mother who you hurt." It was a lecture my mother gave to me once too, when I made fun of a strange boy in my class named Adam, who later became my best friend. I believe my words made my daughter a kinder person. I got that part right. But for her brother, I did a single thing wrong, and I will never forgive myself: I looked away.

17

Charon

She drags me onto the riverbank, where I lie panting in the blue dirt. At last I open my eyes and the shadow-woman is watching me. Seeing what, I do not know. She says at last, *I am just like you. I cannot decide if I want to stay on earth or go into the darkness. My curse will be to row back and forth endlessly.*

I do not understand what she is saying. I do not know if I am imagining things. I know nothing except that I have not drowned. I vomit up river water and it tastes like salt and ancient rot. Now the woman is crumpling into my arms. Is she a spirit or not? I look frantically around, checking for signs. Not knowing what else to do, I comfort this woman. Not with a song, but instead I hum to her, touch her hair. At last the woman looks up, then stands. She has a rounded stomach. I ask her:

- *Why did you do that?*
- *You needed rescue and I am a swimmer.*
- *That boy—is that your—?*

- Shhh.
- Who—are—you? You remind me of someone—who came here—long ago. She had a son—a living son.
- You let her come through.
- Yes—but her life isn't better for it.
- Her life isn't my life. Bring me across to that boy. Please.

- You should go back. You are with child.
- It happened. I wish it hadn't. Let me on your boat.
- Not when you carry life within you that deserves the world whole.
-
- Have you named him?
- Her. She'll be called Marella, after me. I was named for my mother who was named for the ocean.
- What a pretty name to inherit.
- I don't want to go back up.
- I would do anything to go up.
- Trade places with you.
- I have a job. You probably wouldn't like my job. But you could bring me up.
- To do what?
- I'm sure there are jobs above that involve boats.
- There are. But I don't think you want to live where I live. Where I live is water-scarred. Haunted.
- Is there sun?
- Too much sun. I would rather stay here. My son is here.
- Not here. On.
-
- I'm sorry. I'm sorry he's not with you. I know it is not where you want him to be.
-
- I'm just—sorry.

-

- Will you tell me, please, what happens when people are born up in the sun?
- They come out crying...
- Why?
- Because they need air.
- Oh.
- They come out crying and bloody. They begin breathing on some woman's swollen chest.
- What happens in the sun when they die?
- They just...stop. And then I suppose they show up here.
- Let's help each other. I'll get you back to earth where you belong, and you bring me with you.
- But how?

I don't know this script any more than I know life away from my boat. If I do this, there won't be any me. These trips across the river will stop. The souls will gentle into dust and air and plankton, as all souls do in the end. They will not go On. The Auctioneer's industry will stop. It would be for the better if it did. This poor mother must not know about the Auctioneer.

I have a caul in my hand and this woman is here and I feel certain that I can be born, whatever that is, into the sun.

I look back toward the river; I close my eyes, saying a silent good-bye to my boat. I curl myself up as small as I can; I fold like a seedling inside the caul. I look up into the face of the woman, I tell her: *I'll guide you back up the stairs and away from here. Don't let go of me and I will keep guiding you. You won't remember this in the morning. I will be born as your daughter. You'll name her something else, not after the ocean, but for the gray Seer's Sage whose roots become our Underworld trees. The name will just come to you and you'll give it. But none of this will you remember.*

- *That's good. I hope neither will you.*

Now the woman is walking barefoot away from the river and into the lavender trees; she is carrying the caul next to the warmth of her belly, and within the caul, like a husk, she carries me, or the seed of what once was me. My mind is awash with all I have seen.

18

Sage

MARCH

After the cave birth, once I felt sure both Iolani and her baby were doing well, attended by the other women, supplied with enough food and water to last until they left the island in two days' time, and secure with a plan to meet her other children—once I had made sure all of these details were seaworthy, I promised to come the next day to check on them, and then we three said goodbye and climbed back into Pupuka's little sea kayak and he took us back to the cave's mouth. An earthy new energy sparkled between the three of us.

"Look," said Ilya, as we came into the moonlight outside the cave. She took my hands in hers and held them up in the light of Pupuka's headlamp. "Now your hands look like mine."

I stared at my hands in mute astonishment. They did look like Ilya's hands after a birth: calm, unshaking, with rust-colored creases and purplish silt under the nails. That night my hands were bloody, swift, and certain of their work. Even in the dark they had known what to do.

Back at the houseboat, Ilya and I made fast work of the

after-birth: we simmered the placenta with ginger and lemon, set it out to cool. We readied some herbs for Iolani to take. While we worked, Pupuka laundered the soiled linens.

Once we finished, it was only an hour or so before the sun would rise. Ilya and Pupuka and I sat together on the deck of Ilya's house, our feet dangling toward the water. Pupuka asked Ilya's permission to swim, and he stripped to his shorts. I joined him in the water while Ilya walked into the house, leaving us outside alone. We tread water for a long time. Suddenly Pupuka turned to me in the pinking darkness and said, "That was the most amazing thing."

We had just emerged from a crazy night. A birth among births. The water swirled around us. It was too dark to see the expression in his eyes but I could hear the eager sweetness, the sincerity, in his voice, when he said, "I know you will spend your life doing this. You were fearless! I've just seen you in your essential state. I want to see you forever this way."

I swam over to him and we wrapped our arms around each other, treading water in this position until our legs grew tired and we began to sink. Water slid into my mouth. Laughter spilled out. I felt moon-drunk, purposeful, proud to be a midwife.

All the small windows in Ilya's house were beaming light. We got out of the water and dried ourselves and sat on the deck, wet spots spreading from our legs like shadows. Ilya came out to the deck and began doing her morning leg lifts. It was just after six.

"I should get home," I said. "My mother hasn't been eating well and I need to make sure she eats."

Ilya nodded and was about to say something when my mother's car pulled up to Ilya's house. Marella, angry and puffed as a blowfish, stepped from the car and slammed the door.

"You!" she screeched, charging at me with her belly pointed like a weapon. "You! You forgot to come home. You could have killed me with worry and it could've killed the baby—you of all people should know what stress can do to a pregnancy. What the bloody hell were you doing staying out all night without telling me?"

I had told Ilya about my mother's spells—Pupuka of course already knew—but until tonight I don't think she fully believed me. Neither Ilya nor Pupuka moved, their eyes watching Marella.

"Marella," I said in my calmest voice. "I was helping a woman give birth. I'm sorry you were worried. In the future if I don't come home, know that I am probably working."

"Idiotic girl," she said, cutting me off. "Look at you, acting outside of your age. Ilya, this is your fault. And you, filthy boy, I doubt you are helping anything by hanging around. Right now I could just slap you three."

"Don't do that," Pupuka said, standing up next to me. Ilya stepped forward too, and we three faced my mother. She seemed to check herself then, and she turned around, still scowling. A wake of shimmering silence hung about us after my mother got back into her car. She idled for a few moments, watching me, and then drove off.

I started to apologize, but I knew if I finished my sentence I would begin to cry. Both Ilya and Pupuka stayed silent.

"I don't know what to do," I said at last. A few tears came down and I wiped them on my hand.

Ilya resumed her leg lifts. She spoke cautiously, looking sideways at me: "Do you think you can solve her problem for her? After all you have learned?"

I wasn't entirely sure what she was getting at. I was too tired to understand.

"A mother delivers *herself*," Ilya added quietly. "The midwife only watches."

I waited for more, but she said nothing and gave me a single curt nod. An aura of coldness hung about her—and I saw her as if for the first time, cold silver hair, cold ocean-dark eyes. She stared at me for a long moment. "Do you know what to do now?"

Going home seemed the right answer.

Pupuka escorted me back to Nana's house. We did not talk. When we arrived, the windows were dark but I didn't trust it to mean rest.

I dawdled near the waterline and Pupuka asked, "Do you want to go for a swim?"

I looked at the dark waves coming in innocently. The tide was low but still I didn't trust it. "No thanks," I said quietly. I felt a flash of my mother inside me, her hereditary fears. I amended: "I'd love to swim with you, just let's wait until it gets light."

The sun sent spidery tentacles up from the farthest East. The grass stretched behind us for an acre, the endless ocean stretched ahead. The air smelled of macadamia blossoms. Our legs dangled off the long wooden pier and brushed against each other occasionally, sending tiny jolts of electricity through my tired muscles. I said something inane about how pretty the ocean looked. Pupuka looked at me sideways. "Do you want to try kissing?"

Did I want to *try kissing*?

I laughed, and he laughed too. And then he leaned in.

I closed my eyes. He smelled like soap, dirt, and a sort of salt-smell that I could only identify as Boy. His lips brushed my forehead, my cheeks, and finally my lips. They stayed there, soft and closed, and then they parted. Then I began to kiss him back.

I had had kisses before, but this one was different.

There was the hold of his arms around me, stronger and more like a man than I could have expected. Pupuka kissed the way he spoke, sometimes urgent, sometimes quiet, always sincere. When he kissed me, it felt like just one more way of communicating, the way we do when we are underwater; he was saying, *thank you for the cave.* He was saying, *I've liked you for a long time.* I was saying those things back, and more: I was saying, *my god you're a beautiful man,* and *you've made this island feel like home.* I thought as we kissed of all the generous reasons nature would have its animals use their mouths on each other: birds feeding their young, mammals licking each other's injuries.

I wanted the kiss to go on and on. But I heard footsteps on the pier behind us. Light, constant, slippered. Marella. I spun around. "Mother!" I cried. "We didn't..."

She looked furious. "You didn't what. I find you here, on the pier where your brother died, kissing some boy."

"Mother," I said, smoothing my tangled hair and sliding my shirt up my shoulder. "We didn't do anything wrong. We were just *kissing*."

Her voice kept rising until it was just an angry squeak. "Try it! Just try it! Trust someone once and just wait for them to leave you!"

"Just...kissing," I repeated, speaking quietly to prevent our voices from escalating into an arms race. I looked at Pupuka as I said this. I don't know what I expected him to do—perhaps dive into the water and swim home as I had instructed him to do the last time my mother lost herself in front of him. Instead, he stood, straightened his shirt, and placed his hand on my shoulder. Then he smiled his sweet, crooked smile and extended his right arm.

My mother didn't take it at first, and we both watched his long arm, open hand, waiting like a branch in the air. Finally my mother, for whatever reason, met it and they achieved a tenuous handshake.

"Mrs. Brouge," he said. "I am sorry I failed to introduce myself before. My name is Townsend Bora—though my nickname is Pupuka," he added, looking at me.

All I could think was *Townsend*? *The secret name is Townsend?*

"I am happy to meet you," Pupuka went on. "Sage has told me about you."

"Oh great," said Marella. "I'm sure she has."

"Naturally. You are the most important woman in her life."

His sincerity halted my mother. She was probably intending to fume, to scold us, to insult me for being promiscuous. But she didn't. Instead she stood up straight and dropped his hand. And then she broke into beautiful laughter, like a birdsong.

"How do you do," she said to Pupuka. "I hold no grudge against you. You seem fine. One day I might even invite you in for breakfast or lunch. But right now I am furious with my daughter who is flaunting all of the minor rules I have set for her. Come inside, Bird."

I paused, unsure what to do.

"I'm sorry, Mother," I began, and out of instinct I stepped forward to comfort her. Here I was again, trapped by sympathy. The old sympathy, always the imperative *Help her*. How it crept in, dominating the situation, siren-singing the words, *You are stronger than she, you aren't caught in a sad story, you don't have to live surrounded by the thing you fear most*. Sympathy decreed that I stand by her. This was what made her so difficult. She always played such an easily-hurt heroine, and if you went against her, you clearly were the villain.

"Come inside," she said again, stepping away from me in the direction of the house, and I saw the smile in her eyes that trusted I would do as I was told.

Usually I did. Usually I tried to shield her from the things that hurt her, even if it meant tending to her safety over my own. But this morning I refused sympathy's call. Marella was a grown woman and so was I. And my muddy morning brain was finally awakening to what Ilya had been trying to teach me. *A midwife only watches.*

It was not my job to deliver my mother from her fear of water or her grief over Adam. My mother would have to perform her own rescue, and I was hurting us both by trying to do her work for her. In that moment, in that strange half-morning, the mother-spell inside me broke.

"Come *inside*," Marella repeated a third time, a little more shrilly.

I ran to the edge of the pier and dove into the ocean.

I could hear her shrieks from underwater. Her voice came at me long and thin, like a whale's song. A second later I felt a splash and Pupuka was in the water with me. I felt mute with terror, but wildly proud of myself for escaping by water, for swimming while she watched, for doing something that my mother would never have dared.

I held my breath for as long as I could, and when I surfaced I saw my mother still there. "What are you doing?!" she shrieked hysterically. "What in the hell are you doing?"

I saw a light turn on in our neighbor's house.

"Mother," I said in a low voice. "I *know* how to swim."

My mother spit into the sand. We stared at each other for so long that my eyes began to water. Then she twisted her hair up into a tight knot and walked primly back to the house.

I treaded water, staring after her. Slowly I swam back to the pier and climbed out.

"Shall I stay with you?" Pupuka asked. He stood with his wet clothes dripping on the pier, and he looked unsure of what to do.

"No, you go home. Sleep. I need to talk to her."

We kissed again, this time with no interruption. Then he left and I walked across the sand and grass to the back of Nana's house.

Inside the house, Marella ignored me. She was sitting in her purple chair, pretending to read a newspaper while eyeing me. I thought of how many years I had felt terrorized by her, and how today I just felt weary. It was a less epic feeling, a safer one.

I began making breakfast for us both, scooping out yogurt and granola and splitting open a kiwi and spooning out the bright fruit into our bowls. The dark wood of the house was turning bright and glinting gold. I left my bowl on the counter, for I felt too excited to eat.

I brought my mother her breakfast and finally she looked up at me.

"Here's the thing," she said. "If you are having sex with him, we need to talk."

"Mother! I'm not. That was our first kiss."

"Sure. Just listen. For a minute, just listen to me."

"No! Just because I have a boyfriend doesn't mean that I'm going to run off like some dumb teenager and get pregnant..."

I stopped.

"Would you like to continue?" Marella asked, aridly. She had caught my moment of conscience. She was eighteen when she got pregnant with Adam.

"No," I said. "I am done."

It had always amazed me how quickly my mother's moods could change season. Seeing me back down, Marella sat up straighter and grew animated again; her power began to return. She was flushed, petunia-pink, with the tiniest beads of sweat at her hairline, where her widow's peak peaked. Her face looked so young, so foolish, so unfinished. Now she was capable again of being a wild shark of a woman, a scary predator who was trying to make me and my father miserable.

The flowers in the trees outside hung dewy and heavy. Everything felt suddenly too potent, too fertile. I wanted the relief of being in a place where nothing would grow, some place like the cave we had left only four hours before, some underworld where mothers couldn't follow. Suddenly I felt very, very tired.

I considered going to bed. I needed it. But this night, being awake and full of birth and love and energy, it felt wrong to sleep in the same house with my mother. I found my shoes on the back deck and jogged toward town. The last time I went running from this house was when Marella was throwing up and Ilya gave me ginger. This time I wasn't running away but running toward. Toward-town, as Dragon Islanders would say, not toward-water. In my case, toward-Pupuka.

Soon I arrived in the neighborhood of the flat-roofed houses, and I stood in front of the blue house where Pupuka lived, with the yard full of plastic flamingos. I had walked to this house many times before, but never been inside.

Pale light gleamed through some of the windows. If his parents worked for the radio station, they probably got up early. I circled the house, trying to decipher which room was Pupuka's. Around the back of the house, near where a wooden picnic table squatted under a sprawling tree, stood a separate back door. It looked like a separate apartment within the home for a renter or an adult child living at home. Which is exactly what Pupuka was. Next to the door leaned Pupuka's bicycle. I knocked quietly.

Pupuka answered. He was standing in his boxer shorts, holding out a plate with a square of coffeecake on it. "I was reading in bed," he said, as if to explain why he too was still awake. I took the plate, realizing I had not eaten since yesterday's lunch. And I gobbled it up.

We faced each other for a long quiet minute, while he just smiled his crooked smile. He was so clean and almost-naked and I was still in my damp filthy clothes from the cave. Without thinking I stripped them off. I wanted to be clean and naked with him. Then I tugged my hair out of the knot it had been in all night. It tumbled down my back, almost as long, I realized, as my mother's. There was a sink in the bedroom and I washed my hands and face. Then I looked up. Pupuka had taken off his shorts and was lying on the bed. He had a beautiful lean body. He had a dark line of hair bisecting his belly. Of course, I had seen him nearly naked before, every time we swam. But nearly naked and naked are entirely different things. He was a beautiful man, a kind man. I lay down next to him.

We kissed again, but this time we both knew it was a prelude. I felt a buzzing all over my body, an aliveness. He wrapped his hands in my hair and ran them all the way down my back. He kissed my shoulders, my stomach, my breasts. I rolled over on top of him, straddling him, kissing him deeply. I could feel him hardening beneath me. And I thought, *This is it.*

Most of my friends' first times had been clumsy affairs—I was prepared for that. Generally they included a fancy dinner at a Blue Island restaurant or some other wooing, and then a tumble that ended quickly. But as I curled my body toward him, I thought how our preparation had been much more animal, much more grounded in the fundamentals of life and death. Our genesis was steeped in the deepest elements—the work, the water, the cave, the birth, the blood, all my fears faced. This stuff didn't scare Pupuka. Not one bit.

I paused in kissing him and whispered, "Just in case you were worried, this is not a time when I could get pregnant."

Pupuka leaned his neck back and just looked at me. He had a grin on his face and his floppy hair stuck in all directions.

He just smiled and smiled. Then he said, "I'm not afraid of that, if you're not."

"Right now I definitely am!"

We both laughed. Then we kissed again. Then I shifted my hips and he slid inside me. We undulated our bodies and quickly found a rhythm that reminded me of dolphins: how they swell up to breathe and surge back down. It felt like wet slick ocean-mammal play. I got lost in the rhythm and could not tell how long it lasted, but I knew exactly when it ended. It ended with a feeling of warmth spreading up my body and everywhere, and then a slowing, followed by a wild sense of drowsiness.

Then we fell directly into a long light sleep.

I spent the day with Pupuka's family. Amazingly, his parents didn't say a disapproving word about my being there, a strange girl coming out of Pupuka's room in time for lunch. They were standing at the kitchen counter with the twins, making English muffin pizzas while a Frank Sinatra song blared from a radio somewhere: *Fly me to the moon... Let me plaa-ay among the stars...*

They turned around with smiles as wide as Pupuka's.

"Good morning," I said. "I'm Sage." I trusted the radio to fill any silence: *Let me see what spring is like on Jupiter and Ma-aars...*

"Well, hello!" said his father. He gave a little wave of his tomato-sauced fingers.

His mother added: "Are you hungry for lunch or breakfast?"

"Either one," I said, "would be great."

His parents introduced themselves—his mother Riva, his father Kimo—and we took turns commenting on the good spring weather. Then I joined them in the pizza-making and half an hour later we all sat at the wobbly wooden table with "Caterpillar" and "Adopted," who were telling fifth grade jokes in between bites of muffin pizza.

"What were you two up to last night?" Kimo asked conversationally across the table, and Pupuka looked at me for permission, and then launched into the story of the past few days: finding the cave, then the woman inside, making plans to help her, getting Ilya involved, and then the birth.

"Ilya?" echoed Riva. She looked at me. "You know Ilya? She is a saint in the eyes of Dragon Island women. You know that, of course."

"How do you know her?" I asked.

Riva Bora leaned in as if sharing a secret. "None of my boys were hospital-born."

When I finally went home in the late afternoon, my mother was not in her usual spot in the living room. The purple chair had sitting marks on it but was empty—and I saw something small and white fluttering on the kitchen counter, next to my untouched breakfast bowl. It was bigger than a sticky note, and it was not in my mother's handwriting. It was dated March 20, the day before, and written in pencil.

Marella and Sage:

In an hour I will catch a plane to Montana. Thank you for letting me be part of your lives. I'm sorry for the trouble I've caused. There is something special about your family that draws me in, but it is something that I need to get away from. It's not good for me and it is keeping me from moving on and making a life and a family of my own. If you ever need anything, money or things for the baby when she or he comes, I'll send an address when I have one. I will never forget you.

—Lance

On the floor next to the note stood a whittled wooden crib with slats the bleached white of whale bones. It was clearly handmade. I supposed this was Lance's best effort at what a father, even an absentee one, could offer his kid. And I realized that more than any other feeling, I felt surprised that Lance stayed as long as he did. He didn't belong with us. Here was this young, handsome, charming, adventurous guy, so bored with small talk that he created a short-list of answers to get all the questions out of the way; someone who would start an affair with his boss's wife. Why would he stay? Some part of me wished to believe that a man, when fatherhood is impending, would root down and be responsible. But then, my mother still had vast room for improvement in the responsibility department.

Setting the note back down next to the knives and the teapot, I ran my fingers over the ribs of the crib and considered the ways life would be different without Lance around. My poor father would have to find a new fishing partner when he got back to shore. And our house of women would change, and the baby would not know its father. My mother, no doubt, had read the note already. It explained her tantrum the day before.

As these realizations arose and became solid in my mind, I felt a sudden difference in the house. I could smell a familiar scent, fishy and like petroleum. Only then did I notice the rubber boots at the back door. Dad had come home.

That night there was an explosion in my parents' bedroom. Their argument spilled into the rest of the house, tumbling into the living room and unfurling monstrously in the kitchen. I kept moving rooms to try to get away from it, but the argument kept following.

My father thundered around the downstairs. "I've been gone six months and look what happens! Do you need a babysitter your entire life, Marella? Six months without me or your mother and you go and get yourself pregnant and Sage spends her days who knows where and the house falls apart and everything goes out of control."

Marella regarded him scornfully from her perch on her purple chair. "Nothing is out of control. Listen to you. You always overreact."

My dad lost his temper and pounded his hairy fists against Nana's dining table. "Move out," he yelled. "Bird and I will stay here."

"No, you move out," Marella responded with a thin laugh. "Go live on your boat some more."

"I live on my boat because I'm this family's only income-maker!" my father knee-jerked back.

Legally, my dad deserved to stay. In the Charon Islands law adulterers lose their homestead privileges. But my mother was not one to fold so easily. She took a new angle, like a clever snake. "Besides, this is my mother's house. If anyone moves it should be you. I take care of this house and keep it clean."

"If you call this a clean house...." My father began. Then he paused and recollected himself. "Look. I didn't catch many fish, which means I lost money on the trip, and when I come home, I find a note to my wife from my business partner and I find my wife however many months pregnant. I come home to a faithless wife, no fishing partner, a newborn on the way that I don't know anything about. What do I have left? Do I have anything left?"

Marella finally seemed to listen. Her posture changed and she stopped acting haughty. "I don't know. But I love you and I don't want to be blamed," she said. "I want you to see that I am hurting and to try to help...George, I don't know what to do. I feel all alone and abandoned. And now you no longer trust me."

"You made that decision on your own," he said coldly.

I could hear the poison in my mother's silence. Knowing

her, she was deliberating between leaving the room or doing something rash, like biting my father or hitting him, or doing something illegal that might land us all on some terrible television show about families who beat each other up.

But she caught herself. Maybe it was because I was watching and listening, and she wanted to give me the chance to learn from her. Maybe not. Either way, she said nothing.

My father filled the silence. "Look. I have become the career husband you and your mother wanted me to be. We agreed that if I worked, you would keep the home. Since August I bet you've not even made five meals. Sage, would you say she's made…"

He stopped when he saw me shaking my head. I would stand witness, but I was not going to get involved. Anyway, the answer was obvious.

"But I'm overwhelmed," my mother wailed. "Help me. Help me, help me."

She went around the kitchen gathering Nana's mismatched collection of mugs and dropping them one by one on the wooden kitchen floor. As each mug shivered into shards, she said under her breath: "I need more help." Crash! "I need more help." Crash! "I need more help." CRASH!

I crouched on a kitchen stool and covered my ears with my hands, hating that my mother acted this way, and that my father didn't know what to do. It hurt me to think of all those mugs, chosen by Nana, broken by her daughter in a tantrum that you'd think a toddler would be too old to perform. My poor grandmother, who died not knowing whether her daughter would ever grow up.

Outside the big window, I saw one of the elderly neighbors peering across the lawn, open-mouthed, her cup of evening tea in hand, craning her neck to watch our disaster. Serene, domesticated, smugly certain that surely in her house nothing of this sort would ever happen. Leave the violence to the couples who come here for vacation and never leave. The face caught sight of me, and it looked away.

I surveyed the kitchen. All of Nana's mugs were broken, and my mother was sitting among the colorful wreckage, crying. My dad had left the room.

Here again, I thought. I knew these arguments. I had seen this land before. My earliest memories of my mother involved the ring-around-the-rosie of her wanting to run away. Ashes, ashes. Trying to escape and bringing me and her one-eyed boxer Julep, rescuing us—from what? From a peaceful childhood? From my father's clumsy attempts at love? It seemed some elaborate game of pretend. As a child, I thought each fight was the same, but now I saw that each one went a little deeper, revealing more fault lines, more broken glass. The first one I could clearly remember was when I was only four or five and my mother caught the kitchen on fire while making toasted coconut for my father's birthday dessert. ("But I don't even like coconut," he said as the firefighters arrived.) We had to move into a rental apartment while our kitchen was fixed. That house-fire was the catalyst, I believe, for Nana's coming to stay with us.

After tonight's fight, Marella shelled herself into a spare bedroom and turned the radio on loud. It was the local station and I could hear that the radio announcer was Pupuka's dad. His voice sounded just the same on the air as it did earlier that day in the kitchen.

"Sorry the trip wasn't any good," I said to my dad once the air had calmed and we were sitting in the living room while my mother's classical music blared from behind the closed door.

He tugged on his beard. "Thanks, Seabird. The water was rough and the fish weren't acting alive. It may be time to get an inland job."

My father always joked about people who had inland jobs.

Why live in the middle of the ocean, he always said, if you are not going to work on the water? The idea of my dad working on land seemed crippling.

"I see what happened," he began. Then he darted a look at me. "Is it okay for us to talk? I'd really like to talk about this to somebody."

"Sure, Dad," I said.

"Sage, I am not a prudish man. I am not the sort of man to lose sight of the forest through the trees. What your mom and Lance did was temporary, just two lonely people making a mistake. What I need to believe, in order to stay in this marriage, is that Marella won't go out and do this again. If she does, then I will need to move out." My dad's voice was even and steady. "She may not know herself. But soon I'll need to know."

It was strange sitting on the sofa with my dad talking about his marriage. What did I know about this sort of thing? What I knew for certain was that for my new brother's sake I had a vested interest in having him forgive her.

"I think she just needed nourishment," I said. "She missed Nana and you, and then Lance was there. I think she missed you badly the whole time you were gone." I looked at my poor ursine dad, so sad with his spurned husband face. I patted his hand.

During the week that followed, my dad's boots provided clues to the state he and my mother were in. Dad didn't want to sleep in my mother's bed until he had had enough time to work through his feelings about the whole affair, but they didn't seem to do a lot of talking about it, and so nothing came resolved. My dad dug calmly through the bins in the garage, found one labeled "camping gear" in my mother's watery script, took out a tent and pitched it in the backyard. His boots reappeared at the tent's entrance. They vanished the next morning when he left for the fish market.

At night, from my bedroom, I could see him sitting on the end of the pier, dipping his feet in the water as the waves pounded their undertow noise against the old wet wood. When I went to sleep and when I woke, he was sitting in the same spot. He must have slept in between, but not for long.

My mother slept in Nana's giant bed, long nights and mornings as always.

That week I cooked for both my parents, cleaning out the pantry to its very back ingredients, cans of yams, lima beans, baby corn, old vegetables that had been dust-lined there for years; also I thawed plenty of fish from the garage freezer. I made stir-fries for breakfast, lunch, and dinner, because it was the only way I could unapologetically combine so many strange ingredients and call it food. I brought plates to my mother in her purple chair, to my dad in his tent. Each one thanked me politely, as if I were some stranger attending them instead of their daughter.

Marella spent those tent-days creating a small shrine to Adam in the living room. Artifacts went up: baby photos, a small white shirt, a lock of hair. Things that must have been stuck for years inside her and had grown infected. I took pity on her efforts and one night brought down the baby book that Nana had left me. Marella did not say anything, but I saw it opened to different pages each day. It occurred to me that all these years she had been worrying about him in some watery other-world, while she waited on land without him. Adam was the constant heavy clay in my mother's hands, while I slipped through her fingers like seawater. I could see that all of her sacrifices—her friends, her happiness, her former love of swimming—were things she had put on this altar and given up for the boy who died before he could appreciate her sacrifice, before he could grow up.

After a week of these stalemate afternoons I pulled my mother onto the back deck and handed her a towel. She was orbiting herself now, moving in a pregnant waddle. She looked at me as if I were crazy, but still I pressed my demand.

"Mother," I said sternly. "Today you and I are going for a swim."

"Not while I'm pregnant," she said. "No way."

I wasn't taking it. "Pregnancy is the best time. You are buoyant! Come on. We're starting in shallow water, and we're starting right now."

"I don't have a bathing suit."

"You don't need one. You strip down to your knickers and we'll go in near the rocks. It's more private there." My heart pulsed and throbbed.

My mother held the towel firmly and pressed her lips into a thin line. But she obliged me by walking down to the waterline.

The ocean spread ahead of us like a dazzling blue desert. Marella held my arm and I could feel her hand shaking. We waded in knee-deep and she would go no further. It was shallow. But it was a start.

As we walked back, I watched her closely, interested to see if anything had changed in her, grown braver or more vulnerable. She could see that I was trying to form theories about her and so she wheeled out a litany of things that were annoying her.

"I stink!" she complained as we rounded the edge of the lawn and came back up toward the deck. "Why do I stink so badly? Do you know? Do all pregnant women have such gross body odor?"

"No. I don't know. It's probably hormones."

She lifted her arm to demonstrate. She did smell.

"I didn't stink with you or Adam," my mother insisted.

But at that moment I wasn't listening—not fully. I was thinking that if she were beginning to smell this way, she was closer to birth than Ilya had predicted. Her long torso and pretty figure had made her appear less pregnant than she actually was. And I thought back to when her nausea ended. I counted months—then recounted to be certain.

"It can't be Lance's," I said suddenly. Lance was unknown to us when the conception must have happened in order for her to deliver a baby under a month from now, in late April or early May. It had to have been Dad.

My mother watched me, her eyes dark and unblinking, like an ancient eel. Then she pulled the towel around herself and walked back down the steps, to the tent where Dad's boots stood. A few of the neighbor's cats had begun sniffing around the entrance to the tent, looking as if they might sleep there.

My dad was sitting outside the back of the tent, eating an unappetizing snack he had made that looked like it contained shrimp, bananas, and crumbled nori. I saw her squat next to him. Their voices wafted across the grass to where I sat on the back deck. I could see that she was on her best, most tame behavior, trying to persuade my dad to stay with her through the birth of their child and after. But tame had never been her true nature. Soon she stood and began gesturing by the tent like a solitary witch who could command the elements: someone whose feelings ran deeper and fiercer than anything else in the universe. For a moment I found my mother terrifying—I wondered if my dad thought so, too. He sat quietly, listening. His beard made it hard to read the expression on his mouth, but he stood and led Marella into the tent.

The evening world fell silent. It felt as if the whole world was still, waiting for their decision. I could feel a slight tremor murmuring underground. This happened sometimes in the Charon Islands. As a child I used to think it was that my mother's grief shook the earth, the frail roots that tied our little island to the deep-sea bottom. In the close surrounding islands, volcanoes lurked, silent and dangerous; they could erupt at any moment. That is the risk when you live in the shadow of such a volatile thing.

At last, just as night was falling, my parents came out of the tent and stood at the edge of the water, their arms around each other in the darkness. And all I could feel was joy, a strange and mysterious joy and hope that we might face the water again, that my parents were speaking again, and that our life as a family just might turn out right.

19

Ilya

The Auctioneer. How do I tell you of him?

He was certainly not human and had not been human for a long time. Instead he was a bizarre chimera of patterns and parts. His skin—you do not have to believe this except that you will and you must—had the brindled pattern you see on a giraffe. You could see the wide uneven spots on his face and the backs of his hands.

He had, I swear, a snout.

And his head had a lion's mane that fell below his shoulders, and leafy gray ears like a rhinoceros has, and above his eyes he had small bumps like stunted horns. He was a crazy looking beast and a beast who had no kin in his audience, all of whom were people, dead people, but still just people like you and me, Girl.

He wore a blue tailored suit with the silver chain of a pocket-watch looping out of his pocket. He pulled out the watch and checked it.

"Now, ghosts," he said in a thin and swelling voice, "now is time to sit for auction, please." His *please* had a cold-blooded reptilian quality.

The tent had been rolled down all the way to the dirt and I could see nothing outside to my left or my right. I could not see my father. But above the Auctioneer's pulpit rose a giant square window in the tent, and through it I could see the construction. Big trucks carried loads of blue dirt off and away, and bulldozers turned up rocks and more blue dirt. Scaffolding of a round silo was going up next to a line of metallic round silos. I saw the Auctioneer's leafy ears ripple when one of the bulldozers made an especially loud crack.

"Now is time," he repeated. A screen descended behind him, covering the window so the construction could no longer be seen. The screen flashed static, indecisive, and then took shape in the outline of a human body. The Auctioneer cleared his throat; it sounded like a whinny. "Above you, ghosts, are the bodies available: you'll see a schoolboy, a princess, a clerk, sixteen soldiers, two chiefs, a prostitute, a fisherman, three teenage whatnots, a butcher, an artist, a welder, a useless old man, a witch who calls herself a midwife, a schoolteacher..." His voice dissolved into speed and mesmerism as he listed off stations of life as if they were grocery items.

In front of us on the screen, new shapes flashed with each body he mentioned: a parade of humans who would be born today. And the hungry, seated ghosts looked on, deciding which bodies deserved their bid, calculating how worthwhile each particular life on earth would be, and how many years of work they were willing to give the Auctioneer once the body they entered died, and brought them here again.

I wondered then at my trust. How to believe that these bodies will be who they are advertised as being? How to know how their lives will go, or how long they will live? The bodies all carried nothing, of course. They just seemed empty vessels, boats, promising to float on to the world of the living, but really who knew? I looked harder at the shapes on the screen, and as I did, some took form as ancient men or women, while others looked supple and firm in the middle of life. A very few remained children. You could see, somehow, from their posture and the way they held their faces, what their lives might be. You somehow knew what it might be like to be each person, even though all you saw was a flash of their outline. But even so—even if the differences were real—the whole auction still required that all bidding ghosts trust the Auctioneer. He did not seem trustworthy.

In the audience around me, the ghosts rustled. They were excited that they were about to exit this purple world and go back up, and you could feel a change in the air.

The change rustled Adam, who I knew would cry if I didn't feed him, so I pulled up my shirt and stuck him under. As I did, the Auctioneer finished his list and began to speak slowly: "Let us begin." A toddler outline flashed on the screen and stayed. "Bidders for this baby begin at seventy days' work."

Many gray, half-transparent hands drifted up.

"Five months' work?"

Still most hands remained.

"Fourteen years?" One hand still lingered in the air, and its ghost looked around, surprised, to find itself the only one still bidding.

"Sold!" shouted the Auctioneer and the ghost was invited up to the podium to write something in a ledger. "Be ready to leave at nightfall," the Auctioneer instructed, dismissing the ghost from auction.

A hush followed, and again the screen began to flash. The next outline seemed to be a thin, older female body, and everybody in the audience seemed to know something about her that I did not. They sat up. I noticed there was no whispering, no camaraderie among the adult dead. But each one in a separate quiet bubble of their own seemed excited about this ghost.

The Auctioneer sensed this and began: "Six years' work, anyone?"

Hands drifted up.

"Twenty-five years?" He escalated fast.

Still just as many hands.

"Fifty years' work, then?"

Some hands fell, leaving still hundreds.

"One hundred? Only one hand? Going for one hundred years, then…going once, going twice…"

I did not understand this difference between prices. I whispered to the ghost sitting next to me (I did not know yet that adult milk-fed ghosts don't talk to each other): "What is the big difference between those two bodies?"

The ghost sitting next to me did not answer—it was a he, I think, with robust cheeks and a thin chin—but he did something that left me completely off guard.

He knelt down and licked the hem at the bottom of my shirt.

"Milk." The ghost mouthed the word in a soundless observation.

Then another ghost sitting next to him noticed. I pushed down my shirt and stuck the baby back into his sling. But several other ghosts sitting nearby had raised their heads. They had stopped listening to the auction. They were looking at me.

The screen flashed on, but none of the ghosts were interested. Soon the Auctioneer caught on. "What is going on over there?" he inquired in an annoyed and haughty voice.

All of the ghosts had seemingly forgotten their hunger to go back to the sunlight. Instead they were circled around me, hoping for a glimpse or taste of milk. Real milk. White milk. Yes, Charon's words were true. They didn't want my son, or my coins, or the wine I had smuggled down; the ghosts wanted my milk.

The Auctioneer stepped off his pulpit and stood in front of me, blocking me from the screen. He was big, broad-backed. It seemed his shoulders might burst out any minute from his suit. There was a rustle among the ghosts. He took me in: his reptile eyes took in my baby—it chilled me that he could see Adam and my father could not—and he looked closely at my face. Then suddenly the Auctioneer picked up one of my hands and examined it. "Bitten down to nubs," he spat out with scorn. "Disgusting. Nowhere for the dirt to go."

These words surprised me and I looked quickly at his hand on top of mine. The brindled skin, which had faint craters on it like octopus suckers, gave way to surprisingly human fingers—except the nails had been filed into claws. Underneath each of his pointed fingernails there was a line of the glowing blue dirt of the dead. I looked quickly at all of the hands of the ghosts around me. All had lines of cobalt blue beneath the transparent nail, marking them as belonging to this land.

Because I was a nervous girl, a nail-biter with no nails to speak of, and because I had been careful about what I touched, the blue dirt had not gotten under my fingernails. If it had, finally the Auctioneer would have been able to keep me. I would have belonged to him, for he rules the blue dirt. For years my mother had nagged and nagged at me to quit biting. But she did it too, I inherited it from her. The blue paint on my nails kept me disguised, but I knew then that my nail-biting helped keep me alive.

The Auctioneer stepped back and gazed at me with a look that I knew well, a look that my mother often gave me: it was a look that mixed disdain and envy.

"You pretend to be a spirit. I see your blue nails, the nails of your baby. You act like you belong here, and so why do you smell like milk? Nobody makes milk down here but me."

"I'm not going to tell you how. But I have milk to give to all who need it."

His eyes flashed wildly. "You lie!" he hissed. "Do you know what happens to liars here?"

Behind him, the screen continued alternating images. One of the ghosts in the back was standing to auction for a shape on the screen, not noticing that the Auctioneer was otherwise occupied. The Auctioneer reeled around, distracted from me, and sank his fury into this spirit sitting far in the back.

"What spirit do I see back there, trying to bid on this body of royal heritage? Is it Delilah?" His animal mouth snaked into smile. "Delilah, am I incorrect in remembering that last time you bid, you failed to pay in full? Could it be that you are ready to be taken out of circulation? That you are ready to take the shape you deserve?"

I looked behind me. Many rows of chairs away, the ghost-woman Delilah was holding her knees, crunched into a fetal hug, terrified.

Another image flashed on the screen: one of those hard-shelled summer insects that tighten into balls when frightened. "This body has come available," cried the Auctioneer, "and I have been saving it for you!"

And then the Auctioneer performed some strange magic, circling his hands in the air as if he were using a lasso, and the woman suddenly was surrounded by a clear sac as if sealed into a bubble. Then just as suddenly her seat was empty and she was up on the screen, inside the screen, and we saw her body in its sac being tightened smaller and smaller until it merged completely with the insect. Then the screen flashed and the images disappeared.

The ghosts wobbled nervously in their seats.

"Next?" the Auctioneer called. He returned to the pulpit and faced us all.

Nobody spoke. I felt that it was my turn.

"I have come to bid," I said to the Auctioneer in my strongest voice.

He looked hard into my face with his reptile eyes and he lowered his voice. "Here on holiday with your bastard kid and you want a souvenir?" When he spoke, his heavy tongue seemed to get in the way of the words he was trying to form. Speaking loudly smoothed out the thorns in his dialect. Talking to me quietly, he seemed uncomfortable. But I knew better than to let this lull me.

"No," I said. "I have come to take my father home."

"What father would want...?" he started to mutter, while he looked around. My father had entered the tent and was hovering at one end of the front row of seats. The Auctioneer's face dawned comprehension.

"You!" The Auctioneer sneered and began to laugh, a horrible vulture's shriek. "What, you come to me for mercy? You think it's possible for you to go anywhere? You haven't been to work for years." And the Auctioneer kept laughing.

At which point I reached into my pocket and took out the vial Charon had given me, filled with my milk. "Auctioneer," I said, and held it up for him to see.

His face did a strange thing. It didn't blanch exactly, but it changed color to something bluish. Its muscles seemed to ripple. His face itself looked like deep water, but not the safe kind. I had never seen anyone look so dangerous.

"Come close to me," he said, and I stood and joined him at his pulpit. All of the ghosts in the audience swayed in symmetry like fronds of seaweed. It seemed they could all see Adam now that we were standing with the Auctioneer. From the looks in those spirits' eyes as they watched Adam, it was clear that down here babies represent some happily ever after, something all these souls were working long jobs to return to. Babies have long lives ahead, many years in the sunlight. These ghosts would trade anything to become a baby again.

"What do you want for that vial?" the Auctioneer asked in a whisper.

"I want my father to come back as that woman who was just on the screen," I told him. "The valuable one. Before the bug."

He said, "Give me that little bottle now, and I will let this useless man be reborn as that royal-blooded woman."

"And he can stay on earth a long time?" I asked.

"At least seventy years," he promised.

"And you'll assure us safe passage home?"

"You may use the office behind us."

I gave him the milk and he held it up triumphantly and called out, "Auction over for today!"

Then he turned back to me with a sneer on his patchwork face. "You may keep this ghost in this form only until his new body is ready. The body he will enter is going to be born in—" He checked a large clock on the wall written in symbols that I could not read. "Exactly an hour and fifty minutes. Get going," he said, with a terrible look in his reptile eyes.

He took a sip from the tiny vial. Suddenly his horns disappeared and his face changed and he looked not like a demon minotaur, but almost human-like. While I hurried away toward the small wooden annex at the back of the tent, Adam began to wail.

I turned around and saw the most amazing and frightening sight: thousands of ghosts were standing, moving forward. They saw that he held milk and they looked like they'd devour him in order to get it. The last thing I saw—just before we slipped into the Auctioneer's office and closed the door tightly behind us—was a herd of angry ghosts swarming the Auctioneer, the pulpit, and punching ethereal fists through the still-flashing screen.

Three

20

Ilya

I climbed up the tree Charon had told me would be in the Auctioneer's office, scaling its branches like a ladder. Just as Charon had promised, I reached the top and faced a wall of heavy gray stone: the staircase that would take me back up. With Adam on my back and my father's hand in mine, I entered the ocean and swam toward the shore. I could not believe we had escaped.

As I escorted my father's ghost back through the shallow tidewater and onto land, I knew my life would be forever changed from having entered this place, though I did not yet know all the ways. Mostly I felt relief and shock at the value of my milk. The Auctioneer was frightening—anyone who tries to control a world is. But I also felt a strange peace, for I had seen for myself that for souls who do not wish for another lifecycle, and especially for the children, the Underworld was a place of calm, as quiet and unthreatening as the stillness at the bottom of the ocean. It seems, Girl, that the best way to exist in that world is to be without hunger—to be like the children.

When I returned to the sunlight with my father's ghost, he only had an hour, if that, before being reborn. That was all we needed. I tore through the streets to get home to my mother so she could see him again.

It was Sunday afternoon. The trip home took longer than I anticipated. Adam rested heavy on my back, and I was exhausted from the journey, and my father's hand flickered in mine, fading. When we finally arrived at the house, my sisters were in the kitchen. My mother was nowhere to be found.

At first nobody recognized me except my youngest sister—imagine how I looked, streaked with blue soil, terror-eyed but fierce with pride at the fearless thing I had done, and with white hair. White—my hair had been black before. I had read about such ghost-marks but still felt astonished when it happened to me. I had gone underground with hair the color of yours, Girl, but while underground my hair had turned white, the color—almost—of milk.

My sisters dropped their cooking and stared, as our father began to fade and become transparent. He was no longer a person or a parent. Just air.

"Dada?" my middle sister said, just as he disappeared.

The whole time all I could think was that I had failed—I had made this trip and I had failed, I had upset the dead, risked my life and my son's life, and still I had failed. My mother would not get to see the only person in her life she loved.

But across town, at that very moment, ferried into life by the midwife who later took me as her apprentice, a girl was born—Marella Karata Roa—your mother, Girl. The Auctioneer's timing was perfect. My father appeared again as a newborn just after he evaporated in the kitchen. Your mother's birth-time, I later learned, was 6:12 in the evening, the exact time on the clock when the edges of his ghost could no longer be seen.

I never did learn where my mother had gone that afternoon. She was secretive and would not tell me.

It did not matter.

What mattered is that she missed seeing the ghost I had dredged up for her.

What matters too is that through the transfer of that ghost, my spirit-line is linked, Girl, to yours.

When she learned afterward what had happened, my mother was angry at what I had done. She was afraid the ghosts would find me and her. She talked a soft-spined government official into erasing my name from our family in the town record books. Just like that. I never knew such a thing was possible, but she made it happen. Poor terrified woman. As if ghosts would come looking for the living in that way.

But the result of her action is clear: as far as Dragon Island history is concerned, Adam does not exist. I do not exist, either.

So that's all. That is the whole story. It was a wasted effort in some ways, but not in others. I went on to live a different life from my mother. My whole life, since that journey, has been a story of bartering, ferrying, milk, and ghosts.

It was wise of me to have gone then. I was young and did not know better. But I would go again today if I were still a capable enough swimmer. My journey to the ghost auction with my son was a daughter's journey. So you see how I became myself because of her.

All right now, Girl. There's dawn. Go home. Your mother will wake and need you.

21

APRIL

Something was happening with Ilya. Since the cave birth I felt her backing away, pushing me forward to work and take care of the women while she hung back, leaving me alone. A full moon had passed without her taking a swim, and she had stopped making her salves and tinctures. Her kombucha culture languished in the jar like a dead fish.

"Is everything okay?" I asked one morning.

"Sit," she said. "There is something I must tell you, Girl, something that you probably already know. I can feel a cancer that has been spreading through my lymph for months now. I am not afraid. But when my time comes, I need you with me."

"But, Ilya, there are tests and treatments for things like cancer. You're not that old."

She stared at me. "Are you suggesting that I fight against my body? Ignore what the very water that runs through me *knows*?"

"No, but—well, yes, but..."

She shook her head, dismissing me. "When it happens,

you must make sure I die at home. It is up to you, Girl, to keep me safe from the doctors who will try to keep me alive beyond my will. Unlike me, doctors are bound by government rules. They lack the luxury of self-trust."

It was useless to argue with Ilya about doctors. She felt doctors wanted to kill her, and now she was saying that the doctors would keep her from dying.

She went on: "I'll leave you all my tools, my books of course. There will be money too—I trust you will use it well."

I wanted to protest: *Ilya! Why do we have to talk about this? Why can't you at least try to live?* But I knew better. I kept my face as impartial as I could, even though I was afraid. I listened and I promised her that I would step up the midwifery work, and keep up my swimming, keep diving for sea weeds, and always, always, *always* take care of the women.

That night, Pupuka and his younger brothers came to retrieve me at the end of my workday. The twin boys hovered at the edge of Ilya's property until she saw them and waved them in. She began asking them questions and they warmed to her quickly. Seeing Pupuka's brothers play with Ilya made me feel about a hundred years old. Their little arms waggling around as they hoarded sand dollars and the solitary arms of starfish, all the while asking Ilya for permission to take these treasures home. They beamed each time she said yes. Pupuka put his arm around me and we stood swaying on the edge of this island that, before Nana died, I never would've had any reason to call my home. And suddenly the absence of Nana hit me with a fierce pain in my chest and stomach.

I thought of Nana the rest of the evening as I asked Marella whether she had remembered to do any exercise (she had forgotten again) and encouraged her to eat her dinner (she wasn't hungry). Unlike all of the other pregnant women who worked hard to stay healthy, Marella seemed to think pregnancy was a game that she should play her own way—which seemed like an unhealthy game to me. I kept thinking that if Nana were alive, this would be her job. She would be on Marella-duty. All those years, it was Nana alone who had the burden and the privilege to be my mother's handler. Now it was mine.

"Try this," I suggested. This night it was a fish soup with quinoa.

My father always ate my meals with gusto, as he ate this one. Not so with Marella. "What are those grains? They look like fish eyes. Yuck!" she cried, flinging back her hair dramatically.

"Look, Mother," I said, "you've got to eat."

"Obviously, *Daugh*-ter. I'll eat when and what I choose. And, for that matter, why don't you ever call me Mama? How about a simple Mom? Now I hear you say "*Mo*-ther" as if we were living in *Little Women*."

Most of our conversations went like this.

As the birth came nearer, I knew that we would need some material items for when the baby arrived—even though Marella kept insisting that "we don't need any of that junk." We had Lance's white crib; I stowed it away in what would be the baby's closet, because Marella kept getting weepy whenever she saw it. I found in the attic a cabinet that could serve as a changing table. But we lacked bottles and baby clothes, pacifiers and burp rags, and even a pad for the crib.

And that's why my mother and I drove into Middle to go shopping for baby things.

Marella was oddly chatty on the drive over. She talked about where the baby could go to school, who (besides me) might be able to help babysit, and how fun it would be to have a new person in the family. I drove and listened and felt the eternal periphery of the ocean out the window to my left. It stretched on forever, and you could drive around the island again and again—like circling a ring—and always see water.

We parked outside Oceanside Mall in Middle, and crossed the steaming parking lot to our destination, a baby department store called Higgins Hugs. The chill of the air-conditioner blasted us in the face as we passed through the revolving doors. At Higgins Hugs, Marella took an arm-basket and instructed me to do the same.

"Why not a cart, and we can take turns pushing it?" I asked.

"Carts are inelegant," she answered briskly, pulling her basket away from her long hair, which had already snaked its way into the plastic weaving. "Besides, people who push carts fill them. We only need a few things."

She began picking up packages from the shelves, studying them, and placing them gently into her basket. People smiled at her while she walked by. They looked first at her face, then down to her belly, then at me. I looked at her to see if she smiled back, and she did. It was unusual to see my mother this happy.

Women in uniforms the color of Easter eggs floated around my mother like sea anemones. "May I help?" they asked. "May I suggest a new product?"

Marella smiled at them and always said yes, though she didn't buy any of the things they offered. She put them in her basket, nodded thanks, and then slipped them into my basket and whispered: "Put it back." It felt, as things often did with my mother, like a game whose rules were decipherable only to her.

The one thing the department store women brought her that she did keep in her basket was a bright gold baby onesie that had a picture of a green shovel on one side and a sand castle on the other side, and buttons on the bottom to go around the diaper. I personally would not have chosen it—I preferred the blue ones that had pictures of starfish and baby whales.

Eventually we got the necessary items. Marella charged everything on the family credit card, and we stopped in several more stores, getting her a new sun hat, undershirts for my dad, and a new bathing suit for me as I had worn thin my old one.

We drove home the long way, circling the full belly of Dragon Island so that the ocean remained on my left. It was the first time since Nana died that I remembered having fun with my mother. I floated home on that energy. And Marella kept talking about happy things, her voice flecked with hope.

"We might even sell Nana's big house and move back home," Marella said. "I never feel steady when I'm surrounded by water."

I started to disagree about water, to tell her how I felt comforted by the ocean, safe having it visible in every direction. But then I realized that she was offering us a way home.

And just as suddenly and without doubt, I realized something else: *I did not want it.*

As we pulled into the driveway, Dad stood waiting with an anxious look on his face and his beard-hair all wiry, presumably from his pulling on it. "Seabird," he said. "You have a message on the machine."

I pressed the button and heard Ilya's recorded voice. "I lost a baby," she said. "I need you here."

My parents watched me in silence. Then my dad tried: "Can we do anything to..."

"No," I said.

I walked to the edge of the grass. I could feel their eyes on my back as my jog across the lawn sped up to a run through town toward Ilya's house.

The woman was Gala, a healthy woman in her thirties. She was crying on the cot. Ilya had wrapped the stillborn in a towel and set it aside in the bathroom, where Gala would not have to see it. And though Ilya was speaking to Gala in a stream of steady words, I could see that she was twisting her hands and looking ancient. For the first time, I saw men coming into the houseboat on their own. The coroner stepped in and Ilya pointed him toward the bathroom. Gala howled.

Ilya knelt in front of the cot and spoke to Gala in a stern voice, telling her all of the things I knew she believed, saying, "Look only at me. Your eyes on my eyes. Here is what I need you to remember. You never know how long or how short a person is meant to belong to you. All you have is today. You have the water and the trees and the fruit and your body, your husband, your living older son. You have a mind that works and a healthy body that can grow another baby. Tomorrow the trees, the fruit, even the ocean might go away. Your duty is today. Now. Be here for them all. Do not fear losing them. Today they are yours. Use them all up."

"But how can I..."

"No talking yet," Ilya said. "Just look at me and listen. Your body is in trauma and every bit of your energy needs to go into healing. Not talking. Not arguing. Today your job is healing your body, the soreness that lives for a week after birth. And after you are healed, don't look back or even forward, but straight down at your life today. If you lose something tomorrow, you lose it twice if you do not use it well now. Love your living son. Focus on him. That is the only way to heal."

Then Ilya held Gala in her arms, the young and round body in the embrace of the willowy white-haired one, and together they cried until Gala's husband came into the room and helped her to the car. The husband looked Ilya in the eye with molten fury and said, "You'll hear from our lawyer next week."

Ilya said nothing. She waited in silence until they drove away. Then she closed the front door that they had left open and she turned to face me and she cried out in an injured voice, "I am through with this work!"

I didn't know what to say to this.

She added more calmly, "When a person nears the end of

a profession or a life, she can read signs. This death may or may not have been preventable. I have resuscitated babies before. A hospital, perhaps, could have saved the baby. But Gala came to me."

We sat quietly together, Ilya and I, for a long time. The out-of-hospital midwifery that Ilya practiced wasn't exactly legal here. She did it, accepting money or goods under-the-table, because she believed women deserved it; she had given her whole life to the women of Dragon Island. Would a jury be able to see that?

No women came to us for the rest of the week. Those who trusted Ilya were not pregnant, and those who doubted her must've gone to the hospital in Middle. When the call came from the lawyer that the trial would not be pursued, Ilya looked exhausted. We were sitting on the hardwood floor, the afternoon sun painting latticework spots on our legs and feet.

"Aren't you relieved?" I asked. "We are going to be okay!"

"Yes," she said without enthusiasm. "Gala has decided that she is able to bear that particular pain."

I wondered what else was keeping her so quiet. Ilya seemed all out of words.

I approached tentatively. "Are you worried about Gala herself? Or...Gala's baby?"

Ilya shook her head, dismissing me. "The baby is fine," Ilya said. She said it with a casual certainty, as if she and the baby had just gotten off the telephone.

This annoyed me. "Ilya," I said. "The baby is dead. What do you *mean* the baby is fine?"

She cocked her head at me. "He is fine. I know. You know who else is doing fine? Your older brother." She looked smug.

"I'm sorry, Ilya," I said finally. "I'm having trouble following you."

"All right, Girl. Would you truly like to know how I know or will it frighten you?"

"I don't know!"

"Girl! Don't let these things spook you. I am talking about life. We find people as we lose people. Often through the same streams. I lost my Adam to your mother but through your mother I found you. Never mind if my story frightens you. It is all true and you must know."

She rose and walked outside onto the deck. I followed. Then Ilya looked at me with the same anchoring, seaworthy look my Nana and I used to share. I knew that she was right, her death was coming soon. I knew also that—whatever I did or did not believe—I would need to prepare myself for whatever story about dead baby ghosts Ilya was about to tell me.

She said, *All right, Girl. Here is the story I want you to hear. It is as real as the wood on this deck.* And I sat with her, all evening, and listened.

It was deepest night when Ilya finished her story. We both sat silent. I looked across her deck, to the point where high rocks crashed out of the ocean and into a weird formation. To me those rocks had always looked like a turreted fairytale castle. Yet, in that moment, I saw that it was not that at all—the rocks jarred upward in the shape of the petals of tulips. And at once it dawned on me that I knew those rocks.

"Ilya," I said, my heart speeding up. "Is the entrance to the Underworld near here?"

She nodded.

"Where?"

Her eyes flickered toward the rocks and back to me. "I think you know where."

The sun was being born as we sat there, a neon orange dot on the rim of the hazy gray ocean.

"You could go if you wanted," Ilya said. "You know how. But I don't see why you would."

"To see my older brother. And Nana. And visit you once you go there."

"If you wanted. But you know it would not change anything."

"Do you wish somebody had just told you that it's impossible to save your mother, and saved you that trip?"

"Oh no," Ilya said. "Never would I want that taken away."

We sat looking at the ocean and then Ilya added: "But, Girl, you were wiser than I. You didn't have to go underground to learn that we can only rescue ourselves, but that we can love our mothers anyway. We all learn in different ways."

"Ilya," I said, "we left Nana there. In the water around those rocks."

Ilya nodded. "It is the place to exchange spirits. You were wise to take her there."

Then she tapped her foot on the wood of her deck. "Well, Girl, you've learned some things. You can swim now. You know what to do at a birth, and you know where to take the dead. You haven't properly tried to remember your birth, but there's time for that still. All that's left for you to do in the world is live in it. Enjoy the sun until it's time for you to join the ghosts. There is life there just as there is life here. The sunlight is the difference. The sun is the only real thing that's holy."

We watched the sun take shape and brighten the wrinkles of the ocean into oranges and pinks. Then Ilya took a heavy breath. I felt in my bones that she would leave me soon.

"I'm losing her," I told Pupuka the next day. We were sitting under a canopy of young trees in full white bloom. I was visiting him at the school at lunchtime, after he had finished work. On the monkey bars at the playground, little kids shrieked and swung.

"How do you know?" he asked.

How *did* I know? Because Ilya kept talking about death? Because she told me this crazy story that I crazily believed about going on a day trip to the land of the dead? Because people just die? Or because, somewhere in my body, gut, and bones, I just *knew*?

"I don't know," I finally said.

Pupuka was eating almonds and thick pieces of dried papaya, which he shared with me.

"I'm terrified to be without her," I added.

He opened a new bag of papaya and set it onto the bench between us. He also handed me a small jar of pickled fish, which I ate hungrily.

"Why are you so afraid?"

"Because—I don't know, what kind of question is that? Because she's someone I trust and love. Because I'm still learning from her. Because she's a responsible adult and I don't know a whole lot of those."

Pupuka opened a second jar of fish and handed it to me. "But you are a responsible adult."

"Well, so. So." I didn't know how to respond to this. "But aren't you uneasy with the idea of not having anyone to look up to?"

"Never. I will always find people to learn from."

"What if something happened to your parents?"

Pupuka sat in rare silence and began to nibble at his fingernails. "I'd be broken up for a while. Everyone would be, because my parents are great. But they've taught me to be a responsible adult, and I would honor their memory by staying one. As will you, after Ilya. Sage," he said. "I have news."

"What do you mean?"

"College." The answer was simply stated, a fact like a heavy coin.

"What about it?" His sparse answers were beginning to frustrate me.

Finally his crooked smile began to take over his face. "I got into the university on Blue Island. Into their malacology program with a scholarship and a job. September start."

He watched me with his face half-eager, half-concerned. I knew what he was thinking. He was moving to my old home island to attend college, an opportunity I missed by coming here. *Was I uneasy with my decision?* he was wondering.

With a hopeful smile, he added, "But I'll be back. You'll be here. I will come back, as long as you're here."

"I'll be here," I said, feeling both a tightening inside and a hope. As I said it I knew it was true. There was nothing left for me on Blue Island. My work, *my home,* was here. Even if the people I loved were leaving, my work with Ilya served as my promise to this place. My parents were here. Soon I'd be some new person's older sister here.

He took both my hands in his and kissed them. "You have big work ahead."

"I know."

"And when I have a degree in four years, I'll come back and be here with you."

He continued holding onto my hands until the bell rang and the teachers minnowed through the park, calling out "First and second graders!" and herding the students back to school. Pupuka stood and waved at the teachers, indicating that he could help herd. He took my face in his hands and kissed me for a long moment, even with all the little kids watching. A tiny boy said "yuck" and a girl no higher than my hip asked in an inexplicably adult voice, "Have I just witnessed a first kiss?"

Pupuka laughed. "Not first."

Later that night Ilya and I had a birth at the houseboat—it was a woman pregnant with twins, and Ilya had monitored her carefully to make sure that the first twin's head was facing down. Risa, the woman, gave into her pain, howled when the waves bit at her, and pushed out two babies, a girl and a boy, six pounds each, both with full heads of hair.

Ilya and I worked together through the birth like lifelong shipmates who knew the patterns of each other's hands. While I caught both babies, Ilya was at the mother's side telling her how strong she was, what a beautiful job she was doing. The first baby crowned at sunrise, and Ilya and I cleaned up in the early hours of the morning.

It was birth as it should be, and as it most often is. Though I didn't know it at the time, it was also the last birth I would share with Ilya.

Ilya stayed with the mother while I left to check on Marella. And when I returned in the afternoon, Ilya was alone again and the house had been scoured of its birth-traces. The mother and twins were back at their own home with neighbors to care for them. Ilya and I wrote down notes, prepared to encapsulate the placenta. We sat for a long time on the deck.

We dipped our feet in the water, and Ilya asked in a way that seemed almost playful, as if trying to be cavalier, "What do you think of the story I told you the other night?"

I paused, and before I could answer, she interrupted: "You don't believe my story. You don't believe such a world could exist. Such creatures as Charon and the Auctioneer. Girl, if I hadn't made that journey, I'd have felt the same way."

"That's not what I was going to say!" It annoyed me when she ascribed to me words that I hadn't said. "I was going to ask you a question. Ilya, what promise did you make to Charon?"

She circled her feet in the water, slowly, as if she were stirring a pot. "All the bad luck in my life happened because I made that trip when I was your age—younger. All the good luck too. You cannot visit the Underworld without leaving tracks. I didn't know how everything would unfold, but I knew it would. It had to, for it was all somehow part of the barter I made. I knew my life would be affected by my father in his new form. I didn't know that it would be through your mother, and I could not have known the hurt she would do to my son. My whole life changed when I met Charon. She made me promise a single thing."

Ilya took a deep breath and pulled her legs out of the ocean and tucked them beneath her. "That I would spend my earth-life as a ferrywoman on one side of life, and then my eternal-life as a ferrywoman on the other side."

"Oh," I said, not knowing what to feel. Then suddenly I knew exactly what I felt.

"I know what I'd do if I were the ferrywoman," I told Ilya. "I wouldn't bring the souls over. I'd just let them find peace without crossing the river. Or better yet: I'd take them across but warn them about the Auctioneer. If nobody goes to auction, then he's done. Right?"

She got a look on her face. She was now listening to me very carefully. "Yes. Except—"

"What?"

"As long as a single person is afraid of him, he will have some power. He's just like any bully. Certainly, the ferrywoman can control the ghosts. But she has no power over the living who fear him."

I hadn't thought of this. "Is anyone alive afraid of him?"

Ilya paused. "I think so. Someone still is."

"Who?" I asked. But Ilya shook her head. "Please, Ilya, tell me. Who knows about him here except you?"

She stood and stretched out her legs. I knew the signs of a woman being done with a conversation.

"Years from now when I die and meet Charon…" I began, but she interrupted me.

"When I am in the Underworld again, I'll carry on your plan."

We stared at each other for a long time, co-conspirators in the moonlight as it bloomed into the corner of the sky. "Good!" I said finally. "Because then all the souls can be happy—like the children. Just like you said. And like Adam is."

Ilya stood up then—she had had enough—and went inside her house. Through the window I saw her starting to stir her miso and vegetable soup for her dinner. After all these months, it still astonished me that she hardly ate and rarely slept. What this woman needed was a mystery to me.

She invited me to stay and share soup.

"Thanks, but no. I must be home for my mother."

Ilya nodded. Then she put down her wooden stirring spoon and crossed the room and placed her hands on my shoulders.

"You are very, very good at this," Ilya said, looking me straight in the eyes.

It was the first direct compliment I could remember her giving me. I thanked her. And then I left.

When I glanced back from the end of her pathway, she was sitting at her small table by herself, blowing on her soup to cool it, looking out at the sea, the blue light descending around her and making her look supremely alive.

The next morning, in the early hours that Ilya called "panic-morning" because no calm news arrives before six a.m., the phone rang. I was fully awake within a half-second of having been fully asleep: midwifery had taught me that.

"I need you to come to me," Ilya said in a whisper I could hardly hear.

I grabbed my birth bag and rushed over to her. Only when I was halfway to her house did I realize that I had brought it with me.

Hurrying up her front steps, I thought: *how well I know*

this house. The exact number of steps from the road to the front door; and the colors, the salt-washed wood, the winking windows eye-lidded with their gauzy curtains. The dock outside her little houseboat undulated—it was a windy dawn and the waves were knifing under the dock, pushing at the house from all sides.

As I approached the house, the front door opened and a man's stooped figure stepped out. He was wearing a tam hat and had a vacant look on his babyish face. Though I had only seen him once before, I knew who he was. He turned the knob consciously, like a child learning to close doors. He called quietly back into the house, "Love you, Mom." Then Ilya's Adam smiled at me and hurried away in a determined, shambolic walk.

I watched him retreat, then opened Ilya's door. The only reason for both of us to be here was that he, like I, had come to say goodbye.

Inside, there was Ilya lying down on her cot in the kitchen. Next to her was a crumbled pile of thin blue blankets that she had kicked off.

"Ilya?" I asked in a voice that echoed around the walls in the small house. "What can I do?"

Her long silver hair dwarfed her tiny body, spread about her face and shoulders like translucent wings about to take flight.

From her cot Ilya called out in a clear and demanding voice. "Just get me out of here quickly. I do not want this to take long."

I swallowed. Here Ilya was in this transitory state, as vulnerable as giving birth—more so because there are no stories from the other side to tell us how it's supposed to go.

"Sage." She was directing me now, as she had before. "I'm going and it hurts and it's not fast enough. I need you to help. I need the smallest green bottle. Bring it now."

I opened the cabinet to Ilya's herbs, all in their identical glass bottles and jars. None of them were green. I parted the sea of bottles and reached instinctively toward the back of the cabinet, where behind the rows of familiar names stood a green bottle smaller than all the rest and labeled "for the end." I brought it to her, unsure of whether I was doing the correct thing.

"And a glass of water." She tried to sit up but collapsed several times. "Open it," she said, thrusting the bottle toward me, and I did. Tiny dry bruise-colored berries filled the bottle, which she took out of my hand. I propped her up while she drank the water and swallowed the contents, chewing and gulping slowly and with difficulty, until her eyes looked glossy and no berries were left.

"Ilya, what is this stuff you're taking?"

She wouldn't meet my eyes. She was afraid, or ashamed.

Instead of answering my question she said: "I will only leave this place feet-first. Do not take me to the hospital."

"*Don't worry.* But are you sure I can't call anyone else…"

"No." Ilya's voice had a beast-growling quality that I had never heard before. "No one. Anyone else will try to keep me alive. I don't want to be kept alive. I have plans after this." Her agitation contorted her face, and I sat there, waiting.

Then she seemed to calm again, recognizing that I was not working against her. "We all belong there, in her. Do you see, Girl? You, your mother, and I. I'll be gone but you'll hear me in your head; in your past and my future, we are the same ferrywoman."

I felt the pressure of tears behind my eyes as I looked at her sun-browned face, its life-marks, its wrinkles, the long hair resting on the sheets. I felt that I needed to take care of her, but I had no idea how. "It's time, Sage," she said, as if answering my unspoken question. "I'm going under.

Just...float in it," she said in a whisper to herself. Her voice was getting quieter with each word. "Be...in it...That's... all." And with that she closed her eyes and held her breath.

I watched in horror as Ilya tried not to let herself breathe. I didn't know what those berries were that she took, but it was obvious they weren't something recommended by experts for a long and healthy life. I knew that she was trying to hold her breath to the point of unconsciousness, in hope of slowing her system quietly from here into her death. She had gone into labor of a wholly different sort.

And I had a *déjà vu* moment, gutting me and taking me back nearly nine months to that last day in the hospital with Nana.

Just then Ilya locked eyes with me and said: "Mother."

"I'm not your mother," I said, uncertainty flooding my voice.

"Mother!" she cried. "Please."

"Ilya..." Why was I arguing? "Your mother isn't here."

"I—*need* you! Please—come for me. I'm dying and I need you now."

I couldn't speak. My whole body was in mourning for her and I didn't want it to seep into my voice.

And during this, Ilya had begun to cry. It was dry, almost noiseless, but it shook her small body and the thin cot beneath her like dry wheat in the wind. "Please come. Please come, please..." She took a ragged breath. It barely filled her lungs. With her eyes closed, she said in a strange voice: "The construction has stopped. I can see..."

I never knew what it was she could see, for suddenly she seemed to see me, grasped wildly for my hand, held it fast. Then for a sudden moment she recognized me, said, "It's your story now, Girl."

Then just as suddenly she let go. Her straining body relaxed.

I reached for her pulse, feeling nothing.

For half an hour I just sat there and held both of Ilya's dead hands in mine. Even though the dying itself did not feel peaceful, Ilya lay in what looked like peace.

I searched her face, wondering at her belief-system, her ghosts and her Underworld, and all the births and deaths she had witnessed. I wouldn't put it past her to believe that our mothers come to the edge of the next life to escort us on. If mothers bring us into life, they might bring us into not-life, too. Perhaps somebody has to run that ferry.

When I felt ready, I called the coroner—the same one who had come to take away Gala's baby now would wrap up Ilya's corpse. Corpse. I hated that word. I held onto Ilya's hands while the tan-suited coroner came in, surveyed the little house, made a face at the floating kombucha cultures in jars, and set up a flimsy gurney to put her on.

"You the granddaughter?" he asked in a rough but kind voice.

I shook my head.

"Odd," he said. "You look something alike. Same hair or face or something. What *are* you, then?"

"I'm her...we're not...*I don't know.*"

The coroner looked pityingly at me. "Well you must be something to her, or else you wouldn't still be holding her hands." I looked hard at her face for one more minute: the tiny nose, such a small barrier between the air inside and out, her thin lips, her wide-set eyes, all that silver hair...

And then I took my hands away.

The coroner lifted her gently and placed her on the gurney. "You know," he said. "If you want to—you know—do it yourself, I don't have to take her."

I thought of Gala's baby, taken away and disposed of somewhere where Gala could not see. In contrast, I thought of rowing out with my dad and letting Nana go ourselves. If I had the choice....

I swallowed slowly and nodded. He nodded back. He took from his bag of supplies a long tan blanket and a thinly-folded ice-pack and placed them on the floor. Then he gathered Ilya up and placed her on the blanket, unfolded the ice pack, and rolled her up like you might swaddle a baby. Ever so gently, the coroner carried her into the bathroom and lifted her into the bathtub as if it were a cradle. He said: "Keep her there, where it's coolest. But don't wait long."

Sunlight flooded into the house when he opened the door to go. The brightness startled me. It was daytime. Life was starting again for the living.

After the coroner left I got the cleaning supplies out from under the sink and scoured the entire houseboat, with the exception of the bathroom, which I left alone—out of fear, respect, practicality? It didn't matter: no time to stop and reflect. There was so much to do.

I washed the corners, the windows, the floors. I put the thin blue blankets in the washing machine, under the bathroom sink. When I did, I looked sideways at the chrysalis that was Ilya and I thought, in a flash, of her journey underground with the swaddled baby. *Had she reached the river by now?*

I cleaned up everything, just the way we did it after every birth. Like I was preparing for the world to begin or end.

I threw away the green empty bottle, sniffing it once to find a faintly sweet smell, and then scrubbing my hands after touching it. And then I took a bunch of dried sage from a jar neatly labeled in Ilya's script, and set it afire. The smoke curled up the walls, washing out death smells, birth smells, and my ambivalence. I opened the windows so the smoke would mingle with the ocean air. The place felt clean, alive, ready.

Ready for me.

It was 3:30 by the time I finished cleaning, and I heard the bells from across town. School was getting out.

I had one last thing to do before leaving the house. I needed to plan a funeral. I dug into the drawers under the kitchen counter. Always organized, Ilya had set her address book on top of her small box of alphabetized files. I would ask Pupuka—and his brothers, and his mother and father—to help me go down the list, calling each woman to invite her to come to Dragon Island that Sunday—two days from today, which seemed about as long as I could afford to wait—and pay her respects.

At 3:45 Pupuka showed up. He took in the sight of me alone in the house and took me into his arms.

On the phone, every woman said the same thing: *How can I help?* If I said nothing, they pushed, saying: *I have skills, I have a company, I have a husband who has a truck.* The funeral plan came together in that way, with each woman offering some small part.

I felt exhausted in a deep-animal way by the time I got home that night. I was so tired that I almost didn't notice that Marella was not in her usual place, her purple chair. I slunk down and sat on the floor next to the empty chair.

"Mother?" I asked into the quiet air. "What are you—oh."

She was walking downstairs slowly, holding Adam's baby book: the book that had initiated my search for Ilya many months ago. She did not ask where I had been. I knew she knew.

"Who told you?" I asked.

"Who didn't? You couldn't walk into the yard without being told. There is no such thing as a secret on an island this size. Are you all right?"

I nodded. "But I don't want to talk about it tonight."

Marella sat down in her chair, setting the baby book onto the table next to her. She looked at the floor while she spoke. "We didn't make a baby book for you. I wish we had. Nobody could focus on anything."

"It's fine," I told her. "I know. It's not a big deal." Months ago, it would have mattered. Tonight, there was only Ilya in my mind.

Marella tried again. "I can remember things. I just didn't write them. Hey! I could record them now, try to make you a late baby book before this new one comes…"

I was exhausted. I did not want to be part of this conversation of regret about a baby book. "Mother," I said. "Let's please drop it."

"But isn't there anything you want to know? Your favorite toy, your first word?"

I think I must've fallen asleep on the floor. I don't remember what I answered, if I answered. But I heard her voice repeating the question.

"Sure," I said speaking through the deep pull of sleep. "Tell me my first word."

She patted my hair, an act so unfamiliar that I might've flinched if I hadn't been so tired. "It was strange. Maybe it was because you had been spending time out on the boat with your dad. But your first word wasn't dog or mama. Your first word was *row*."

22

Marella

I did not want to come back to Dragon Island to watch my mother die, but my father had died already and no daughter can let her mother die alone. I wanted you to stay away, go to college, but you were eighteen and could not be forced. The thought of being somebody's mother on this island again made me spring leaks. I'm afraid here. How could anyone not be afraid, with so many places a person can disappear off the edge of the earth, and with so much danger crowing at the center of the soul, just crowing and clawing and pressing its beak against the vena cava, pushing it almost to bursting point?

It is August 18th when Mortalis and I speak again. We are in a taxi on the way back to Mother's house from the hospital on the day Mother died. It has been over thirty years since we first spoke on the beach. I see his face in the rearview mirror. He is sitting in the center back seat, between George and you.

Mortalis is paring his nails and listening to every word George and I say. He catches sight of me noticing him. He smiles. His eyes are as cold as the bottom of the ocean. He has a blond shadow of stubble, prickly and succulent, as if he's just missed a shave. He is young. Or he appears it. I look around to see if anyone else notices him. George's eyes are on the ocean outside his window. You are asleep with your head against your window. Mortalis looks straight ahead to the road but his ears are alert. He has produced a newspaper and opened it to the crossword puzzle.

When we stop in town for lunch, he vanishes; I think he may have slipped out of the sun-roof. *Does he have a job*, I wonder? *Hobbies?* What is he doing following us?

Now we are back in the car and George and you are talking about my mother. "Do you think her death was painful?" you ask. George frowns and says that the nurses didn't think so.

I look into the rearview mirror again. He is there, trying to cross his long legs into the narrow middle seat. I knew he would come back. "What do you think?" I mouth in a silent whisper, knowing that Mortalis, if he is real and not a phantom of my imagination, will hear.

Mortalis shrugs. He does not appear interested in this sort of thing. He flips the crossword puzzle open. "Know a nine-letter word for homesickness?"

It hits me with a pang: my mother would have known. She loved puzzles, loved crosswords, had a thousand word-born hobbies. She would've answered without any hesitation. I inherited her love of words, but not of games or puzzles. For most of her life, Mother could beat anybody in any game. That was one of the things my father loved best. He could never master her.

We arrive back in our neighborhood and get out of the car. Mortalis slides out too, tips an imaginary hat at me, and begins to walk with a cocky stride out into the street. I lower my voice so that my family will not hear. "Come back," I whisper.

"I want to ask you something."

He pauses but does not turn. The newspaper is rolled up under his arm. "I don't care about the puzzle," I tell him. "But I need to ask you a few questions about death."

"Answers are not my commerce," he says in a voice that is clipped and haughty, full of the crispness with which foreigners enunciate words in a second language.

Suddenly it hits me that the word he wanted is *nostalgia*.

The next time I see him I am shopping downtown at the farmer's market. George is preoccupied trying to hire a fishing partner. You are who knows where. I am at the flower stall, surrounded by lilies and baby's breath, when I notice a beautiful woman about my age at the next stall over, buying fruit. She has hair that is fox-colored and she is heavy-pregnant, wearing a long black dress with her belly bulging low. She seems so peaceful, just filling her basket. I see a rustle at the edge of the fruit stall and there is Mortalis, dapper in a sun-colored suit and hat, and he says something to the pregnant woman. She places her hand on his arm; she looks into his face. There is, it seems, an understanding and I feel unexpectedly jealous. I begin to walk away, hoping I will not be noticed.

Then in a flicker, Mortalis stands at my side. He touches my arm, stopping me. Then he plucks a sprig of baby's breath from a bouquet and says, "Would you like to get a drink with me."

So simple. Barely even a question. I say yes.

It turns out there is a hotel only one block from the market. I have never before noticed it. He holds the door open and follows me in. Inside, there is jazz playing, dim blue light making the afternoon feel like an evening full of possibility. It is another world, a blue musical nighttime world. This world is the opposite of home.

Mortalis brings us a pair of martinis. "To chance meetings," he says. *Clink*!

He wants to know everything about me: what brought me home to Dragon Island? What is my favorite stand at the farmer's market? How old is that pretty daughter of mine? What are the hardest parts and best parts of being a mother? What are my favorite games to play? His questions are good questions, not your typical yes-no, true-false questions, and my answers fall together like dark uneven beads: *I lost my mother / the coconut toasters / eighteen years old / the paying attention, the paying attention / I don't like games.* I forget about my drink as well as my manners. Steadying myself, I ask him about himself.

Mortalis, it turns out, only wants to talk about games. He produces a shoulder bag apparently out of the air (perhaps he was holding it under the table?) and begins rifling through it to show me his collection. He has so many. Every board game of my childhood, and then some. And then many. The bag seems endless and deep, like a magic trick.

But it is more than just games. There are a thousand and one things this man says he does for fun: folding boxes, balloons, frogs, foxes, and swans out of origami. Crocheting, needlework. Any sort of hobby with string. Building Adirondack chairs and bookshelves and canoes: chopping down the trees, planking the wood, polishing it until it gleams, then snugging them together, joint by joint. Cooking. Throwing pots on a wheel. Bonsaiing trees, snipping the branches into perfect stunted shapes, like bound feet, that will live for thousands of years without ever growing tall. It is clear this is something that especially interests Mortalis. He speaks of it with a gleam in his eyes. He gave up on having pets, he says, because the job is never done. I think I know what he means, how the clean dog runs straight for a pit of mud to roll in… but Mortalis has beaten me to it. "I mean," he says, "how much fun can it be when every time you finish bathing a creature, it dies on you? Dogs don't bide time very well. It was getting discouraging. I give up things that discourage me."

Listening, I tell myself: *do not look deep.* For now, I think, the thing to do is just enjoy him, look to the surfaces. Mortalis has the smooth skin of a person who has just been born, yet his hair has streaks of silver. He has a perfectly symmetrical, half-amused smile and perfect posture. His hands are tan and clean. There is something about him that strikes a woman like a match. My husband is handsome but not like that.

We say goodbye, and I am flushed and drunk for the rest of the afternoon. I walk home past the farmer's market and once again I catch sight of the beautiful pregnant woman holding a bounty of fruit in her basket. I am surprised she is still shopping. She looks at once otherworldly and deeply familiar and I think: *I want to be just like her.* And I ask myself: *what am I doing here, wasting time with this man, when I could be peaceful like her instead?*

"What did you do this afternoon?" George asks later, over dinner. He has cooked fish and rosemary roasted potatoes. I eat the potatoes but I am tired of fish.

"Not much," I say. "Took a shower." I hate lying to him, but what would I say, that I have spent the afternoon at a swank bar with Mortalis? When, of course, it is all in my head.

Then only a week later, my trysts with Mortalis harden into a purpose.

It happens the day before George leaves on his fishing trip, and I look out from my window to see you sitting on the pier with some strange island boy, and there is Mortalis standing by, waving at me but looking straight at you, and I run to you...and the boy swims away...and Mortalis watches, frighteningly engrossed, while George carries me back into the house. This is when I think that perhaps if I can seduce him, then I can overpower him, and with that power I can get his answer to my single question.

We meet in secret every day while George is gone. We meet at the market, in cafes, on the streets. He kindly never invites me to meet him by the ocean. I want to know him more deeply but each time I ask anything he brings the conversation back to games. I see why he must be lonely. This is not a topic that can last for long. We keep going for dates, to the bar, to the hospital to look at people being resuscitated, to the movies, to the carwash, to the farmer's market, where I see the beautiful fox-haired woman again, still pregnant, still calm.

I ask him general questions about death and he gives me answers with the pieces missing. Mortalis and I are getting tangled in each other's lives, and I cannot seem to help it. And I begin to see something about him. Whenever we walk down the street, people around us seem to pause with vacant looks of worry—and when they do, Mortalis lurks closer, basking in their fears as if it is the sun giving him a tan. I make note of this. I see how he feeds off the panic of fools.

"*J'adore les fous*!" he says in a giddy voice, after I tell him this. We are downtown and he is admiring a yellow pair of gloves in a store window. He bows his head and says with delicate secrecy, "I'm just the awareness of mortality. I'm all bark and no bite."

I'm not sure if I believe him. I'm not sure if I believe any of this.

He keeps stopping by the house when I am alone. I am dizzied by him as I once was by Zach in high school, and as I once was, what feels like forever ago, by George. We go to the tiny Dragon Island Zoo, a place I haven't been since childhood. Being there I feel like a child surrounded by birthday balloons. All around us are families, young doe-eyed parents with their newly hatched broods on a weekend outing. Mortalis is a mostly silent companion and so I make conversation, narrating the animal description at every cage we pass. Our zoo has a young male lion and a covey of birds of prey. The birds of prey loom at passersby; we eye their long flexing necks and hard red glares. They want us dead so they can pick at our organs. I tell Mortalis this.

"Unattractive," he says. "Stop being so morbid."

The lion sleeps, unbothered by us or the birds or the heat. I read aloud the information on his metal plate next to the glass. His name is Samson.

Near the zoo's exit are three stuffed black bears, a taxidermy family. The largest bear's mouth is opened in mid-roar. The smallest bear is hunched over and its paws are batting at an imaginary fish. Mortalis circles around them. "Well," he says, at last breaking his own silence. "Risk is how you pay. These animals are safe from me, but look at them. As long as they lived they had to wait and wonder. But here they are. Taxidermied. Perfect. Gorgeous. Dead."

I cannot help it. I ask the question I have been harboring for eighteen years. "How will she die? Please tell me. I need to know."

He smiles at me with his sharp teeth. "Don't ask questions whose answers will horrify you. But if you come home with me, I'll give you a hint."

I weigh my choices. *How much do I fear the answer? / How much do I need to know?*

I need to know.

I follow him to his apartment, which feels far from downtown. All the while I know that I am not supposed to be doing this, this is not where I belong, but this man has answers and he might be able to allay my unceasing fears. We are on our bicycles and we ride past the highway overpass that runs toward Middle, through badly maintained parking lots with bright weeds breaking through the asphalt. We do not talk much. We arrive shortly at a low set of apartment buildings, gray stone, that look like they just grew up out of the moldy ground.

"Here," he says gently. I follow him through the gate. A small frog pond burbles with false cheer. It is the most depressing lodging I have ever seen. The courtyard opens to countless tiny avenues, each leading to the apartments themselves, and I know for certain, as we pass unnumbered doorway after unnumbered doorway, that I would never find this place again without a guide. "Here we are," he says, pulling a giant wad of keys from his pocket. The room we walk into is nighttime black, and I can see a candle burning in the next room over.

He whispers, "May I take your purse, dearest?" And he smiles and shows those teeth like the mouth of a shark, razored and overlapping and infinite. I think: *Why have I followed him here? Will his answer make me stop worrying? Or will it be at the expense of my life or hers?* I think this is what he is thinking, too; I see it in his smile.

We walk further into the room, and I almost trip over a set of low stairs taking us down a level. Mortalis holds my elbow to make sure I don't fall. Then the lights switch on! The blindness I feel for a moment staggers me, and if he weren't holding my elbow I certainly would've toppled down the stairs. When my eyes adjust I see a den with built-in bookshelves. But instead of horizontal shelves, his shelves are vertical, and in each column he has piled game upon game upon game upon game: Yahtzee and Scrabble and Monopoly and Cranium and Uno and checkers and chess and Chinese checkers and Taboo and in a basket in a corner next to a fireplace, there are hundreds of decks of cards. Across the room is an enormous cage and it is covered by a pale green velvet drape.

"Oh kitty," croons Mortalis. "Are you hungry?"

From the cage I hear a low purring roar.

I see at that moment something I have been trying not to see for my entire life: that I am a coward. I am someone who acts out of fear and has always acted out of fear, and here is where fear has taken me.

"Well, dearest," he says softly. "What game shall we play first?"

"Won't you show me around a bit?" I try this, knowing it won't work.

"Oh no," he says, smiling. "I only entertain my visitors in this room. This is as far as I'll let you explore today."

He challenges me to a game of chess. We play halfheartedly. He wins, of course.

"Well that wasn't very exciting," he says. "What next?"

Then I have an idea: how about hide and seek?

"What are you, a child?" Mortalis mutters with a hint of impatience. But you can tell he is taken by the idea. Of all the games he has lining his shelves, none of them are child's games, the kind you just make up as you go along, the ones that teach the secret rhythms of being human.

"Fine," he says. "You hide first. But stay in this room."

He begins to count to a hundred. I look around. There is really no hiding place except the cage, and I know better than that. I stand next to it and pull up some of the velvet and flap it over me. I wait.

He finds me quickly and with great glee. "Let's just look inside, why don't we." And he pulls the velvet off the opening of the cage like a magician doing a trick, and I gasp. It is a grown lion inside, sleeping lightly. *This is not a game,* I think.

"Oh, sure it is," he says, even though I have spoken no words aloud. "Once it was the only game. Fighting, darling. It was how heroes were made in the earliest days of civilization. It would be ungentlemanly if I didn't pay homage. I borrowed the beast from the zoo. Would you like to take a closer look?

Not now? All right, dearest. Your turn to seek. I'll hide."

I count to a hundred. Mortalis is silent. And then I hear a squeak and a tiny latch sound, and I know he is hiding in Samson's cage, waiting for me. I cry out, "Ready or not!"

Then I look around the room and know: *this is my chance.* I scan the room for a bar of some sort, and I find a domino. And I run over to the cage, peek in. "You found me! Come on in," Mortalis says. But instead of opening the cage door, I thrust the domino into the lock, wedging it shut. Then I run off into his hallway.

I open door after door. They are all closed. A kitchen, unused. A bedroom, no bed—but a leather couch in the center—a bathroom, a second bathroom, and finally—the study! I let myself in, locking the door behind me. Then I look around.

I can hear him roaring my name from the other room. He has figured out that I have trapped him. But surely his magic is more powerful than that; surely he will find a way out before I can even cross the threshold of his apartment and get back to my bicycle, my family, my life. But I have to look first. I came all this way for answers.

23

Sage

APRIL — MAY

I woke in my bed, though I didn't remember walking myself there. When I came down to make breakfast, both my parents were watching me with solemn curious faces: Marella in her lilac bathrobe, my dad half-dressed in his fish market gear, wearing rubber pants and suspenders but lacking his socks and shirt. My dad gave me a sideways hug, lingered long enough to make sure I was acting like myself, and then grabbed a handful of trail mix and headed out to work.

My mother perched on a kitchen stool and waited until I was half-finished preparing an omelet.

"So," said Marella at last. She searched me with her dark eyes and I could feel her looking for sadness that could match her own.

"I'm okay," I said.

She stared at me.

"Really, I am."

She was silent. Then she burst out, the shrapnel of her

grief peppering holes in the air. "You're lying! No one's okay. Death is terrible! Death is everything wrong. We would be a perfect family if only...."

I flipped the omelet and patted it down and waited for her to finish. I collected my thoughts, and when the eggs were cooked through I had my words ready.

"Marella," I said, in the same stern voice that I had heard Ilya use. "Death is just the next womb. Our mortality is a certainty, but it becomes a tragedy if we spend our life obsessing over it. I miss Ilya. I loved her and spent time with her. As much as I could take her with me, I did. But there is no tragedy. Ilya used life as well as anybody could have. And I don't feel sorry for myself because I made sure not to waste her." My voice wobbled, but I was telling the truth.

I sliced the omelet and placed it onto two plates.

Marella was toying with her hair while I spoke. Her eyes darted between me and her Adam-shrine in the corner with all of its memorabilia: the lock of his hair, a finger-painting he did with what looked like coffee, photos of him beginning as a baby and ending before age one-and-a-half. A stunted shrine.

I steadied my voice. "Marella, what is the hardest part about outliving Adam? Is it that it is not the natural order of things, or that you miss him, or that you put in so much energy to raise him, and now it's all wasted? Or that you wish you could have known him better?"

"All of it," she answered slowly. "I hate that I didn't see him grow up. I wish I could know who he would be."

"Who do you think he would be?"

She shrugged. "An engineer, perhaps. He loved George's tools. Or a doctor. Who knows. We will never know. All I know is...he would have been perfect," my mother finished in a whisper.

"Marella, no. You say that about Adam because he is only

a theoretical. But here I am, and here you are about to have another baby, and we are all the perfect you are going to get. Adam belongs to the ocean now. We belong to the earth."

"I don't think you have any idea what you are talking about," she said, steadily watching me. But her voice lacked fire.

She was right. I didn't know anything for certain. I could guess, but it was all just a story, one story among many stories. All I knew was that fear had loosened its grip on me, and unlike my mother, I felt free.

She swept majestically out of the kitchen, took her omelet and ate it upstairs in her room. I ate mine slowly, alone, on the back steps facing the water. The sea had a certain purple violence that morning. It showed me something different every time I looked. This morning felt like Ilya's ocean, like the ghosts she knew were rising to welcome her home.

The day passed in a blur of calls with women about the funeral. In the back of my mind I was thinking about Ilya's Adam: whether to find a way to get him to his mother's funeral. I knew he had said goodbye to her. I didn't know if drawing it out and bringing him there would make his life any better.

Still undecided, I went about my tasks. I invited Marella to keep me company on a trip to the store to get some food for the funeral. She didn't want to come the first time I asked, but I asked a second time and she agreed.

As soon as we got into the store, somebody she knew from high school waved at her and said in a chitchat-making way, "Look at you, once more with child! You looked the same twenty years ago."

Marella did not answer, so I smiled obligingly at the woman and kept walking. As we pushed our small cart among the mangoes and the imported cheeses, avoiding the fish counter completely because we had so much fish, too much fish, frozen into inelegant slabs in our basement industrial freezer, my poor panicked mother looked like somebody had forced her into a net. She was looking around wildly for an exit. It was not a good call for me to bring her.

I took her elbow and led her into the rice and beans aisle at the dinky little island grocery with its two brands of everything, one fancy and one generic, unlike the vast stores on our old island, supermarkets that held the whole world inside.

Employees restocking the aisles smiled at us: a mother and a daughter out shopping. Marella leered at one woman with such force that the woman fumbled and dropped a carton of yogurt and apologized in the air to no one. I left Marella at the checkout and ran back to the paper goods aisle to grab five hundred paper plates and cups. When I returned Marella was fumbling with cash; it was clear that she had reached her boiling point.

"I can't do this!" she yelled out in frustration. I went to her side, thinking of how many layers of safe blubber I had built up between the frustration of "I can't do this" and the need to yell. How many layers every person in the store had, too—what a marvel we are—and then here was my poor mother, thin-blubbered and upset. Petulantly, she gave a shriek. Then she said to me in a loud voice: "I have changed in the last twenty years. Just not for the better." Shoppers' heads turned.

"You wait outside," I told her, and she obeyed. At that moment it was beyond my comprehension how this woman could function as a grown-up for yet another child. But I felt sorry for her as much as I felt irritated: while I had had the chance to grow up in the past two decades, she was still pregnant, still trying to launch into adulthood, still afraid to face what the ocean and her body would bring.

I took us the quiet way back through town, not through the busy streets where she'd see people she knew, but through the alleyways Pupuka had shown me, giving Marella a chance to calm down. Passing through Squid Ink Alley, I saw that the art had evolved and the green and purple graffiti shark was finished and snacking on one of the tentacles of the squid.

As we walked by Ilya's Herbs, which looked even more derelict than when I first went in, I saw a face inside, looking out through the dust-mote sunlight. Adam.

He was standing at the counter and smiling. When he saw me through the window, he held out his hand.

My mother didn't recognize the face through the glass, so I took the opportunity to guide her into the store. "What are we—?" And then she saw Adam and stopped.

"Adam," I said, "there's something I must tell you. Now that your mom has..." I stopped.

How much did Adam understand about death? Would I have to explain a funeral? I felt that I should explain gently.

"She has gone to the ghosts," Adam said in a deep and echoing voice.

His candor caught me by surprise. "Yes."

"She said she'd go there again."

I didn't know what to say next. I waited for him to speak.

Adam looked into the sunlight for a long moment, then said: "Don't worry. She likes it there."

Then he turned and peered vacantly at my mother, who was still attached to my arm and pulling backward like a terrier. I knew she was afraid of seeing Adam. But in the wake of her unshelled moment in the supermarket, I wondered if she would feel less different from him, less finished.

"I don't remember the ghosts," Adam continued, as if turning the silence over slowly. "But she said I liked it there too."

"Adam," I said slowly, "do you remember Marella?"

He smiled at her. "Always."

Marella stopped pulling away from me. "Always I remember you," she said back.

They stared at each other goofily, like kids on the first day of school. Adam kept smiling. Marella looked frightened, but she touched his hand. He smiled wider. "Thank you," he said.

"For what?" my mother said quickly, taken aback. She was looking awkward, not angry or frightening, just scared and guilty and out of place.

"All things."

Adam began moving crystals around on the counter and pulling down the blinds to the store. "Closing time," he said. "Home to your mother's for dinner." He gave a soft laugh. And he pulled on his little tam hat, nodded at us both, and locked the door after us when we left.

Marella was silent all the way home. I let her be.

Then the next morning my mother, dad, and I woke early for Ilya's funeral.

Women flowed onto Ilya's lawn, bringing their gifts. Several helped cater. Many brought flowers. One woman had her officiant's license and performed the service. A woman who had four babies in Ilya's house owned a rental company and provided tables and folding chairs. We used all she had and still they were not enough.

Women came from all nearby islands and even from other countries, on boats, airplanes, foot. I got chills when I saw the mother of one of my old school friends from Blue Island. I had no idea Ilya's influence had stretched so far.

Women came from all over Dragon Island, wearing their hair in traditional celebration twists, with island flowers tucked in. The grass outside Ilya's house transformed into a great outdoor room full of women, women bearing flowers, women holding hands of children, women holding hands of husbands, women holding hands of women. Old women, young women, mothers, daughters, infants, girls. They swelled around the houseboat and spilled out of the tent that we had erected in the front yard.

Many of the women brought garlands of flowers, woven with purple orchids and red roses. They dropped their garlands to form a mound on Ilya's wooden deck. Before the funeral even began, flower necklaces cluttered the windowsills and were starting to fall like leaves into the sea. At high noon, when people were beginning to leave, the rain came, washing her steps, dispersing the petals; soon the water around her house filled with floating flowers, like red and purple lifeboats, like perfect placentas, like the lopsided hearts of women, floating out to sea.

The afternoon after the funeral, there was one more thing that I needed to do. I needed to deliver Ilya to the ocean resting place. I had hoped somebody else might do it, but who? I was the person she left responsible. I knew where to go. And already I'd borrowed my father's skiff and asked Pupuka to come with me.

Pupuka wore a life jacket and insisted that I did too.

We were silent the whole rowing out. The day was still and the rowing was easy. Ilya's thin suntanned body lay sheathed and nestled on the boat's bottom. It took half an hour to row out, and when the rocks shaped like tulips came so close we could swim to them, Pupuka lifted her into my arms.

It would be up to me to let her go. Unlike with Nana, this time I was in charge and I would have to choose when to stop looking at her and give her up to the ocean. Six months ago, such a responsibility would've seemed impossible. Yet once I accepted the fact of it, I felt a strange ease.

Because Ilya held no fear of the deep. Some part of her lived there, all along.

I let go, turning my head away so I wouldn't have to see her sink.

I started to row back but then changed my course. Pupuka did not say anything but looked confused. I said to him, "Wait here."

I took off my sandals and life jacket and slid into the water still wearing my dress. Using the powerful strokes Pupuka had taught me, I swam toward the tulip rocks. The water here was deeper than any place I had swum before. I focused my mind on the task, not on what could be beneath me. Just as Ilya taught me to do during a birth.

I reached the rocks and began to tread water. How to know which one held the entrance? I swam into the center and looked around. The rocks blocked the sun, and that or something else made the water in the center ferociously cold. I might have chickened out if I didn't see it immediately—but I did. There on the side of one of the tallest slender rocks, I found the mark. A mark in the shape of a canoe.

I took a breath. Diving under the rock, I felt a glimpse of the terror Ilya must've felt, doing this with an infant. I counted the seconds I held my breath, and it was fewer than fifteen—but the heavy stretching fact of the rock above made it feel longer, made me fear it would not end. And just as Ilya said, I came out on the other side into a full dome of air. *Like just-dampened fire.* I could almost hear her voice.

I found the entrance easily, feeling above me in the thick blackness. It was a smooth opening, like a hole in a piece of fruit or the mouth of a giant snake. I had feared it might be jagged like the rocks themselves. Still it took all the courage I had to hoist myself inside, trusting it. Inside the hole my vision got lighter, and soon I could see the staircase, going down, down, down. Being at the edge of life and death didn't feel spooky, just necessary—I was simply taking the trip that Ilya took. Was I testing to see if she told the truth? Was I trying to bring her back? Did I want to see her on the other side?

It felt automatic. Some place I had to go. Like I was sleepwalking.

How long the descent took, I could not tell. I made it to the bottom, to the bruise-colored light. I saw the evergreen trees and their weird coin-needles. I saw the line of souls. How to tell one from the other? They all just looked blank.

I looked beyond, saw the river, at its edge a boat. And then I saw Charon. She was kneeling, untying a rope, her face away from me. I wanted to see—I was afraid to see—and then she turned and I saw.

The ferrywoman had Ilya's face.

Unwrinkled, ageless, but unmistakably Ilya's. She had Ilya's long hair too, but it was black, not white. She shimmered in her bigger-than-human body, the size of four living Ilyas. As I stared, Charon looked up at me and her hands rose as big as brooms, sweeping toward me.

Away, she mouthed. *Go.*

But I could not turn back. Somehow I had to go to her—some wild force seemed to draw me closer to her—across those coin-spangled banks....

I began to walk forward as if pulled by a magnet. Turning away felt impossible. I had the strangest feeling as if I were looking into a mirror, trapped by my reflection. I had to go forward. I had to. The face of Charon was stormy now, an angry thing of the Underworld. I needed to get closer, to see it more clearly...

Go—back, it said. *Now.*

But I couldn't. It felt like there was only one direction in the world and it was toward her.

And suddenly I felt a familiar pair of hands grab my arm with an unfamiliar roughness. They pulled me backward, and I did nothing to fight them; they picked me up; they carried me as if I were a baby kitten.

Through the trees, up the stairs, through the darkness, under the rock. Backward, forward, it didn't matter, it seemed. I was in the hands of stronger forces than me; let them decide my fate.

The air of our world woke me from the trance. Back in the cold ocean at the center of the tulip-rocks I saw that our little skiff had been tied to one of the small rocks at the edge, so it wouldn't rock away farther than we could swim.

And Pupuka had not let go of me. We were in the water now, nearing the boat.

"You didn't see her face, did you?" he asked as we made our awkward swim, his hand still holding my arm.

"Yes, I did. That ferrywoman was Ilya. I was going to talk to her…"

Pupuka looked exhausted. He had hauled me up all those stairs. The moonlight fell in odd creases on his face. His mouth a small firm line. He was shaking his head.

"It was! I saw her—you didn't see…"

Finally he set me in the boat and sat down behind me. He began to row.

"I saw her face. She was you," he said. "And I think if you had kept going, you would've become…"

He stopped shortly. I began to shiver all over.

Pupuka just kept rowing with a grim look on his face. "Sage, don't do that. Don't go to non-human places. I'll go anywhere with you—like the cave we went into where that baby was born—but this is not a human place. This place could get us into real trouble."

He didn't speak for much of the journey back. When I reached for his hand at arrival, he took it, inspected it—as if looking for dirt beneath my nails—and at last his face softened. "That scared me, Sage," he said. "I thought you were gone."

"I'm *not*."

"I'm not scared of your mother," he said. "I'm not scared of your midwifery. But I've been around these island myths a long time, and some are more than myths. I don't know what magic was playing down there, but that huge woman by the river had your face. I swear she did. Stay up here. With me."

"I will," I said, and I meant it. "I promise."

I woke in the morning sore from the swimming. My arms and legs felt a hundred years old. I woke up knowing too that Pupuka was right. That I needed to stay away from that place. Ilya had said something on her deathbed that I didn't understand but couldn't shake: *We all belong there, in her. You, your mother, and I.* Ilya had gone to the Underworld to save her mother—and made a barter that changed her fate. Did this mean that my mother had gone too? I could not imagine her going that deep into the water. Maybe she did it to try to save Adam? If so, no doubt she made some barter that changed her fate too, because you don't go into the Underworld, it seems, without bargaining away something.

So then, why did I belong there? Were Ilya's words what provoked me to go? I thought and thought about this. I think I went because I was curious. Because it felt like my turn. But I left—rather, Pupuka yanked me out—before I could barter anything away. If he hadn't yanked me out…so then what?

I did a lot of worrying that week. Worrying and sleeping. I felt creeped out by the Underworld, confused by what I had seen, and I wondered, in the days afterward, what exactly had really happened.

I wanted to ask somebody—some adult who knew more than I did—but did not want to sound crazy. But Pupuka had seen it too. He knew it was not made up. But whatever it was, he wanted nothing to do with it.

I craved the simple sadness of missing Ilya, as I had missed my grandmother. There were tears, but rarely. Instead of feeling sad, I felt guilty. Guilty for letting life move on, for being its accomplice. I felt worried too that I would not be able to rise to the task of all the births. Ilya had chosen me to take over her practice. Despite all my training, I felt amateurish and unprepared, as soft and undeveloped as the pink under-shell body of a hermit crab.

Pupuka came over every single day during the week following Ilya's death. His visits stood out clearly in my mind even though the rest of those hours blurred into sand. My parents gave us space to be together; several times my dad even brought us meals which we ate in the loft of my bedroom.

When I told Pupuka how I felt, the guilt and its subdued tentacles, he said, "It's because you have the biological imperative to keep living. You're being a good animal, see? And you've got to run her business, so you're looking ahead."

It wasn't the response I expected. It helped, it didn't help, I was too tired to know.

Having Pupuka visit put me at peace, but it also reminded me how much work lay ahead. I had never done a birth without her. I had never talked with a doctor as an equal. I had never resuscitated a baby, even though she had explained the ways to do it. I had never ground herbs without her supervising my proportions. I had never even looked through her massive *Book of New Life, Herbs, and Mammals* without her standing right beside me, her quick eyes guiding mine to find the right words on the page. The enormity of my task swelled like high tide and for the rest of that day, I slept. I didn't even notice Pupuka leaving. But when I woke it was evening and he was gone.

So then what?

It was the last day of April. I had been sad long enough. I had been sad for the loss of some much-loved woman, it seemed, all year. It was time for life to move on. *So then,* I told myself sternly, *you do your work.* Not in the Underworld, but here. If fate must be changed, let it be here, on earth, through the work of my hands. Through my own life's work.

This thought propelled me out of bed and into my clothes and my shoes. It was time for me to re-open Ilya's houseboat for women.

It was a slow and deliberate walk from my house to Ilya's. I arrived near sunset: the extravagant purples and oranges made the wooden sides of the house glisten, and her roof carved a silvery silhouette against the sky. I stood at the shoreline, admiring—as I still do, each time—how much the land really does curl around the bay like a sleeping green dragon, its low head resting in the water, tall trees spiking its neck all the way down to its black-rock nose. From Ilya's house, you could see practically the whole dragon.

I knew that she left her house unlocked for women to use. She never wanted to close them out when they might come seeking help, solace, or sanctuary. I opened the door.

The salt and vanilla smell of Ilya hit me hard. I could not have articulated her smell until it resided here, without her. It suffused the wood of the house. The shutters had been left closed, the screens uncovered, and I went around opening windows, letting the sea breeze in. I felt comforted by her smell but also found it eerie and distracting—sort of the way it felt to listen to Nana's dead voice on the answering machine.

I looked around the room. It was spotless, gleaming, as Ilya always kept it and as I had left it on the day Ilya died. The herbs needed harvesting and the aloe plant looked ripe with serum. I began to do my work, and I even called the phone company to place a line in the tiny Dragon Island directory with my name and underneath it, "Medicine Woman, accepting enquiries."

I saw Ilya's copy of *Book of New Life, Herbs, and Mammals* high on its shelf, where it belonged. I took it down. I knew all of the things with my hands that she had wanted me to know, and the book was here for me as it had been for her, to give information beyond what my hands knew. I saw that a bookmark had been placed in the book since last I held it. The bookmark itself made me laugh aloud—it was a paper urine testing stick. I opened to it. It was the page about "Caul."

The first definition was all history: who the caulbearers were and other myths. A long and witchy section about how in seventeenth-century rural Europe, some caulbearers gathered and called themselves the Benandanti, meaning Good Walkers. At night, they flew out of their bodies to battle evil spirits in order to ensure good crops for the coming season. How a caul signified luck and knowledge, and many caulbearers were thought to be witches and put to death by fire. They were burned because it was considered a punishable crime to shed the blood of a caulbearer.

What followed was a highly practical section on how to remove a caul without harming the baby: "In the case that a piece of the caul sticks to the baby's head, make an incision at the nostrils so the baby can breathe. Afterward, remove loops of caul from behind the ears. Peel or rub gently with cloth so as not to leave scarring."

And then I saw a note in her handwriting: *See Charon.*

I turned ahead a few pages. Charon's entry was a single sentence: "In Greek mythology, an old man who ferried souls of the dead across the River Styx to Hades." Ilya had crossed this sentence out, written another note. *To Sage*, it said. *Your caul is in the red box in the closet above the linens. PS – ask your mother who Charon really is.* As if in a trance I found it: a dry piece of tissue from my body, pinned flat to a piece of cardboard, covered with plastic wrap.

My thoughts raced at the foolish impossibility of her saving this thing: if we had stayed where I'd grown up on Blue Island, she would've never known me and this caul would've belonged to nobody. But she kept it. Why, I may never know. She must've had a vision for my finding it and left the bookmark in the final few days of her life. Whatever the reason, she kept it for me and at that moment I knew exactly what I would do with it.

Before returning home, I looked through Ilya's tools. I chose the ones I needed and packed them into my bag, adding a few other things of my own: Tincture of Lady's Mantle. A more modern Doppler. My bag was packed, and I stashed it at Ilya's—at *my*—houseboat.

That night I walked home, energetic and awake and carrying my plastic-wrapped caul under my arm. When I arrived I crept into the baby's room. It was half-set up, just the crib and the changing table and a few unsorted boxes of clothes. I made a trip to the garage to find supplies and then spent an hour at work with the hammer and nails. When I was finished it was nearly midnight. My caul hung on the wall, pressed between two glass panes, above the baby's crib.

It was a superstition, a myth. If you didn't know what was inside the frame, it would be impossible to diagnose whether it was modern art or a specimen. My caul could not keep him safe forever. But it was something.

The following afternoon, a client called. It was Delia the baker, who came with a friend.

The friend, Neda, said, "I am pregnant with my second, and Delia told me that this is the place to come. Are you the primary midwife?"

"I am." I invited her to sit on the cot and asked how she was feeling.

"Sick!" she said, with a laugh. "Sicker than with the first." I gave her a small bag of ginger gum. And I felt her wrists. She said, "I've heard that the pulse can tell you if the baby is a boy or a girl."

"Some people believe that," I told her. "Not me. I've seen predictions go wrong enough times. If you really want to know, you can get a sonogram in the hospital in Middle. And if you want to know without going there, you can ask yourself—what does this baby feel like? The mother's first strong hunch is the best non-medical indicator."

Neda and Delia looked at each other and laughed. "It's a boy, then. I've been speaking to him in my mind since the beginning. If what you say is true, then it's definitely a boy."

Delia took out some yarn from her purse and held up a blue bundle, making Neda laugh again. Then Neda lay down and rested while I felt her abdomen and blood pressure, and then asked her all of Ilya's questions. Neda would be my first client. She would be the first of many.

I kept my work-days short when I could, so that I could be ready for Marella. After Ilya died my mother called the hospital to register her due-date. The hospital was what she had pushed for initially and with Ilya gone, there was nobody to persuade her otherwise. I urged her to go in for a checkup. "You don't want to waste time giving them your medical history when you are in labor," I advised her. She ignored me. She was thirty-nine weeks pregnant.

She was in waiting now. Soon her life would undergo another sea-change. She was excited, she was nervous. Her yellow sticky-notes tripled, spilling out of her bedroom into the hallway and pattering down to the floor like cicada shells. She washed her hair compulsively, twice a day or sometimes three times. The kitchen gleamed. She would not let anyone wear shoes inside the house, so a pile of our flip-flops grew in the mud-room and began to stink. She jittered around the living room, dusting things, rearranging books and photos and trinkets. When my dad came home at night, she dictated chores to him: make sure the windows are in good condition, recheck the freezer to make sure we have enough fish.

"Why don't we go for a walk?" I suggested to my mother one morning at the end of the thirty-ninth week.

She balked. "I have far too much to do. The nursery still has no mobile!"

"The baby will not care!"

We went back and forth like this for some time. Finally my mother agreed.

We set off toward town. I had thought we'd go for breakfast at the bakery where Delia worked. The waves were low that day and the sun was bearing down on our backs. I thought of how strange it must be for a baby, existing only in darkness for so many months, suddenly to see the sun.

We spent breakfast talking about baby names and gossiping about people we knew in town. It was fun. The highlight was when my mother said that, as the adult sister, I could choose the baby's name. My mind flickered to Ilya and her hopes for her son.

"I want to name him Ola," I said. A word for life. The name Ilya wished to give her son, if things had gone the way she wanted.

"And what if it's a girl?"

"He won't be."

Her dark eyes glistened for a long moment; she did not argue.

And then on the walk home, it happened. I had not expected it so soon. Usually there are signs, there have always been signs, but for Marella it happened too quickly.

"Oh no," my mother said, stopping suddenly on the side of the road in a patch of dry grass.

"What is it?" I asked. I looked at her feet to see if something had stung her: an insect, or a fox-head. But she was clutching her belly.

24

Marella

The ceiling of Mortalis's study arches like the top of a rock cave. All of the walls are covered in metal file cabinets, their fronts labeled with neat small letters, so the room feels like a vault of alphabetized secrets. I spring toward the B's. I pull the drawer open, but the files are not in a form I recognize: there are names written on paper, as I believed there would be: one name for each person who has lived. But the papers are tiny circles, and they are speared into spindles: stacks and stacks of circular sheets of paper, each like a notepad impaled by a stem.

I pull open several other drawers, and each drawer is thick with bunches of these papers, like great bouquets of paper flowers. I feel for the bottom of one layer and find another layer—I suppose they fill the drawers endlessly, going all the way down. Each name has beneath it a pad of paper a hundred sheets thick. I find my own notepad easily, and look down at the writing:

The top page reads: *Birth canal: loss of oxygen.* What—? Obviously, that did not happen or I would not be standing here now.

I flip to the middle of the stack: *Coral Reef: catches bathing suit.* But I haven't swum in the coral since I was a teenager.

I flip it and go to the next. *Sailboat: suicide after loss of friend.* First this one seems ludicrous, but then I remember that I had thought about it—

I flip down further: *Zoo: bitten by a poisonous snake.* But I have only been to the zoo twice in the past thirty years, and both times the snakes were safe in their terrarium.

I peel back the next page: *Marketplace: run over.* I remember earlier this spring when a truck ran a red light near me, but I simply waited until it passed.

I search for other files. I notice something strange, that the files inside are clustered around family. I see my mother's name, my father's, the names of my grandparents. Each one has a stack as thick and vertical as mine. Desperately, I reach to the bottom of my mother's stack. *At hospital: gave up.* But—not cancer? The cards above it, above it, and above it, all offer different—all incorrect—situations.

A metal door rattles. He has escaped the cage and is looking for me.

Let him. He can't hurt me.

He cannot hurt me. Deep in my body I know that death at the hands of this man is not anywhere in my cards.

And only then do I understand: Mortalis is not death.

Mortalis is only the fear of death, and all of these files are his games, the many ways he watches while humans torture themselves by imagining false deaths, consequently dying over and over until the real one comes.

I look in my file again, looking at all of the deaths I feared meeting but didn't meet. *Avalanche: crushed on way to party.* I wonder if this party could have been the birthday of George's sister in America who had years ago sent an invitation to us all. But I declined to go…because I was afraid.

I reach down to the bottom of my stack to see my final death. But my last page is blank.

On every page before it, scenarios have been written. But that blank page at my very end gives me pause. Could it mean that my fate has not yet been assigned, not yet imagined? And then it strikes me that is the answer.

These are all just branches of possibilities. There will always be possibilities.

Mortalis doesn't know. He only hopes, and these rolodexes are lists of his many hopes. And when you live through that first possibility, you can peel off the top sheet and wait to see how you will negotiate the next. And the next. But it's worth it, isn't it, to be alive, with the mortal sentence listed there, in plain legible writing? Standing there I ask myself the question I have been avoiding all along: *what will it take for me to stop seeing Mortalis everywhere?*

And then I find my daughter's file.

I can look if I want. I am here to look. I could see all of the answers, every way that my girl might be yanked off Earth like an actor being pulled off stage by a cane. But I look away. And I realize that that is my answer: *stop looking*. In the grand list of possibilities, one will be worth it. Of the thousand ways for a person to die, we only have to undergo one.

I hear Mortalis clanging around in the other room. At once, he gives a frustrated yell, and I hear the sound of something—a stack of games?—falling.

But I don't fear him anymore. I close up his files and walk out of his study. In the living room he stands staring at me; the lion is back in its cage. "Dearest, what game are you..." he begins, then he quiets when he sees that I do not intend to answer.

I face him as if he is any ordinary man. "You visited me once when I was a child. You've followed me since she was born. Why?"

Mortalis looks diabolical; his hair is rumpled from our hide-and-seek and looks almost like horns. In his anger at me, all the blood has rushed to his face; his handsomeness is gone and he appears like something else, something ugly, terrifying, and not at all mortal.

I get the chills all over; I take a step back from him. But still I wait for an answer.

"Because you stole my ferrywoman," he says in a low, reptilian voice. "*And until I get her back, there is no life after death.*"

"Maybe there shouldn't be," I say. "Maybe this life should be it. Everything there is."

I speak before considering whether what I say is true, but then I believe, suddenly, that it is. I have spent Sage's childhood afraid of losing her. Would I do it all over again with this new child? Could I bear it? Then could I go on to the Underworld and try to find my children there, or wait there for them...

No. No.

"NO!" I yell at Mortalis, who jumps back in surprise as I walk quickly past him through the room and toward the front door.

Mortalis's face dims. He sees that he is losing me. His bright ocean-colored eyes are turning gray and his chin is losing its angles; his face is dribbling into some anemone blob, no longer chiseled full of secrets whose answers I must know. Still he follows, he tries to draw me back: "You come here looking for Death," he hisses. "You want to know what Death is like? You see her every day at the market. Eat your heart out. You know exactly who I mean."

And the picture flashes inside my head. Yes, there she is. I know exactly.

He sees me reach for the doorknob—this is not how he planned it, and he changes his voice so that it sounds like the roar of the surf. "Don't you want your son back?" Mortalis taunts. "Don't you want to see him? I can show you. I have him…I have him…"

Behind him, there is the purr of the caged beast. How have I come into this place? A memory comes to me from early in my daughter's life, when Ilya visited and said, *As long as you cling to life, he's got you. As long as you're afraid.*

I cannot be. I need to show him that now. He cannot rule me anymore. "No," I say, even if I am about to cry. Even if I am bluffing. I say it again. "No!"

He straightens out his shirt and tugs the chain of his watch. It falls out of his pocket, and I can see suddenly that its hands are gone—it is just a blank face. He sees me noticing and covers his watch with his hand. His hand no longer has skin on it—it has instead something that looks like scales. He sees me notice this too—and he thrusts his hands in his pockets.

"So what if you don't fear me now," he jeers, his eyes slit and lethal. "You will after you die. We'll see each other again. If you want to come back to life, you'll have to bargain with me."

"I won't bargain with anyone," I say. "I'm done with the bargains. Done! I have been down there, and I won't fear you now or then. And I'll tell the others there not to fear you. I'll tell them all!" I yell at him, my voice rising. I am not sure that what I threaten is possible, but I feel that I must summon everything I can to tell him that I finally understand.

"Took you long enough," he says, trying to sound nasty, but I can see that he is now the scared one. He is melting into something else, something small and afraid. Mortalis, this man who is bigger than me, is beginning to shrink. Clothes and all, he gets smaller and smaller until he could fit easily into my pocket. Out of some instinct that I still do not understand, I grab him and hold him tight.

In my hand, for a moment, the whole world pulses. I see the Underworld again, in its eerie lavender light. I see the turbulent river that once I swam in. Then I see things I do not recognize: factories with smoking chimneys. A stage. None of these make sense. And then I see children, everywhere, happy children playing games, and something deep inside tells me I need to get rid of this thing in my hand once and for all. I squeeze tight, then thrust him through the bars of the lion's cage.

"No!" protests a little squeak of a voice. I guard the cage. No escaping. I hear nothing at first. Has he vanished? Then I hear the soft thud of a paw catching something. Then the crunching sound of the great cat eating.

I open the front door to the now-silent apartment, then close it behind me. I take a few steps, then turn around. The door to his apartment—that I just a moment ago closed—has vanished. Now there is just a long blank wall, like the empty face of his watch.

I ride my bicycle back home past the market, feeling calmer than I have felt in years, perhaps in my entire life. I feel certain that I won't see him again. He is gone. He is not in the world anymore, and even if he were, his trick won't work on me anymore. His trick of trying to get you to lose life before you really lose life, so that you might let go more easily.

The Saturday market is full of young families with baskets on their arms filled with flowers, kale, melons, carrots with the tops still on. And then I catch sight of her.

Her long auburn hair falls around her, glinting in the sunlight, as she leans down to smell a basketful of cantaloupe. I watch her closely as she fills her bag with mangoes and a lemony Buddha's hand. She strolls with the most enviable, still, quiet, and unworried grace. Her belly looks about to burst; she cannot possibly see her toes. Death looks up and finds me looking. Her smooth face opens into a thousand-year-old smile: ripples cast out across her fine cheekbones. I can see in her smile the earth curling out, a small beginning from the semen of some ancient creature, and I can see the earth's final explosion into fire. In her smile I see the twitch of a fox-tail, the hollow black bones of a bird carcass spinning into the air like a naked planet, the benthic sadness and happiness of a boat-woman who sees both sides. She keeps smiling, and I smile back, for a long time.

Should I speak to her, should I say, *I wish you could have pushed him back, told him to go back to his mother, not let him run out of air?* She is walking away from the market, away from me, her satchel of fruit and flowers and dark root vegetables bumping against her hips. I think of following her.

Then I don't.

This is the ending—you see how it ends. I will try to be like Death, always on the verge of bursting with some new life, always looking ahead toward beauty. Picking up a melon and turning it around in my hands. Facing life so that when it is time to go, I have not wasted it.

You are the first person to hear this story. I feel better after telling it. I will tell it to the baby, too, when he grows up. I see how keeping Adam, both Adams, in the past was never going to work. They would come back into your history and mine, and that's how it should be, for stories rinse out the cave until our pasts are washed clean and can no longer infect anybody. We're okay now, I think. It's a relief to put these fears to rest by shaping them into sense outside my body. When I think of the day we lost Adam, I hear only the seagulls crying as they dove the waves for fish. But it could be worse. There are worse things to hear. I know that now.

After leaving the market, I go home and I look at you. You are nearly nineteen and I have never noticed how dark your eyes are, and that you have a mole below your left eye where my mother had one. You are busy making dinner so you do not appear to notice how hard I am looking. I gulp you in like fluid. I look and I look and I look.

Once you go to bed, I write George a letter telling him everything. He may think I am crazy, but he has promised to stay by me and all these years he has. I will leave it by the bed, or read it to him if I am feeling brave over breakfast. And this night, I do one last thing: I slip into your room while you sleep and place my hand on your forehead. Instead of batting me off or waking, you sleep on. I feel your mammal-warmth, remembering when you were born, your molten baby heat against the curve of my arm. Your liveness.

Your arm is flat next to your side. As I watch, you move your arm and reach out your hand to see if I am still here.

Still here.

25

MAY 5

A long minute passes. We are crouched in the grass. My feet are itching from its thin dry fronds, but I cannot think about that now. I search the previous day for early signs of labor: there have been no contractions. No water has broken.

"Are you feeling okay?" I ask my mother.

"I'm fine," she says. "This might be it, or it might not be."

We squat next to each other facing the ocean at low tide. Cars pass by on the dirt road beyond the trees. I am rubbing her back and she is silent. I am calculating how far along she might be, whether it is smarter to flag down a driver to get a ride to the hospital or stay here and see what happens. I am not prepared for a birth—my birth bag is still at Ilya's house.

"I'm all right," Marella says.

So I stand. "All right," I say. "Let's keep walking."

We walk past the post-office, past Gillas Governor's Mansion, and at the end of the street my mother groans.

"Are these different than normal cramps?" I ask her.

"I'm not sure. I think—I don't know." Then suddenly she rises and begins walking in frantic circles. She sits down a moment after.

"Does it feel like your stomach is being put through a pasta-maker?" I ask her. I remember hearing a woman say something to this effect.

She glares at me. "How would I know? We don't make pasta." She holds her belly in silence, eyes closed. Slowly she nods. "Yes. Yes, it does. I need to rest here a minute."

If she were an ordinary woman and not my mother, I would tell her with confidence to keep walking. But I feel myself losing confidence. She has been through birth before and I have only watched it, and when she drops her purse in the gravel and leans back against a tree, shuddering, all I can do is check the time. She had wanted to go to the hospital. I am not her chosen midwife.

11:08 a.m. This contraction is harder than the last, I can see in her face. I wait.

Above us the squirrels are chasing each other in ringlets through the trees. "Here," I say, "drink this water." And she drains my water bottle dry.

11:13. "Eiiiii!" squawks my mother, rising from the ground to spin in the strange pain-faced dance that women do, hunching her shoulders and grimacing and moving her feet. I know this dance, this effort to move through the pain as if walking away from it. It speeds labor up, but it makes it more intense.

She is silent again. She sits on the bright spongy grass, holding her purse against her chest. At 11:18 she groans again and begins her dance. Then at 11:22. Then at 11:26. I ask, "How painful are they, between one and ten?"

She won't answer.

Another one. 11:30.

Think, I tell myself. Think fast. Her contractions are gaining rhythm. Could we make it home, then to the car, then to the hospital?

11:34, another one.

No.

I look closely at my mother. Her long hair is sticky on her shoulders. She has begun to sweat. Next to us the ocean rolls at low tide, above us the sun peaks in the noon sky. Over the edge of the trees, I see a slanting metal roof.

Ilya's.

"Marella, you must stand with me. We're going to walk."

She obeys, and I carry her purse and support her with my arm around her waist. We walk at a snail's pace. Every four minutes we stop so that she can dance again.

Silently I am beginning to panic. What will I do when my mother gives birth? How could my first birth alone be *hers*? I feel a childish need to get to Ilya's house, to use the phone, to keep my mother calm and get her into somebody else's hands.

A half-block.

Pause: dance.

Another half-block.

Pause: dance again.

I need to slow my mother's labor down. The walking is only serving to speed it.

At last she speaks, and her words surface as a roar. "This is excruciating! Why don't people talk about this?" My mother is going under now, into herself, and all I can do is to keep her walking.

The waves that crash through her body, up and down her spine, are coming now every three minutes, and she is whirling in her dance more frantically.

Things are happening so quickly, both in her body and in the flashes that keep coming to me, so that it is not life flashing before my eyes, but all of the events that have come before leading up to exactly this and making this moment the only answer.

I see the pain in her face come and go away. Birth like death.

Just as I saw in her own mother's face when we came here ten months ago. *Was it only ten months?* How I had my flimsy degree from an island high school, college spread out ahead like a promise, but I could not abandon my Nana here, could not leave her with my mother who didn't know how to love, and then I could not abandon my mother here, not without my father nearby. But no—that's not the full truth. I could've gone back to Blue Island, enrolled in college late. My staying in Dragon Island wasn't a choice I made for Nana or my mother alone. I made it, in part, for me.

We arrive at Ilya's front steps and I help my mother inside the house. The cot downstairs is made, fresh white sheets and military corners—always ready. I help my mother onto it. Then I raid Ilya's refrigerator and find—relief!—many cartons of juice. I bring my mother mango juice and instruct her, "Drink this now, because you won't want to later."

"I don't want to now," she says. But she gulps it down and then asks for water, which I have ready. She rests quietly for a moment, then groans and dances. 12:20.

I call the number for the fish market where my father is. No answer. I know Ilya's cupboards by heart, where she keeps the raspberry leaf and the placenta tincture, but still I feel at a loss for tools. Do I call 911? I have been at so many births, but my mother wanted a hospital, a doctor. Even if I called 911, it is a long way to Dragon Island Hospital.

Breathe, I tell myself. You know what to do. You have done this before.

My mother is groaning again. 12:22.

I am panicking. I am alone with a birthing woman, with

my birthing *mother*. All I have to help me is Ilya's birth kit, her compresses and her book and her tinctures. The birthing tub is empty and there is no way I can get it full before the baby comes—it takes nearly an hour to fill. Already I am failing to do my job, failing at being a midwife. I cannot even get my mother into a bath, to stall labor until I can bring in help. I have seen birth before, caught babies before, but never unsupervised.

Then an epiphany hurls itself onto my chest: for all births starting with the cave birth, Ilya stood beside me, but she made sure I did the work. My hands would remember what to do. A woman knows instinctively how she wishes to birth, if you just leave her alone and let her do it.

My mother is dancing again. 12:24.

"Would it feel better to keep moving?" I ask.

I am no longer trying to stall her. The birth is happening here, in this house, with me as midwife, and all I want is to get my mother through it safely. And I know that walking will get the baby in the correct position more reliably than lying down.

She nods. She is not speaking now, just obeying or disobeying. I offer my arms and help her up. She stands, looking intensely focused, and at 12:26 when the next wave comes she spins around, twisting her body and running madly in place. When it ends, she goes still and sits on the edge of the cot.

The contractions come again and again, faster and faster, and each time I watch my mother dance, her body trying to hold the impossible pain at bay.

It is high tide in my mother's body, and each wave that comes swings her deeper into motion, rocking her body in circles across the room, bending and curling to a rhythm of her own. She is never still, not once, when the waves hit, and they are becoming almost continuous. She dances and dances. In the moments between waves I offer her food, water, juice.

"No!" my mother cries, shaking all over. Then she runs out

Ilya's door and vomits into the sand.

I ask my mother to lie down inside, quickly, so that I can check her dilation. She does not have the focus to take off her skirt, so I wriggle her out of it. It is like undressing a child. Another wave hits, and she springs up, tearing her shirt off. When she completes that round of dance, she is naked. I direct her over to the cot.

"Mother, I'm going to check you, get ready for my hand." I reach between her legs. It is too late in the game for modesty or any other emotions that might plague me during a quieter time. I feel the dilation, my fingers' span wide. Ten centimeters. And I feel the baby's head, hard and round and ready to come out.

Working quickly before the next wave hits, I pull out my fetoscope and listen for the baby's heartbeat. A tad slow, but still normal.

"The waves don't stop!" my mother cries. "At first there were breaks. Not anymore."

"Marella," I tell her in as calm a voice as I can summon. "You are about to have this baby. You are completely effaced, ten centimeters dilated. It is time to get ready to push."

"I need a break," my mother pants. "Just a rest."

"No rest now. There will be rest after."

"No—"

"Yes," I say firmly.

The dance comes again and my mother howls this time. "Water," she cries, "water water water water water."

I push the cup at her. "No. A bath."

There is no bath. There is no way of having a bath. I have nothing, no water except for the ocean.

The ocean!

"Mother," I say, during her next brief moment of rest, "you must come with me outside."

She dances through the next contraction and I guide her from Ilya's cot to the beach outside Ilya's cabin, grabbing the birth kit as I go. My naked mother is fearless, she has gone into herself deeply, and I help her into the knee-deep water. It is warm, bath-temperature.

She calms immediately, sinking into an animal crouch. When the next contraction comes, she dances through it again, and then the next comes, and she is smoother, less panicked, more determined. She is fully in the water now. I am carrying the fetoscope and testing the heartbeat every minute. The heartbeat is lowering, a sign of distress. The baby needs to come out now.

I know that my mother's next rest will only last thirty seconds at most. I tell her, "When this next one comes, I need you to push."

Then, splashing the water frantically, my mother dances another ringlet of her churning, private dance, and then collapses on the ocean bed on all fours. She pushes weakly, and greenish purple water explodes out of her into the ocean. Her water has broken at last, and it is not clear water. I know from Ilya that dark fluid means meconium: unborn baby feces that the baby will likely try to breathe in. We have to get this baby out and into a hospital now.

I kneel in the water and face her. We look deeply at each other. I try to channel Ilya, the way she spoke to women in labor. "Marella, you are brave. You are doing so well." My mother stares at me and I keep talking. She is caught now in one long contraction, no more rest, and Ilya's voice is pouring out of my mouth and there is nothing I can do to stop it. "You are doing so beautifully well, and I am so proud of you. Mama! You are almost done."

My mother's body peaks like a triangle, her head and hands pinned together, her legs wide open. I move to stand behind her. "Push again," I tell her. "Hard."

"Oh God," she cries, "when will it stop? Be calm, be calm, be calm, be calm." She howls like a panicked animal. "Be calm, be calm, be calm."

"Push again," I command with more urgency.

My mother pushes, then roars with the effort.

"Now take the deepest breath you can. A long one."

My mother breathes in.

"When I say so, close your mouth and push with all of that breath you've saved."

My mother looks pleadingly at me. She draws in her breath. "It's time," I say. "Now push."

My mother pushes.

My brother crowns, the amazing red moment when the hard grape of the baby's head pops out of the vessel, and then the shoulders slither out afterward. I catch my brother and my mother collapses in the water, crying, splashing, dragging herself weakly through the shallows to shore.

I slide alongside her, Ola in my arms. My mother drops onto her back, panting, the water lapping her shoulders and hair.

I put the baby on my mother's chest, Ola's pink skin against my mother's tan. They heave together in the shallow water, tainted purple with my mother's blood.

I watch them for a short moment. My mind swims with thoughts and wonders and miracles and fear and love, all at once. Then I notice that the baby's color is draining out. He is not screaming.

All of a sudden I feel Ilya, I just feel her, her hands calmly and swiftly guiding my hands. It is as if she were whispering in my ear: *This baby does not have enough air.*

I flick his feet. I rub his back. Still his breaths are shallow.

"I need to take the baby from you," I say. Ola is losing his color and starting to turn limp and white. I know what I have to do next, and I do not want to do it—the cord is still pulsing, not ready to be clamped. But I have to get him free. I do not want to separate my mother and her baby this soon, but more so than that I do not want to lose another brother.

I clamp the cord an inch from my brother's small slimy belly. Then I root in the birth kit for the scissors, which I cannot find. Did they fall out? How could I have forgotten to check for them, or at the very least keep with me a knife for cutting?

But there is no time for these thoughts. I do what midwives for centuries before me have done: I bite the cord with my front teeth, biting down and twisting it until it breaks, breaking him free from my mother. I spit out blood. The cord pulses less and less, going still and becoming a dead object.

I lay the baby on his back between my mother and me and put my mouth to his, breathing air into his tiny lungs, trying to help him breathe. Marella rests next to us, bloody and exhausted and too far gone inside herself to realize what is going on.

He breathes. But not enough. I speak to him, loudly and firmly, striking his chest and feet in little slaps, and saying, "Ola! You need to hear me. Wake up. Wake up, you need to use your lungs." I turn him over and tap his back. I keep talking to him. "Breathe, baby brother. Breathe."

I try the bulb syringe in his mouth. It draws out the sticky meconium, colored like a sick and viscous shade of tar. I use the bulb again and again, until finally the fluid that comes out from his lungs is clear. Then I put my mouth to his and try breathing for him. In between breaths I cry out to nobody, "Help us!"

Nobody comes to this beach. Nobody will hear me.

"Right now," I say to Marella, trying to keep the fear out of my voice. "You need to talk to him. Say, 'Breathe, baby.' Tell him you love him. Tell him to stay here with us."

Marella does not move.

"Mama!" I raise my voice. "He needs *you*." I rest him flat-backed on my mother's chest, breathing into him, between breaths instructing Marella, "Talk to him! Stroke his chest, his feet," and praying that she will cooperate.

Marella hears me, at last. She looks at the baby on her chest, cooing tentative encouragement, flicking him, rubbing him, her hands and my hands at work, coaxing life to stay in his tiny body. His breathing increases, but I know we are not yet safe. I tell her: "Keep doing what you're doing. If he slows again, breathe for him. I'll be right back."

And I sprint up the rocks into Ilya's house, toward Ilya's phone. Desperately I press 911 and when I hear a voice, I call into it: "A baby was just born who is not breathing." And I give them Ilya's address.

"What time was the baby born?" the voice wants to know.

I forgot to check! The wall clock says 12:52pm. Could all of this have happened in the past five minutes? I guess. "12:48pm. A boy." And I hang up, feeling fraudulent because I have fabricated my brother's birth time. But then comes a green seedling of hope: I have facilitated his birth.

And just then, I hear from the beach outside the sound of a baby screaming.

The scream! The air it took for Ola to make that noise is the most hopeful sound I have ever in my life heard. I run back to the beach. He is breathing now, on his own. He has brought himself back from the edge. He is still lying on Marella's bare chest, and they are alone together on the damp sand—she is half-laughing, half-weeping. I cover them with a blanket and let them rest.

There would be more work ahead: I would have to get Ola nursing, and I would have to get my mother to push out the placenta. I would have to call 911 back and say that it was a false alarm, we don't need them after all. These would happen before the end of the hour. But the hardest work is done. *My mother is okay. Ola is alive. The tides have lapped the blood away, and the water around them has cleared.*

My dad arrived within the half-hour. He had gotten my voice-message and come straight from the fish market.

"Seabird..." he said shakily over and over. He swallowed a few times.

Together he and I carried my mother, Ola still on her chest, into Ilya's house, where she would recover. Blood trickled on the sand behind her as we walked. Dad and I helped her into bed. Even birth-bruised and labor-spent my mother was beautiful: her skin shining, her legs limp and together, her long hair matted with sweat. We carried her the way in storybooks people carry mermaids.

"I forgot how much it hurt," she said as she settled into the cot. She was murmuring in the post-birth daze, to my dad, to me, to herself, to no one. "Did Adam hurt that way?" Then she said in a small voice: "I wish my mom were here—but Sage..." She turned to me, and I realized it was the first time in memory that she had used my name. She smiled weakly. "You were here instead."

She kept talking for a long while. My father sat in the birth-chair, not knowing it was a birth-chair, looking unsure of what to do. I worked quickly at the after-delivery jobs, tending to my mother's body, leaving Ola alone. Marella kept talking. It was as if all these things were coming out of her, along with Ola, along with the placenta—all the sad and helpless stories she had kept stored up for so long. I caught fragments of what she said: "What is it about my boys? So close to death. Sage and I, never. But Adam...and Ola...and George at sea...and my brother—what, do I have a curse on me? But my women. You, me, we, just fine."

Yes. Yes, I thought, half-listening. We—our family, our women and our men—we will be just fine. Just fine, our whole family together in the little houseboat. A bright beautiful cloud of us.

That night we drove back to our house and everyone fell into fast, deep sleep. I tried to will myself to sleep. You will need to help her to help him, I told myself. But sleep was nowhere. As I tossed in my bed, I heard a voice inside my head say, *Well worked, woman.* And I knew without doubt that it was Ilya.

26

Charon

My mind is awash with all I have seen, a great parade of souls towed one-way across the river. I have helped humans die, and now I will help them be born. Someone will replace me, man or woman, some other deliverer. It will not matter who rows the boat. I will go on, I know, ferrying women as their legs open and a dark river pours out, dividing one world from the next. But first I must lead this shadow-woman out of my world and into the ocean, into the place where there is no smell, only sound and taste and touch. A place both peaceful and terrifying. I will come alive holding the water of my river still around me, carrying memories so deep I will have no words to say them. I will know everything when I am born out of the ocean again. I will remember.

27

Sage

MAY 5 (DREAM)

I will forget everything when I am born, I am certain—if only I could cram this knowledge of the other side into every cell of my body, big as it is and small as it will be. I know I am unraveling into forgetfulness. It is a solid hard fact, as certain as the fact that I am going to be born. The forgetting is part of it. I know.

But I know one thing even as the others slip away:

She is in pain, and she needs me, and I have the cure for her. I have it! I know that I have it! It is me, I think, as I hear the crash of waves and a wash of sounds, voices, water, her voice in pain, so many sounds that they deafen me. I am so certain that I am her cure. But how will I remember this? I don't want to be empty of knowing these things. But somehow I know that I will forget.

Here, there is no smell. There is only sound and taste and touch. Here is the most peaceful place. I rock back and forth on the lifeboat of her hips. It is a perfect warm, blood-warm.

Food comes constantly. I have nothing to do but grow. She gives light and love and water and patience and I grow, grow, grow! Fingers, toes, tooth-buds, ear-drums, lanugo, eyes. Something new each week.

There is a lot of sound. I know her voice from the start and now I know his, too. I love the heat of her voice and how lightly it dances, like something flickering bright and red-hot. There was a younger voice too—then it stopped. It just went away. Her voice became damp-sand all the time, and something changed in her—and somehow I know—I just *know*—that she is scared of water. And scared of me too. For I am all made up of water, bobbing around inside her, seasicking her from inside out.

Of course she is afraid of water. She has lost people to it. I know things about her. And at the same time, I know that I will forget each one. For that reason I am a little frightened at the thought of being born.

Now everything is ocean.

Now there is the hum of undertow, the roar of the waves coming in hard.

Now there is pressure pushing my head down.

Now her voice is in pain.

I cannot see anything and yet pictures come to me complete. On earth, the man who is my father sits, his legs heavy on the floor. And I know somehow that he loves the water. He flips around in it, all joy. He comes to her dripping wet, happy. She tells him to dry off. Coldly. This is her dark voice.

In the room also is her mother, an uncomfortable stiff sitter in a chair. She doesn't trust the stout bearded man sitting next to her. She hopes I will be her creature more than his.

Now my mother writhes on her bed, saying, *I want up, I want up!*

Now, the doctor shoots drugs into the base of her spinal cord, and she lies still and quiet. Now, there is a knock on the door, and a soft voice. A halo of a question. *How do you want to have her?*

My groggy mother stirs. *I don't care. Just get it out.*

This new voice does not belong in the hospital. It is made up of moonlight and seaweed and boats that feel every curve of the ocean and potions in sea-glass bottles and silver long unnetted hair. The hospital is made up of silver technology and doctors in masks and hairnets, containers with tops shaped like squares, long hallways that lead to dead-ends, telephone conversations and counselors to comfort the aggrieved. No, this woman should not be here.

The doctor's voice is gone, he must have stepped away, while the woman mixes something: a few powders, some drops. She gives it to my mother and within an hour her baby will be born.

An hour from now, I will leave my mother's ocean and howl into the air. During that hour my mother will push hard with this woman whispering to her: *this is a do-over, you will be okay, you can stop fearing water, you will finally have a child who lives.* An hour from now, the amniotic sac will hold like a bubble around me, a final reminder of the river from which I have come. An hour from now, the silver-haired woman will catch me and tell my mother: *your daughter is in the caul.*

28

Sage

MAY — SEPTEMBER

Late that night I would finally get to sleep—heavy and well. So would Ola. So would my mother. That night I would dream the birth that Ilya had for so long insisted I remember.

And then the next morning I would get to work: file the birth certificate with fudged birth-time; give Marella a bath; feed Marella dried fruit and urge her to go to the bathroom; model for her how to urinate after birth, how to stand above the toilet with her legs close together, letting a little leak out at a time. Marella would giggle but obey. I would show her how to bathe Ola, touching him as if he were made of lace, using only water on the softest handkerchief. And I would cook my mother's placenta and dry it and grind it and sift the powder into capsules. I would instruct her, and she would remember, to swallow a pill each morning and each afternoon, taking back her own nutrients, her own iron.

My father would watch in awe and revulsion. "Did you use the coffee grinder for that, Seabird?"

"What, Dad? It's just meat."

"Sure," he would say. "But it's meat made of your mother."

The first week would pass in three-hour rounds of milk-diaper-sleep, milk-diaper-sleep, all hands on deck tending to this new person. My mother would at last agree to stay in bed all the hours she normally did, devoting fifteen nap-checkered hours toward sleeping her usual seven. My father would look at me like a lost dog and say, "Tell me what to do," and I would give him a list that he would follow for the rest of the month—he would learn how to make Fenugreek tea, how to change a diaper, wash a diaper, check a diaper. Each night we would work in shifts, taking turns bringing baby Ola to my mother's bed.

And neighbors we never knew would leave dinners on our doorstep, and my mother would eat them in full—we would fill her plate again and again, and she would keep eating, metabolizing it all into milk. Ola would eat and eat and eat, hungry for her, the strong current of his mouth oceaning her like an undertow. Often it exhausted her and I found them both in her bed, asleep.

Through all of this my mother would keep changing. Marella would grow solid, less ethereal, under the glow of her baby's gaze. While Ola would sleep easily in my arms and make sweet faces at my dad, he always would want to look at my mother. My mother's body would thin quickly into its old shape, with only the *linea negra* remaining, the long brown line bisecting her belly like a beetle-stripe. Soon that, too, would vanish. Something would change in Marella after this new baby, something expanding her to be bigger and more brave, and I would realize at last what it was, that Marella was becoming less of a myth, more of a woman with skin and fingernails and fat and muscle. She would be born again as Ola's mother, as my mother, as herself.

In the evenings when Ola's thin nights stretched longer and longer, four hours, five, six, I would hear the sound of my parents laughing through their bedroom door, my mother's laugh rising, airy and effervescent. My family would feel peaceful in a way I had never known us to be—something temporary, a spell—all of us aware that soon fishing season would return and my father would go away, soon my mother would rustle and begin her life out of the house, soon Ola would hit a new plateau and need different things—one day he would walk, speak, run, go to school, grow up, marry, work, and one day, die. If all went well, he would get to do all of these things. But for now, all we would know was that he was here now, and it was our job to love him and observe him and do our best not to miss anything.

One day, not long from now, something in Ola would change and I would remember how Ilya once observed, "The spirit baby leaves at six weeks and the human baby takes its place." When she had said it all those months ago, I thought she just meant that the baby was becoming more cognizant of the world. But after what I had seen, I wondered if there really was another life, another world, that Ola was shedding and forgetting as he learned to open his eyes longer, to grab at real objects with his clumsy hands, and to look up at me and recognize someone, not a mother, but someone who would matter in his life. Another life that he knew well, but would forget before he learned to speak.

In a few weeks Ilya's lawyer would come by the house, telling me that there was more than just the houseboat, that Ilya had saved many hundreds of thousands of mora, and that she had left it to me and what did I want to do with it? And I would call my father into the living room and say quit the boats, retire the company, because now we can afford for you to be home with Marella while you look for a job that keeps you closer to your wife and son. And I would save the rest, as Ilya had.

My mother would surprise me one morning with a bright shyness in her face and something small held in her hands, and she would give me a book hand-bound with thick sewing thread, a book as slender as a knife handle, a book she had written as a gift for me. The title would be, *What the Raftswoman Knows*, and inside, in her handwriting, it would be dedicated, "For Sage, a story told to me but meant for you."

And I would read the first line—*My name is Charon and I am a boat woman*—and wonder what other mysteries were there for me to understand, or not understand, that my mother and Ilya knew?

And then Ilya's money would arrive in the form of a single check, and I would make the choice to drive to Middle twice a week and take part-time community college classes in nurse education, giving me time to stay on call for the Dragon Island women who needed a midwife. Pupuka would begin studying his snails and mollusks in September, and evenings we would talk on the phone from where I sat in the loft of my houseboat, for soon I would stop calling it Ilya's house and know that it was mine. Mine and all of the women's who would ever come in need of it. My dad would stay at home for six months and then hook a job as a harbor pilot that would give him an eight-hour work day, and my mother and Ola would bike over and meet him for lunch.

Which would leave me. Me, nineteen. Me, watching my mother do it all over again. Marella and George rewriting their lives as young parents. Crazy that, if I wanted, I could have a baby and it would be practically the same age as Ola. But I wasn't ready for that yet. Who knows when I might be. All I knew was that, for now, I would keep learning and helping women; I would go on to set an example for my parents and my younger brother. I would watch in awe as my family's landlocked world turned back toward water, toward life.

And one ordinary evening I would step onto the back porch and find two glistening black slugs on the doormat and I would know that Pupuka had come home on break from college and that I would see him before the night's end, just as I would see him every time he came home, and know that his plans were to come home, afterward, back here for good. And that night I would turn in his arms beneath my ocean-facing bedroom window and tell him how it all happened, tell him yes to his question, yes to the question he kept asking me with his eyes and body and his words—

And we would sleep long and whole that night, wrapped up in each other, and it would be the first full night of sleep I had gotten in a long time, and I would wake to feel nourished by the pink sunlight out my bedroom window…

But before all of this could happen, there was something I needed to do first:

On the second night Ola was alive, when the bushes and flowers around the driveway swayed in the light wind and a stillness hung about the house, I went to say goodnight to my mother.

She was leaning back in her purple chair, which my father said he would reupholster in a fresh color. Ola was nursing in his sleep, the ocean outside the window making a perfect iambic pentameter, like a heartbeat. It was the same sound, I realized, that he had known as long as he had existed, the first music every mammal hears. Naturally he was lulled by the sound of the ocean, the same ebb and flow of blood through some universal mother heart.

My mother was looking out at the ocean as the sky darkened. She was stroking the baby's forehead and looking thoughtful. She was staring at something invisible in the darkness, a bird or a spirit. When she saw me she smiled.

I knelt down and whispered to her, "I am going to write down your birth story this week, before I forget anything."

She turned her head toward me. "I have missed so much," she said so quietly that I could hardly hear.

I took her into my arms, and together we three made a nesting doll with Ola as center. It was true—there was much that she had missed. But my mother is young and there are many years for her to explore. I told her this. I pushed her long dark hair out of her eyes and kissed her forehead and I spoke to her—first soothing, reassuring, and then a hint bossy, just as Ilya taught me—and I said, "Tomorrow. We will swim again tomorrow. We'll go to the part of the ocean where Ola was born."

"Yes," she whispered. "And tomorrow, Sage, I have a story I've wanted to tell you. It's a story about water and fear—but it has a good ending."

"Yes," I whispered back.

And then I picked up Ola and carried him out of our house into the strong sea air full of salt and moisture, past the steps where Lance first stopped by on his bicycle, past the mat where Pupuka first left his slugs, tiptoeing between the palm trees down to the beach, where the surf droned on, low and gentle and invisible in the dark; the moon was brand new and the only light came from our porch light and from the stars—

I knelt in the shallows and took off the baby's swaddle and let the warm water lap his legs and bare bottom. I seemed to remember that in baptism some mark should go on his forehead, but not knowing what, I ended up wetting my finger and drawing a wet heart.

"Look Ola," I said. "This is water."

Then I rubbed his tiny back and whispered to him stories of the sea—about the lobsters who are bluish grey underwater, and about the brown bottoms of the boats that make shadows on the ocean floor when the sun shines above; how friendly the scuba-divers are in their rubbery wetsuits, like orcas, and how they wave and smile and blow silent bubbles; and how the coral looks like thin bones, and how the shimmery pink jellyfish contract and release. And how the slender eel waits loyally in the rocks like a dog.

I told him how swimming feels like flying, and how clear the water gets when you go out far—and how much space there is, open space that goes on forever and ever and ever. How it is peaceful and still and silent, and how soon he will learn to swim. I told him about fish, how some live in the darkness and others are made of clear light, and how they are all beautiful and one day he would get to see them. How most sharks won't come near you, and how in the end there is nothing to cause you fear of the deep—there is just you alone, swimming toward the shore.

Fin.

Acknowledgments

My gratitude runs as deep as the ocean to Lynn, who read every draft; to Lanie, who spent countless hours teaching me about structure; to Gill and Melanie, Roosevelt Writers and wise readers; to Lesley, Laura, Kimber, Kelli, Karen, Paula, Anna, Catie, Sarah, and Kristi, who believed in this book from the beginning; to SEMO Press, for selecting this book as a semifinalist for its Nilsen prize; to the late poet Gary Cooke, who taught me to look everywhere for beauty; to Julia Sippel, ferry woman extraordinaire, for remembering this book when it was waiting on the riverbank and for asking the questions to move it across; and to Paul Dry and the whole team for bringing it into the world; to my parents, who when I told them I wanted to write books never once tried to talk me out of it; and finally to James, who took care of our young so many early mornings so that I could write, and who listened deep into the night while I told him this story.

About the Author

CREDIT: FIONA MONTAGNE

ELISABETH SHARP McKETTA grew up in Austin, Texas. She holds literature degrees from Harvard, Georgetown, and the University of Texas at Austin and teaches writing for the Harvard Extension School and the Oxford University Department for Continuing Education. She is the author of eight books: *We Live in Boise, Energy: The Life of John J. McKetta Jr., Fear of the Deep, Fear of the Beast, Poetry for Strangers Vols. I and II, The Creative Year: 52 Workshops for Writers,* and *The Fairy Tales Mammals Tell. She Never Told Me About the Ocean* is her first novel. Visit *elisabethsharpmcketta.com* to learn more.